FOREVER MARKED

JESSE LORENZO

WORDS THAT LEAVE THEIR MARK

TABLE OF CONTENTS

DEDICATION

To my three beautiful daughters,
Jazlyn, Veronica, and Marcela:
Dream big and reach for the stars!
Mommy loves you!

FOREVER
MARKED

PROLOGUE

Now was her chance. She took advantage of the momentary distraction gifted to her and wrenched herself from his vice-like grip. Fighting him off, she clawed her way to her feet. Her short nails ripped painfully in her effort to get away. Mustering up all the strength she had, she raced to get out of the tiny room. She didn't get very far, her momentum suddenly halted when she felt a punching blow and then a dragging pain slash down her back. She shrieked out as the intense burning sensation traveled through every nerve in her body. Only then did she realize that her flesh had been flayed opened, exposed.

A draft cooled the warm flowing blood as it soaked her shirt. The horrific realization of what'd been done momentarily froze her forward progress. She heard him stumble from the barbaric force of his blow. It's now or never! Adrenaline flooded her system, sending a jolt of energy to her frozen legs.

The sudden rush helped to propel her forward. She sprinted through the door and raced down the hallway as fast her legs could carry her. Panic rose up inside her when she heard his heavy footsteps pounding on the hardwood floors, gaining on her fast. She knew that if she couldn't make it out of here now, she'd never survive. That debilitating fear twisted inside her gut, making her feel sick. It didn't matter how fast she ran, he was always right behind her.

His powerful presence echoed around the eerily empty house as he chased close behind her. She shook uncontrollably when she made it to the stairs. If she could just reach the door, she might have a chance. Reaching out, she grabbed the railing with both hands, using the leverage to fly down the steps. She skipped so many steps, it felt like flying. Her heart hammered inside her chest painfully as it worked hard to push her broken body to its limits. Her ears throbbed as he screamed out her name over and over. He was right behind her. She could smell his rancid panting over her shoulder, the stench stung her nose. She risked looking back. His large black eyes, fierce with anger, were just a few feet behind her and closing in quickly. He was close enough to grab her, a monster zeroing in on his prey. Hyperventilating, her lungs stung with the effort to forcefully pull air in and out. Oh My God, this is it! *He reached out... And...*

Ellora jumped up and almost fell out of her seat, gasping in the air she must've been holding. She pulled in several more deep breaths and took a look around. *Everyone* on the plane was openly gawking at her. They looked shocked and disturbed. Realization dawned; she must've shrieked out in her nightmare. Extremely embarrassed, Ellora turned her attention to her clenched fists, still clammy and shaking. "Get a grip, Lor," she muttered to herself.

It took several minutes more to calm her nerves. When the embarrassment subsided, she let her eyes roam around the cramped cabin in coach. The tight seating used to feel so uncomfortable and annoying, but at a time like this, the crowded seats gave Ellora a much-needed sense of security. Relief washed over her as she realized that she was halfway to her destination. She was headed to Scotland, as far away from Syracuse, NY, as she was able to go, to the place where her parents were born and raised.

He shouldn't be able to find her there. After all, her mother and father were very tight-lipped about their upbringing. With their passing, and Ellora being their only child, no one could tell *him* either... *He* couldn't find out!

Ellora hadn't stopped looking over her shoulder since her brutal attack. Every time she turned a corner, she couldn't help but think he would jump out at her and finish what he had started. Her anxiety rose as she thought about the monster who nearly killed her. Did he know she left? Was he on this very plane, just biding his time until he could get his hands on her? The very thought of him hiding in the shadows, watching her, made the hairs on the back of her neck stand to attention.

Closing her eyes, Ellora secretly willed the plane to go faster; the sooner she got there, the better her chances were of hiding herself away. She thought back to all the events that led up to her escape and prayed she hadn't left behind any clues as to where she was headed in her hasty escape.

The thought of starting her life over from scratch, and doing it alone, frightened her. "You can do this, Lor. You're almost there," she chanted to herself. After all, starting from zero was easy when you had nothing left to lose.

Inverness, Scotland
Bus Terminal

Exhausted from the long flight, Ellora was actually looking forward to the scenic bus ride. As she waited for the Citylink bus to come around, she took another look at the pamphlet in her hand. It read: *The Isle of Skye is world famous for its natural beauty, history, romance, and legendary folklore. It offers a truly unforgettable experience -- a real adventure among jagged mountains, sweeping moors, and dramatic waterfalls.* In two hours and thirty minutes, the bus would arrive in Portree Harbor, the largest town in Skye, population two thousand five hundred. Plus one. Ellora's new home.

"Damn it! What am I going to do now?" Ellora complained to herself. Her pace quickened as she navigated her way down the pier on Quay Street. The sun was setting, and the cold, icy rain drizzled down, drenching her. Cold, miserable and starving, Ellora desperately needed somewhere to hole up while she tried to figure out her next viable option. She tried every B&B on the harbor, but there were no rooms available. She just about gave up hope, when she spotted a run-down looking pub. It was situated at the end of Quay Street and the corner of Beaumont Crescent. *Grady's...* It looked like there was more to the sign, but the rest had long since fallen off. In comparison to the rest of the Portree Harbor row buildings, this last one wasn't at all bright with color and charm; it rather looked like a dreary afterthought, and a dismal one at that. "Well," she mumbled to herself, "there's no point standing out here in the rain."

Of course, she tripped on the damaged doorstop, letting a few un-ladylike curse words fall from her lips. Frustrated, Ellora roughly dragged in the wet luggage behind her -- definitely *not* the grand entrance she was hoping for. She looked around the dimly lit bar, and sure enough, she'd captured the attention of the locals inside. They all wore curious, amused expressions. Ellora smiled, inwardly laughing at herself and thought, *I must look like a complete fool.*

"Grady, ya old goat, give us a spot more o' that ale. The day's been a long 'en." Old man Grady finished drying some more mugs and shuffled over to fill up the guys' mugs. He'd been daydreaming all day, worry creasing his brow. The pub was falling apart, and he was behind in all his payments. His wife used to be in charge of all the business and goings on there. All he was good for was pouring a mean drink. With her passing, he'd let his grief take over his life.

Catie had been barren, so they hadn't children to dote on. He was truly alone. Grady ran his calloused, over-worked hands through his scruffy un-kept hair, and blew out a frustrated breath. Catie would've given him a fierce tongue lashing at how he'd let this place go. After all, the pub had been her pride and joy. He was thankful for the help that'd been given to him since Catie's passing.

His younger brother, Gerard, had been running the kitchen when folks ordered something more than the liquid meal. Gerard's wife, Kristy, ran the B&B next door. She'd been helping Grady with the bookkeeping mess he had ignored for so long. Only Grady's loyal regulars came around anymore. The dilapidated pub wasn't appealing to the tourists visiting the harbor, especially since there were plenty on the pier to choose from.

Grady looked out over the bar at his devoted regulars and friends. Every night, come rain or shine, six-thirty at the earliest, the same four guys started pouring in to wind down the day. Behr operated his own ferry boat to and from the mainland and islands for the tourists, and the occasional local. Gavin, Behr's longtime friend, was kin to the owners of the Portree Harbor Ferry terminal. Lachlan worked at the

Portree Medical Practice on Bank Street. Last, but not least, there was Patrick, Grady's ol' friend from childhood, who worked at the Portree Fire Station on Martin Crescent. Yep, if his ship was going down, these fine lads would go down, too, with a drink in their hands no doubt.

No, no, no! Grady thought, mentally shaking his head. He won't let down Catie, or these fine folks. He was just going to have to get off his miserable arse and think of something. Grady heard the pub door fly open with a crash and the mumbled curses that followed. He glanced over the four lads on their stools to a curious sight, the same four following his gaze to the door.

Fumbling over the doorstop, dripping wet with equally drenched luggage in tow, was a lost tourist if the looks of her were any indication. The lass looked around, gave a slight tilt of her head, and smirked. This was going to be an interesting night. By the look in her eyes, she was definitely no ordinary tourist. She lifted her head up and squared her shoulders before strolling across the room, mindful of the tables while struggling to maneuver her luggage around them. She successfully made her way up to the bar and set herself down on a stool in between Gavin and Behr.

She was a wee petite little thing, not more than five feet and four inches. Aye, and a pretty lass she was, with her raven black hair. It was long, straight, and shining like sheet metal. He took her in as she positioned her belongings close by. The lass was blessed with elegant features; her fair skin was the color of warm cream, with the palest hint of freckles, maybe four or five lightly dappled on each cheek. She blushed when she caught Grady staring, as did he.

The wee lass looked Grady straight in his eyes, dazzling him with hers. They were as green as the Isle countryside. She confidently ordered a hearty ale. Grady shuffled about, getting a pitcher and a dark rich brew to warm her drenched bones. Aye, a pitcher will do just fine, as he could see there was an interesting story to be told. He poured her a glass and placed the pitcher down by her mug. While she removed her damp overcoat, Grady found that she carried a delicate frame about her as well. She was thin but not skinny, with subtle curves that gave her body a softness he thought every woman should possess -- softness his Catie used to have.

With a look about, Grady could see he wasn't the only man interested in hearing about the wee lass' story. Even Gerard and Kristy were peeking their heads 'round the back, awaiting her tale. No one more so than Behr. Sitting to her right, a look of concern crossed his eyes, as did a flicker of attraction. He took his time and searched over her, from top to bottom. With that obvious gesture, Gavin flashed Behr an amused crooked smile. Grady smiled as well. Aye, there was something different about this girl.

Patrick nodded at their wee guest. "Ya movin' in, lass?" He chuckled dryly.

"With any luck, I just might," Ellora mumbled under her breath. Geez, wouldn't that just solve all her problems...

Ellora's Mother told her years ago that this small town was friendly with tourists, but guarded with any newcomers. She was going to have to open up to their curious questions and answer as honestly as she could. And just maybe, they would accept her enough to offer up a place to stay for the night. Otherwise, she was going to have to get real cozy on the bench seat in the corner. *Here goes nothing*, she thought. Taking a big swig of the rich, dark brown ale she'd been offered, she put on her most charming smile.

"My name's Ellora Belle Sutherland." She extended her hand to the short man with the balding reddish hair and kind blue eyes.

"Grady's m'name, Grady McAndrews, an' this 'ere's m'pub." He reached out and grabbed her hand, giving it a firm shake, and nodded his head in greeting.

"Aye, what's left o' it," teased an older brawny man that sat at the end of the bar.

"Aye, Patty, and there won't be much left o' you, if you don't mind your tongue," Grady snapped back.

"So, tell us your tale, lass. Should be a good 'en. A young filly like you hardly comes strolling into this pub, nae alone," observed the younger man to her left. He wore a crooked smile and had a cocky air about him. He was definitely a handsome man, almost too good looking. Definitely a pretty boy. He was tall and lean with an athletic build. Winking at the new girl flirtatiously, he ran his hands through his thick, brown unruly hair, the action making it stick up in spikes. Ellora was used to her parents' thick accents, but she found herself struggling to keep up with their fast-paced dialog. It didn't help that they kept interrupting each other, either.

"Geez, where do I begin?" Ellora asked out loud, mostly to herself. "My mother and father grew up here. They used to run a Bed and Breakfast right here on the pier. Whe..."

Grady interrupted her before she could even finish her sentence. "Is that right?"

"Well," Gavin butted in, "the only one running the B&B around here is Kristy, an' she's back there."

"Aye, that's the truth," Patrick jumped in. "You must be lost, woman, or sick with the rain soaking ya. So whatcha' doing 'ere?"

"Well," Ellora rushed, in a hurry to get the words out before she was interrupted again. "They left for New York when my mother found out she was pregnant with me. I think the B&B next door was the very same one my mother worked in. It looks just like the one she showed me in a picture once. I am a fool, though, for thinking it might still be vacant after all this time."

"Is that so?" Grady mumbled, deep in thought.

"Hmmm..." He rubbed his chin, looking up to the rafters then back at Ellora. He stared for an uncomfortable moment, searching for some unknown thing in her eyes. "What's the name o' your da and ma, love?" he questioned thoughtfully.

Ellora hesitated for just a brief moment before answering him. "My mother's name before she was married was BonniBelle MacLeod. My father's name was Joseph Michael Sutherland."

"BB and Joe, aye, so they did, twenty years or so ago. Patty, you remember, don'tcha? BB worked the Bed and Breakfast, and Joe at the hardware store. Aye, Joe could fix up anything that was broken faster than the rain could fall. High school sweethearts they were. I thought I recognized you a bit. You have the look of your ma, but I can see a bit of your da peekin' out," Grady observed excitedly.

Patrick gave an assertive nod. "Aye, they were good people. Many 'ere were sad to see 'em both off. Did they tell ya why they left so sudden, and hadn't even left a soul in charge?" he pressed her further.

Ellora was instantly relieved that these people not only knew her parents, but used to be good friends with them as well. Now that she wasn't blinded by her nerves, she actually remembered some of their names from the many stories she was told growing up. Responding to Patrick's previous question, she shook her head. "No, my father just told me he wanted his child to have more than what he had growing up. But my mother said it was his dream to go to the U.S. There were bigger and better opportunities that awaited him. She, on the other hand, loved it here. She told me so many times, and also how much she wanted to come back. She spoke of this town so fondly, which is the reason I decided to come here."

This answer was mixed with the truth and a lie. She had practiced her answer many times in her head, knowing she'd be asked. It was the truth, because her mother really was enamored with this town and always promised she'd bring Ellora here someday, and because she had always wanted to move here. But, it was a lie because those weren't the reasons she was standing there now.

"Didja nae bring 'em back with ya?" Gerard inquired as he came up from behind the kitchen to join the group. "I've a lot o' fond memories o' 'em growing up. They were a lively bunch."

Ellora's throat tightened up as she slowly shook her head. "They passed away a year ago," she choked out, trying her hardest not to cry in front of all these strangers. She squeezed her eyes shut as fresh tears threatened to fall against her will. The effort it took to force them back stung. Even the mention of their untimely death ripped Ellora's aching heart wide open, the agonizing pain still raw and never seeming to fully heal. No matter how many times she practiced or how hard she tried, Ellora would never *ever* get over their death.

"Jesus, Mary and Joseph," gasped Kristy, joining Gerard behind the bar. "May I ask how, sweeting?"

"Car crash," was all Ellora managed to reply. She dipped her head low so that they couldn't see the traitorous tears that snuck out against all her efforts to hold them back. After taking a few deep breaths to calm her nerves, she looked up.

"I'm their only child. I never quite felt like I fit in there, so I thought I would make a new start here. My mother's heart was in Portree, so I felt like she would be right here with me." That was half true. The other half of the reason was that Ellora was on the run from a true *monster*.

The man to her right, who she barely noticed because of how quiet he'd been, suddenly let out a low grumbling huff. He put his hands on his temples and leaned on the bar with his elbows. His jaw muscles ticked in frustration. Slowly, he picked his head up and looked right at Ellora, studying her from head to toe. His eyebrows pinched together as he searched for something in her eyes. Ellora nervously fidgeted with her hands under the heavy weight of his intense scrutiny. His eyes seemed to penetrate through her bullshit story and see the truth. His attention made her extremely uncomfortable. After a few more breathless moments, a look of familiar grief showed in his haunting pale blue eyes. Relieved, Ellora convinced herself that she must've imagined the whole encounter.

"I'm truly sorry for the loss o' your parents, and the

grief it has caused you, love. That's a terrible thing..." He trailed off. His voice was so alarmingly deep it almost startled her. Finally, Ellora was able to take in the stranger next to her. She realized for the first time how huge this man was, easily reaching six and a half feet tall and at least two-hundred twenty pounds of powerful muscle. His physique proved that he was no stranger to manual labor. This man's powerful build was obviously the result of working very hard his whole life. He had broad defined shoulders and a wide sculpted chest that could be seen easily through the thin material of his long sleeved shirt. Ellora continued to stare as he pushed his sleeves up to his elbows. She watched the movement, her gaze traveling up until she finally met his eyes. He stared unabashedly back at her, the intensity of his stare so powerful she had to look away. She could still feel him staring in her peripheral vision. Her face grew warm as a blush crept up her cheeks.

He turned away after a few tense moments ticked by and gazed off at nothing, a far-away look shadowing his eyes. Ellora took in the rest of him without the scrutiny of his stare. He was an extremely attractive man. His thick, dark brown hair was shorter than Gavin's spikes, which he wore lying down and brushed forward. His straight angled nose and square jaw, donning a bit of trimmed stubble, gave him a rugged yet clean-cut look. Unlike today's pretty-boy man-scapers of the world, this man was the ideal, all-powerful alpha male that women drooled over. But his eyes were what captured Ellora's attention. They were pale and hauntingly light blue, made even more striking with the help of his thick, dark lashes. She could get lost in them.

She had to know his name. When she remembered that she could in fact talk, she stammered her question timidly. "Thank you for saying that, Mr...?" With eyebrows raised, she waited for him to tell her his name.

This magnificent looking man slowly turned his head, and the soft look he gave Ellora made her feel as if someone sucked the air out of her lungs. "M'name's Behr, Behr Buchanan, Miss Sutherland." When he smiled at her, the whole world seemed to stand still.

"Please, call me Ellora... Behr? Your name's Behr?" *Geez, with a name like that, he was destined to be big*, she thought, inwardly giggling. Ellora was startled when the others started talking. She had completely forgotten anyone else was there.

"Aye, his mum could think nae better a name for a ten pound babe." Gavin poked fun at Behr, reaching around her to jab his friend, laughing. Ellora smirked at the both of them as the room lightened up with an up roarish laugh. She was grateful for the change in subject. The conversation had been heading in a dark place she didn't want to open up about. Any topic was better than her personal life.

"Well now, m'sweet, where'll you be stayin'?" Kristy inquired with a kind motherly tone.

Ellora let out a frustrated sigh and broke the news. "I

don't seem to have anywhere to stay. I've walked up and down the Pier, both Quay Street and Beaumont Crescent. I'm told that the spring season is when all the tourists flood the area, and most places are booked through summer. I guess I might check other lodges around town tomorrow, but I'm not sure what I'm going to do tonight."

"You're in luck, m'dear. All these row buildings 'ave three or four floors to 'em. This 'en 'ere your standing in has three floors. The second floor has two cozy flats, and the third is one large flat. They're nae modern in their furnishings, but all's clean and well kept. Aye, and one o' the best views in town, she has. It'll do just fine," Kristy asserted, not bothering to ask Grady for permission.

Ellora looked over to Grady; she didn't want to get too excited over the offer. What if Grady didn't want any guests? She didn't want to over-step her bounds. "I don't want to trouble you …"

Kristy interrupted her and insisted sternly, "He willnae refuse you, sweeting. You're nae trouble to anyone here. Now, you are our guest, so relax yourself. How 'bout something hot to eat? You are soaked to the core, and I dinnae want you catching your death." Ellora's stomach picked that moment to growl so loudly that Kristy's eyebrows flew up in surprise. She shook her head and snickered. "Aye, that answered ma' question sure enough. I'll 'ave some hot stew brought out for you, dear."

"Gerard, you heard the woman. Best put that apron on

an' get to it, man," Patrick shouted, egging him on.

She sat up straighter and called out after them, "No, please, you don't have to do this. I have no way of paying you for room and board, or the meal. I was hoping to find somewhere vacant to crash for tonight, and go into town in the morning to try to find myself a job." There, she finally said it. Now, hopefully they wouldn't kick her out on her butt altogether. But just in case, Ellora gulped down the rest of her delicious brew.

"I'll nae 'ave BB's only borne soaked an' starving under m'roof," Kristy stated with her hands on her hips, like she was offended by Ellora's statement in some way.

Grady moved around the bar and stood in front of Ellora. He gently grasped her hand in his and put his other hand on top. Patting it gently, he confessed in a warm fatherly voice, "I've got this big ol' place, ya see, and nae a soul to fill it. With your da and ma gone, God rest their souls, I would be proud to look after you for as long as you need. Joseph would do nae less for any o' us, had we needed him to."

Ellora thought of her father's kind and generous nature at that moment. She could almost hear his voice whispering in her ear as she looked around the bar, noticing its sad state, and got an idea. She knew exactly what he'd do if *he* was in her shoes. "Thank you, Grady. I'm grateful to you, and touched to know my parents knew such great friends. But, I guess I'm too much like my father, because I cannot accept handouts. So, I was thinking we could work out a trade."

Grady raised an eyebrow at her, so she took that as a sign to go on.

"My father was a wonderful handyman here, and when they moved to New York, he expanded that skill into becoming a very knowledgeable and successful contractor. He renovated old warehouses and factories in downtown Syracuse into beautiful apartments and condos, and he always took me on site with him. When I was old enough, I worked side by side with my father on every project. I could fix this pub back up to how it ought to be in return for meals and a place to stay."

The bar went quiet, and all the patrons looked at one another. Patrick and Gerard looked down at their hands or drink with disbelief in their eyes. Gavin, the man to Ellora's left, just winked at her with a cocky grin on his face. Behr's eyes warmed over the broodiness he'd been sporting the whole night. He smiled appreciatively and nodded his head, as if he liked what he heard. Grady smiled a big toothy grin and opened his mouth to say something, when Patrick interrupted. "Grady disnae need his toes painted, lass," he instigated, laughing gruffly. "He needs a renovation, an' I dinnae think your nail-file is up for the task."

Gerard joined him in mocking laughter, but was just as quickly rebuffed when Kristy shot him a menacing scowl.

"Aye, and the next thing you're gonna tell me is

you 'ave a pretty pink tool belt," Patrick ridiculed.

Ellora's face reddened, in embarrassment and resentment. But she put on a smile, remembering her mother telling her stories about how Scots loved a good taunt and a challenge. *Ha! Two can play at this game*, she told herself.

"Actually," she proclaimed, lifting her head high. "I do have a pink tool belt that my father gave me, but I was looking to get a different one. Pink is more *your* color than mine." Ellora eyed him up and down in a calculated way, trying hard not to laugh. "I'll give it to you and teach you a thing or two about how to work power tools while I'm at it." Stroking her chin with her thumb and forefinger, she made a point of staring at his mid-section. She pointed at his gut then and swirled her finger. "Looks like you could use the training exercises, too. And, no, liquid workouts don't count! That spare tire of yours will definitely get in the way of the truly magnificent belt. Let me know when you're ready to man up, and then I'll walk you through it." Ellora winked at him teasingly.

Patrick threw his head back and roared out a hearty belly laugh, as did everyone else.

"Ah, Ellora, a smartass ye are. You'll fit in 'ere just fine." With a crooked smile, Patrick nodded at Grady. "She's a wee feisty lass. She'll fit in 'ere just fine. Patrick's m'name. I work at the Portree firehouse. Aye, I do know a thing or two o' tools, but red is more m'color, lass."

"If Miss Sutherland is anything like her father was, I'd wager a bet she could 'ave this place turned 'round in the blink o' an eye. Aye, I bet she could do just that."

Ellora turned her head in the direction the voice was coming from, to a neatly put together man in his mid-thirties. His dark chestnut hair was cut close to his head and smoothed down, not a hair out of place. He was clean shaven with an average height and thin build. His features were very classically handsome, she decided, as he strode toward her from the other end of the bar with a professional gait.

He reached out his hand. "I'm pleased to meet you. M'name is Lachlan Sinclair, miss, and I'm the head doctor over at the Portree Medical Practice. It's good to get a fresh new face to brighten the town o' all these old buzzards here." He smiled as he grasped hold of her hand, and in a professionally polite manner, he shook it.

"Thank you, Dr. Sinclair. Please, everyone, call me Ellora."

"Aye, and you may call me Lachlan. Well, since you will be staying 'ere with us for a while, let me hang this damp coat up for ya. It's doing you nae good keeping your lap wet, an' I willnae need any late night patients keeping me from ma' bed tonight."

He seized her coat, folded it over his arm neatly, and marched over to the front corner of the bar. Old rusty hooks hung precariously from the wall. Lachlan placed her coat on the middle one then turned and bowed his head. "Well, lads,

I best be off. I've a busy day in the morn', but I'll see you all at dusk.

"G'night, doc," Grady tossed at him, before he shuffled back behind the bar to start his cleaning-up routine.

Lachlan met Ellora's eyes. "I know I'll be seeing you, too, Ellora. 'Ave a good night." With that, he lifted the thick collar of his trench coat up around his neck and stepped out into the rain.

Ellora's head was spinning from the long exhausting day and the overwhelming banter at this pub. She was relieved when Kristy snatched the bowl of stew from Gerard and set it down in front of her, and she was convinced that nothing in the world smelled as good as this stew did to her. Ellora was *starving.* She noticed, as she looked down, that her hands were shaking, having not eaten since late the night before. Rushing to get the first flight out of Syracuse was obviously more important at the time. But as of right now, she was ready to eat her own hand.

"Just look at her. 'Ave you not eaten today, m'sweet? *GER!*" she shouted before Ellora could answer her back. "Fetch her some o' that fresh loaf you've got back there."

Ellora wolfed down her meal, hardly tasting it in her hungry state. She just sat back and listened to the guys laugh and taunt each other. Their voices rose as they all relived the stories about the crazy things they used to do growing up. One story in particular had Ellora's ears prick up and listen; she remembered her father telling all the same exact stories. But, this one in particular was one of his favorites.

Gerard looked over at Ellora, capturing her attention.

"One long lazy summer night, we were all hangin' about, bored and looking for trouble. Well, your mother," Gerard pointed directly at Ellora, "as well as Catie and Kristy over there, all dared each other to break into the high school to go skinny dippin' in the indoor pool. O' course, they threatened us to stay put and keep our peeping eyes to ourselves or they'd cut off important parts o' our anatomy." He and the others laughed heartily as they recalled the memory.

"Well, in order to get there quicker, we had to cut through several backyards. The last house shared a fence with the school, and belonged to *the crazy guy*. We never knew his real name, but the whole town called him that. He was bat-shit crazy and used to talk to himself, yelling at people who weren't really there. When the girls tiptoed through his yard, *the crazy guy* came running out, shaking his fist at 'em and threatening to kill anyone who walked through his yard again." Gerard mimicked the movements and shouted belligerently, making the story all the more entertaining.

"So, the girls made it over the fence and in the school, making good on their dare. O' course, then we lads snuck in after 'em to enjoy the view, threats be damned! It was Patty's idea here, to steal away their clothes and make a run for it." Patrick lifted his head up high and raised his mug, obviously still proud of his idea. Gerard imitated the girls squealing their surprise. "They jumped out, wrapping towels around 'em as they went chasing after us. We raced back through *the crazy guy's* yard, drawing his attention through the window. By the time the girls made their way through his yard, BB got her bare feet stuck in the mud. *The crazy guy* came bolting out after 'em, threatening to yank away their towels as punishment for ruining his grass."

Ellora laughed so hard at Gerard's very vivid account of the story that she spit some of her soup out of her mouth. She thought that was his goal all along.

"Well, there was no way on God's green Earth that Joseph was ever going to tolerate anyone else seeing his girl's naked body but him! Coming to her rescue, he scooped her up and ran as fast as his legs could carry him. *The crazy guy* ran after 'em, hot on their heels and screaming like a lunatic. Joseph double-timed his efforts, running so hard he ran right out o' his shoes!"

Ellora was laughing so hard her cheeks burned from smiling so much. Gerard told this story just like her father used to, with over-exaggerated details, sound effects, and lots of flailing hand gestures. After the laughter died down a little, Gerard concluded the story. "We got away, o' course. But the next time we went by his house, *the crazy guy* made it a point to march around the border o' his yard wearing Joseph's shoes!"

Ellora took in the lively group belly laughing around her, finally feeling the first real sense of family since sitting at the dinner table with her parents. She decided to jump into the fun, especially since Gerard left out the funniest part of the story.

"Yes, my father told me this story many times. But I'm surprised that you left out the best part… when Kristy was left with only a hand towel to cover herself. It barely covered the front of her, and the rest of Skye saw her bare behind as she ran through the neighborhood." Ellora laughed harder when Kristy snapped her head so quickly in her direction, she thought for sure it'd snap right off.

Kristy gasped in an exaggerated high-pitched tone, blood colored her neck and cheeks. "Oh no, she dinnae tell you that? She swore she wouldnae tell a soul. Aye, my bum was much better to look at back then."

"I certainly didn't mind the view!" Gerard bravely confessed, dodging Kristy as she tried to slap him.

They all resumed their taunts and teasing for the remainder of the evening. A few insults were hurled at Ellora as she scarfed down her food in a very unlady-like fashion. She barely heard a "don't mistake your fingers for chips, love" or something along those lines. All she could hear was the loud crunching and slurping noise in her ears as she chewed. She should've felt embarrassed, because she probably looked like a hobo, scarfing down her food like she was.

In that moment, she thought of how her mom would've slapped her on the side of the head and *tsk'd* at her for not being lady-like. One of the only arguments they'd ever had was of her tom-boy ways. She would've rather been in the garage with her father than playing Barbies and dress-up with her mother. God, she missed her mom terribly. Once again, she felt a devastating emptiness inside of her. She would never get over their loss. She felt truly alone in this world. She had no one.

She slowed down when her stomach began to feel full. Ellora realized that she was hovering over her bowl, as if protecting it from being taken away. Finally remembering her manners, she sat up straight. That's when she noticed that Behr wasn't talking animatedly with his hands and laughing with the others, but sat turned toward Ellora on the stool. One arm rested on his lap, his thumb tapped a rhythm only he could hear, while the other arm leaned on the bar by his elbow. He ran his hand through his hair repeatedly, staring straight at her, and making no move to hide it, when she looked back at him.

"Umm, sorry," Ellora mumbled low enough that no one else heard her.

"Why the apology, love?" Behr asked in a deep husky voice, just above a whisper. His eyes searched hers, then all around her face, which made her blush.

"For my disgusting manners… I was just so hungry. Umm, that *is* why you are staring at me, right?"

He tilted his head slightly and slowly shook his head *no*.

"Okaaay," Ellora remarked, dragging out the syllables. *His mom should've taught him that it was bad manners to stare*, she thought to herself.

"Why you runnin', love?" he questioned curiously, a serious look plastered across his face.

Whaaaaat! She almost spit out the stew. His comment threw her completely off guard.

"What do you mean, Behr?" She could feel the blood drain from her face.

Behr leaned forward, getting uncomfortably close. Their knees touched as he confessed his suspicions. "I mean, you flew all the way out 'ere, to a place you've never been before, from America, without even booking accommodations to stay in ahead of time. All your hopes rested on a building your mother worked at twenty or more years ago. You hoped it would still be vacant or abandoned so you could sleep there. You've nae money for your visit, and it's clear you 'avenae eaten in a long while. Besides, you mentioned you 'avin' to start looking for a job in the morn'. These are things people plan in advance, so they are settled when they get to where they're goin'. It seems to me, you up'd yourself and left in a big hurry. The way you've been holding on to that luggage o' yours with a death grip, I'd venture a guess that it holds all the belongings you 'ave."

He'd caught on. Ellora was relieved that he said this in hushed tones so that no one else heard his presumption, which was spot on, and that he was the only one who noticed. Yet this was a story she couldn't tell. She took a deep breath and did her best to fake nonchalance.

"What are you, a cop?" she forced a snicker.

"Nae, lass, I'm no copper."

Still very wary, and a little paranoid after all she'd been through, Ellora decided to choose her words carefully. These people automatically gained a bit of her respect, because her father had always trusted them, but she still struggled with *trust.* Ellora decided she'd only give a sugar-coated version of this story, especially to this man who kept catching her off guard. She'd definitely have to watch herself around him.

Ellora gave a non-committal shrug and sighed. "I was just sick of where I was living, and all the people there. With my parents gone, there was no reason good enough to keep me there. I felt overwhelmed with all the reminders I was getting on a constant basis, still living in that house. It was emotional torture for me. So I made a rash, spontaneous decision to leave and start over. Just as they did, when they left here."

Behr's face said it all; he didn't like the idea of Ellora being all alone. She could read his expressions as easily as she could read a book. This man held nothing back. "Is there nae man in your life, love, that cares for you?" She just scrunched her eyebrows together at that question, and he continued. "A husband? Boyfriend?"

She snorted out a laugh at that question, then responded. "No, neither." Not if she could help it anyways.

Behr nodded his head and chewed on his lip for a

moment, as if considering Ellora's answer. He looked up at her and asked, "Did they nae leave their only daughter anything at all to live on?"

Ellora's stomach tied itself in knots from the direction their conversation was going. Nothing seemed to get past this guy, and some of the others were looking their way, curious of their private conversation.

"I... I get my inheritance when I turn twenty-five. My father set this up in the hopes of me finishing college by then," Ellora stammered out, worried the others would join in on the interrogation.

"Is that the way o' it? Hmmm, and how old are you, love, if you don't mind my asking?"

"Well, it hasn't stopped you yet," Ellora bit out, irritation clear in her tone. "I'm twenty-three." She shook like a leaf at his line of questions. Talking about herself was completely out of her comfort zone.

Behr nodded once more. He looked around the bar, then back at Ellora, and winked. "Aye, we better find you a job then, eh, love?"

She sighed a breath of relief as Behr let the subject drop. The tension in her shoulders eased a little.

Kristy slapped her hand on the bar top and yelled out at them, "Hey, dunnae you go scaring off our girl, Behr. I dunnae know what you're telling her, but she's got the look o' a ghost on her face. She's so pale. Aye, she said she's stayin', so she isnae gonna disappear on us this night."

"Aye, Grizzly, you can flirt with her in the morn'," Gavin teased his friend. "C'mon, you big grizzly bear, let's be off."

"Nuh uh, oooooh, no ya don't. And just where do the two o' you think you're goin'?" Kristy commanded.

Behr and Gavin shot each other a sideways glance and looked back at the authority in the room.

"Where's your manners, lads? You're gonna help Miss Ellora to the second floor with that heavy luggage. And you, pretty boy…" She swiveled, causing her curly hair to whip behind her as she gestured to Gavin. "You will bring the food I set aside for Ellora, and bring it up to stock her fridge. I'll bring up clean linens and other items she'll be needin' straight away."

Ellora took a few more bites of her food and wiped her mouth. As she got ready to stand, Gavin and Behr walked up behind her. Both reached out for her luggage to help. They stopped short, and the stand-off began.

"Nay, brother, I've got it covered. You and Ellora go on ahead. You can show her the way," Gavin insisted with an arrogant lopsided grin.

"And sprain that delicate wrist o' yours, pretty boy? I'd think better o' it if I were in your spot. You've got all that hard back-breaking labor awaiting you t'morrow at the terminal. Aye, n' a hard job o' typing and answering phones you'd have with such an injury."

Towering over him with mock challenge, a smile

tugging at Behr's lips as he arched an eyebrow. Behr grabbed the heavy luggage and tossed it over his shoulder like it weighed no more than a bar towel.

"Aye, smartass, that be the plan I had all along. Come, Ellora, I will show you the way."

Gavin dropped both hands on Ellora's delicate shoulders, and the unexpected contact made her jump up and flinch away. Gasping, she sucked in a quick breath then blew it out forcefully. She silently cursed herself when a whimper escaped her lips. She was still so skittish, not ready for any kind of contact yet. Especially from a man -- no matter how kind the gesture. But she also wasn't ready to explain why she felt that way either, so in the meantime, she was going to have to school her emotional reactions and remain guarded. Hopefully they would get the hint.

A growl-like sound came out of Behr's throat. He shot Gavin a hard look. Gavin held up both hands in surrender. "Sorry, Ellora, I didn't mean to give you a start."

Gavin and Behr shared a look. "Is everything all right, love?" Behr probed in a gentle voice.

"Yes, I'm sorry. It's just been a long crazy day. I just need some sleep, that's all."

Behr walked over to Ellora, carefully watching her every move. "All right, love, this way." He shifted the luggage onto his shoulder, and lowered his other arm to the small of her back. This large imposing man gently led her to the back right corner of the bar. They walked down a narrow hallway that led to an old set of stairs.

"I'll go with Kristy and gather up the food," Gavin shouted out to them as he made his way around the bar into the back.

The steps were steep, narrow, and dark. She couldn't see Behr behind her, and she couldn't imagine how he was even able to fit in there, let alone handle the luggage. They made their way to the landing. To her left, there was a long hallway with an old carpeted runner and two doors, one on either side of the hall. Straight ahead of the landing was another set of stairs that led to the third floor. She walked down the hall and stopped in between both doors.

"Oh, I forgot to ask Grady which room I could use." Behr stopped directly behind her and set the luggage down.

"You have your pick, love." He smiled. Leaning down to her ear, he acted like he was telling her a big secret, saying softly, "I'd take the one through this door." He motioned toward the one on the left. "It has the best view o' the Harbor, and has newer furnishings." His breath tickled her ear, raising goosebumps on her skin.

"SOLD!" She clapped her hands excitedly. Reaching up above the door jam, Behr grabbed an old dusty key. Ellora wondered how long it'd been since anyone had used this room.

Behr unlocked and swung open the door. They both stepped inside, and Ellora walked past him to stand in the center of the room. Turning in a wide circle, she looked at him and laughed. She quickly covered her mouth with her hand to stop herself. "I thought you said it had new furniture."

He laughed, too. "I knew you'd say that. Aye, it does. The room 'cross the way has furnishings far older than this, and no view at all."

The furniture and décor was old, worn, and dated. But the flat had a warm, cozy, lived-in feeling to it. Ellora beamed with excitement. "I love it!"

Turning her back to Behr, she looked out the three large windows. They were evenly separated, with frilly, pale yellow curtains that cascaded down to the floor. Underneath each window was a padded window seat. On the opposite side of the room, floral wallpaper with yellow daisies covered the wall. In the center was an antique queen-sized bed, facing the spectacular view. The frame was a rich dark wood. Thick, ornately carved posts stood guard on all four corners. Two side tables, small looking in comparison to the bed, were placed on either side. Tall, skinny lamps sat on top. Above the bed was an oil painting of the colorful pier houses and the harbor at sunset.

Ellora slowly walked in a circle, taking in every detail of the room. The hardwood floors were in desperate need of sanding and resealing. They were cracked, splintered, and dry with thick matted-down throw rugs draped over them. When facing the windows, a door to the wash room was to the right. It housed a tiny stand-up shower, toilet, and a pedestal sink. A kitchenette consisting of a tiny fridge, sink, and cooktop was located to the right of the washroom.

This was home. A burst of excitement tingled through her for the first time in a long while. Ellora turned, remembering that she left Behr standing in the entryway with her luggage. He stood watching her with a warm, genuine smile on his face. She smiled back at him, and slowly looked away when she realized he wouldn't.

"You look pleased with this room. There's a bright, beautiful twinkle in your eye, love." Ellora's stomach turned with unease from his attention. Before she could comment on his compliment, he quickly added, "Where would you like me to set your stuff down?"

"Anywhere is fine, Behr. Don't trouble yourself. And thank you."

Ellora skipped over and knelt down to unzip her large luggage. Reaching in, she felt around for what she was searching for. After a moment, she yanked out her neon pink tool belt. Placing it on the nightstand, she shot a devilish grin up at Behr.

"Aye, you werenae kiddin' 'round when you said it was pink, were ya?" Chuckling, he ran his large hands through his hair.

Ellora shook her head side to side playfully. "Nope! I plan on getting right to work tomorrow."

Behr rubbed his stubble with his thumb and forefinger, deep in thought. "Why'd you bring a tool belt with you on your travels, Lor?"

Ellora took a moment to appreciate the nickname he used and how much she enjoyed hearing it fall from his lips. Her father used to call her that, too.

"I plan on staying. This is my home now. I wasn't kidding when I said I'd be looking for a job, so I'll need this. I plan on fixing up this place first, since it desperately needs it." Boy, wasn't *that* the understatement of the year!

Behr stood silent for a few more moments, analyzing her, trying hard to figure her out. He proudly wore his expressions out in the open. He clearly had no fear of holding them back. Ellora suddenly felt naked under his intense inspection. She trembled as time seemed to stand still. A heavy foreboding weighed her down as she finally realized that they were all alone up there. After everything that'd happened, she didn't know what was worse -- being there all alone *with* him, or just being all *alone.* Those feelings warred inside of her, because on one hand, she liked the feeling of having another person around her. It made her feel safe. But on the other hand, she also felt very anxious and apprehensive when alone with someone else. The last time she was in a room alone with someone, she barely made it out alive.

Reading Ellora's growing fear, Behr released her from his paralyzing glare. He blinked several times, snapping himself out of whatever thought was in that head of his.

He sucked in a deep breath, letting it out in a big huff.

Slowly, he walked toward her. Warily, Ellora stepped back. Her eyes grew wide, silently begging him to keep his distance. Not to be detoured by her reaction, Behr cautiously inched closer. The look in his eyes was assuring and careful, promising her that he meant no harm. Her retreat halted when her calves hit the back of the bed. Panic grew slowly inside of her as he continued forward. She did not like the feeling of being trapped or cornered. She had to keep reminding herself over and over that that's not what he was doing. Ellora's breathing rapidly increased, making her dizzy. Feeling the presence of a man this close caused her stomach to churn. Her fear took over as she became increasingly lightheaded and nauseous; she was getting very close to passing out. Noticing her distress and growing discomfort, Behr held both his hands up in a peaceful manner. Ellora fought to gain control of herself, breaking out into cold sweats with the effort, mentally repeating to herself , *keep calm... don't freak out*, as Behr approached in her personal space.

Tilting his head to the side, Behr gave her an assertive nod. She had to crane her neck back to look up at him. Behr was unnervingly close, so close she could smell his rustic cologne waft all around her like a warm blanket. The scent was sensual and somehow familiar, comforting in a way. It soothed her frantic nerves and helped her get herself together, because deep down, she knew this man was of no threat to her. She didn't know how she knew this -- she simply did -- but her body's natural reaction to this situation was a different story. She steadied her breathing by taking several large gulps of air and forcing it in and out slowly. Her heart was pounding hard and fast, like a bass drum, and she was sure Behr could see it hammering inside her chest.

He placed his hand on her shoulder. The moment of contact had Ellora instinctively holding her breath. She froze on the spot, like a deer in headlights. Behr softly ran his hand down the length of her arm. "I dinnae know what's got you runnin' in a scared panic, love, but you'll be safe here. We take care o' our own, and just as your parents were, you are one o' us." His concerned statement thawed a piece of ice off of her heart. It was exactly what she needed to hear in that very tense moment.

It took all of her willpower not to shake his hand off of her. Oddly enough, she didn't *want* to pull away from him. She was confused. He searched her eyes, unwillingly sucking Ellora into his soulful gaze. The tension between them switched from frightened apprehension to something else... something completely foreign to her. Longing maybe? Behr softly ran his thumb in lazy circles on the inside of her elbow. Her heart skipped a beat at his tender touch, and fluttered away inside her chest. She felt heat spread across her cheeks as she blushed. She *never* blushed. This had been such a weird day.

Behr leaned into her. "Ellora, I..."

Just then, Gavin and Kristy burst through the door

noisily, with supplies in hand.

She quickly stepped to the side, breaking the physical contact she shared with Behr, and ran over to help Kristy with the linens.

"Are we interruptin' you, Behr? Dinnae stop on my account," Gavin teased, wiggling his eyebrows suggestively.

Ellora's face had now turned crimson; she could feel it brighten like a beacon. Behr grit his teeth and stalked out the door without another word. Gavin walked over and set down the food on her small kitchen counter. Turning to go after Behr, Gavin stopped short and turned around to face the girls. "Dinnae let the Grizzly confuse you, lass. He's nae used to being 'round a pretty sort like you. He's nae the datin' kind."

Shrugging her shoulders, Ellora told him that it was really none of her business.

"Kristy, darlin', I'll see you t'morrow, and a g'night to you, Ellora." Gavin stepped backwards out the door, saluting.

"Out with ya, Boyle," Kristy shouted at him. She finished putting fresh sheets and pillowcases on Ellora's bed like a doting mother. Once the boys were out of the room, Kristy walked around the bed, grabbing her hand. "You know, after that skinny dipping fiasco, your mother n' I were grounded for a couple weeks." She turned her head as her eyes started to water. Looking out the window, a small smile crept across her face. "I used to sneak over to her house next door, when it was her father's B&B anyway. Bonni would throw knotted sheets out the window so I could climb up on, just like in the movies, so I could spend the night. We did this almost every night while we were supposed to stay locked up in our rooms." She paused for a moment to wipe away a tear. "She was m'best friend, her and Catie both. I'm so glad you're here with us now."

Kristy gave Ellora a brief, tight hug and kissed her on the cheek before high-tailing it out of the room. Her motherly hug and kiss didn't bother her so much. She realized that these people didn't believe in personal boundaries, and they were all testing her patience by continuously invading her space. Maybe their overly-friendly ways would force her to get over her fears. Making her way into the washroom with her sleep shorts and cami, all Ellora could think about was getting some sleep.

After Ellora's heavenly, steaming hot shower had calmed and soothed her rattled nerves enough, letting the water slowly turn cold, she reluctantly stepped out. With the speed of a stubborn turtle, Ellora got ready for bed. *Finally.* She was more than ready to turn in, and her dated bed looked like a precious gift sent down from heaven. Her lids drooped heavily, and her full stomach had her practically falling asleep while standing. As she crawled into bed, a knock at the door sent her jumping out of the bed and hiding in the corner. She let the dark shadows hide her as she sat shivering with her adrenaline kicked into high gear.

Ellora looked around the second floor apartment, frantically looking for a way out.

Another knock sounded. "It's just me, love. Sorry if I woke you."

Behr. "Oh thank God!" Ellora whispered to herself, sagging against the wall. It took a minute to relax her breathing and regulate her heart enough that Behr wouldn't notice her moment of panic. She walked on shaky legs to the door. Opening it a tiny hairline crack, Ellora peeked out of it. Behr was running his hand through his hair, his roped muscles flexing with every move. He leaned on the door jam with the other. He was obviously deep in thought, because he hadn't noticed her peering out at him. After another moment and one more deep breath, Ellora cleared her throat, capturing his attention. "Yes, Behr?"

Behr snapped his head up at the sound of her soft voice. He dropped his hands and straightened his posture. "Is everything all right, love? I thought I heard you cry out. I hope it wasnae me who frightened you?" He narrowed his eyes through the tiny slit in the door, worry written all over his face.

"No, everything is fine, Behr. Thank you for asking. Can I help you with something?" Ellora added the last question quickly, because it looked like he was going to drill her with more concerned inquiries and she didn't want him to be distracted. She wanted to know why he was back up here.

Behr lifted up one dark brow, knowing full well that she was avoiding his concern. He let it drop. "Well, I thought, after all the excitement from today and overwhelming people downstairs, that you'd be reluctant in coming down the stairs in the morning." He paused for a moment and smiled up at her. "So I thought you might 'ave a need for your very own coffee maker." She watched as the large man bent down to pick up the beloved machine. That machine paired with his smile did funny things deep in her stomach.

Ellora couldn't hide the extremely elated smile that spread across her face. How did he know that coffee was her obsession in life? Caffeine was a necessary evil if she even wanted to think about starting her day off on the right track. "Oh, Behr! Thank you so much. This is perfect. I appreciate this more than you know."

Ellora was going to tell him that he didn't have to do this, but quickly kept that to herself. She didn't want him taking it away from her. After all, coffee early in the morning was a necessity. Behr lifted an eyebrow as he stood there holding the machine, waiting. She didn't want to let him in this time. What if he started in on the intense questions and concerns? He obviously saw through all her bullshit stories, and she was too tired to make one up on the fly. "Umm, could you just leave it by the door? I'm in my PJs over here." Ellora cracked a satisfied grin when Behr's face reddened.

"Oh, yeah, o' course, love. My apologies. I'm sorry if I woke you."

Ellora giggled breathlessly at the sight of Behr. He was obviously beating himself up. "No, I was headed there… but, hadn't quite made it there yet." Ellora watched as Behr nodded and set her heavenly machine on the floor. When he stood, he was rubbing the thick stubble on his chin, looking like he was having an internal debate about something. Her curiosity got the better of her. Besides, she didn't want him scaring the crap out of her later, if or when he decided to come knocking to ask. "What's on your mind, Behr?" Her voice was a soft whisper, as sleep was pulling her under even as she stood.

"Ellora, I will be right down stairs with Grady for most o' the night… If you need anything, anything at all, coffee filters, mugs…" They both smiled at his attempt to lighten his very serious offer. "Please, dinnae hesitate. Just ask me, and it's yours. Whatever you're going through, you dinnae 'ave to go it alone. I'm 'ere for you, to help in any way I can. All right, love? 'Ave a good night's sleep Lor. I *will* see you t'morrow."

Ellora watched him walk down the hall through the crack in the door. When he was out of sight, she opened the door and picked up the glorious liquid-heaven maker. She couldn't help but think about the big magnificent man that just marched his way into her life. Her stomach flipped nervously when his smiling face entered her thoughts again. She hugged her present tightly in her arms. What was she going to do about him? She couldn't wait to find out!

3

Symphony Place Hotel and Condominiums Downtown Syracuse (Former Hotel Syracuse)
Top floor high rise office
10:37pm

Dalton

A buzzer sounds.

"Yes, Susan?" he barked into the line.

"Mr. Antonelli is here to see you, sir."

"Thank you, Susan. Show him in."

A tall blond in a light grey blouse and pinstripe pencil skirt led the gentleman into the office. "Mr. Antonelli, Dalton Ramsey Claiborne III." Susan made the introductions.

"Aaah, Dominick Antonelli, thank you for coming so late, and on such short notice." Dalton clapped him on the shoulder.

Dominick nodded with authority. "Mr. Claiborne." They shook hands firmly, and Dalton turned to the blonde.

"Thank you, Susan. You may go home for the night."

"Yes, sir." She hurried out of the room, closing the

door behind her.

"Come, Mr. Antonelli, have a seat. I've called you here today as a matter of extreme importance. You have always been my top investigator for high risk business negotiations, but now I need your services on a personal matter."

"Whatever you ask of me, Mr. Claiborne, I am at your disposal. What do you need me to find for you, sir?"

"Not a what... a whom," Dalton corrected. "She's the daughter of the recently deceased CEO of Downtown Renovations and Corporate Development Opportunities Group. We were planning a nineteen-million dollar rehabilitation project, using a former office building that was scheduled to be refurbished into *Metropolitan Lifestyle* condos. He was the best corporate rehab developer in the city. When he died, all my investors walked away, fearing incompletion, and took my initial investment with them. I have planned assets that are tied up with that girl. Unfortunately, she has disappeared. I need *you* to track down her whereabouts immediately!" With an arrogant stride, Dalton walked over to his desk and grabbed an envelope.

"Yes, sir, I'll start tonight," Dominick agreed. He could always use the money. It'd been a while since Dalton called on him for anything.

"Excellent." The self-important suited man tossed the thick manila envelope at Dominick. "Everything you need to know about her is in there." He crossed his arms over his chest with confidence.

Dominick opened the envelope and took a quick look inside. "Ellora Belle Sutherland. Hmm… not a problem, sir. I'll get right on it." This case already sounded more interesting than what he usually did for him.

"Thank you, Mr. Antonelli. I trust you can see yourself out." Dalton pointed at the door, not caring in the least if he came across rude. Dominick was beneath him, after all, and Dalton loved to go out of his way to make that clear with everyone he came into contact with.

"Of course, sir. I will contact you when I have any new leads or news." With that, they shook hands, concluding their meeting. Dominick swiftly marched out, happy to be out of the presence of this asshole.

Dalton walked around his chair, behind the immense mahogany desk, dragging his fingers aimlessly along the massive expanse of bookshelves, deep in thought. He strode past the entire wall of books behind him, where he paced methodically back and forth along the wall of windows at the back of his office. Irritation morphed into blind anger, his blood pressure rising as well as his temper. His rage sent a prickling sensation up the length of his spine and into his scalp. Seething, Dalton ran both hands through his hair, slicking it back in frustration.

"Damn bitch!" he hissed through clenched teeth.

Dalton took his frustrations out on his expensive suit,

attacking the buttons roughly. Stripped out of it, he tossed the jacket over the back of the club chair in the center of the room.

"You just wait until I find you, Ellora. You'll learn what happens when you try to run from me!" he gritted out through clenched teeth. He rolled up the sleeves of his designer shirt, anger elevating his temperature.

"You made a big mistake turning down my proposition... *No. One. Refuses. Me.* If it's a game of cat and mouse you want to play, let the games begin! I *never* lose."

Stalking over to the windows, Dalton clenched his fists into tight balls. Staring outside, he watched the busy people flood the downtown hotspots, cutting loose after a long work week. Lifting his arm above him, Dalton leaned on the glass, gazing at the men and women crowding the sidewalks below. He thought back to when Joseph first introduced him to Ellora, when they decided to merge their businesses together.

She was fresh out of high school, full of ambition and driven to help her father's business grow more successful. Joseph was taking her out on the job with him and teaching her all she would need to know, teaching her all he had learned. At first, Dalton didn't think much of her besides, of course, how stunning she was. Plenty of glamorously stunning women threw themselves at him all the time, though, and Ellora was hardly lady-like or glamorous. Their first project finished successfully; the newly renovated factory they had turned into apartments sold to the highest bidder. To celebrate, Dalton arranged for both companies to come together for an early Christmas party.

Dalton was running fashionably late. Once he strolled into the convention center, there she was -- a crimson silk strappy dress wrapped around her irresistible body, ending just above her knees. It swished and swayed with every move she made. Her hair, not in the usual messy ponytail, cascaded down her back like a forbidden black waterfall. The darkness of her outer appearance, mixed with her fiery spirit, was what awoke his carnal desire for her. She was sultry, alluring. Her astonishingly brilliant green eyes were intense and mysterious, drawing him into their tantalizing depths.

Dalton was used to seeing her wear the usual contractors' garb of steel-toed boots, cargos, hardhat, and gloves. He'd never really paid her that much attention, but at that moment, he wanted nothing else in the world more than to have Ellora underneath him. How could he have overlooked such a desirably enticing masterpiece? She was the center of attention, and everyone flocked around her, listening intently to her stories and laughing at her jokes. Needless to say, her drink never ran dry that night, and she was endlessly being offered up every appetizer they had.

There was just something about her that made him want to take her, possess her, and show everyone there that he always got what he wanted. Dalton knew that he was the best man to be had, and she would soon belong to him.

Sure, she was pure and innocent as a result of an overprotective father, but it didn't take much to destroy innocence. Even a light as bright as Ellora's could be dimmed. Maybe there was a little wild cat hidden deep down that would fight him. The challenge and the promise of a fight was what excited him the most. Dalton would enjoy breaking her into becoming his docile little pussycat.

Dalton strolled with a suave gait, right over to where she stood. He made his way through the throng of guys that surrounded her. Leaning in as close as she would allow, he brushed a finger down the length of her arm. Ellora's skin was exceptionally soft, and Dalton couldn't help but press against her side suggestively. He wanted all of her, underneath him, right there. He asked if she wanted to go somewhere, someplace where they could be naked and alone. This became a pissing contest. He wanted to make it obvious to her and everyone else what he wanted from the start. As he followed the lines and contours of her delicious body, he licked his lips with hungry desire. Dalton nodded his head toward the exit. Damn, he was eager to taste her.

Being in his uniquely well-off position, getting girls had always been relatively easy for him. All he had to do was just show off the wealth and the panties start dropping. So Dalton didn't think the daughter of an extremely fortunate contractor, a glorified handyman, was going to be any different. They were beneath him, after all.

Even now, his blood boiled, remembering the look on

her face -- a look of complete and utter disgust.

She made a noise in her throat, mocking a gag. "You have got to be kidding me right now. I don't know what kind of easy bimbos you hang out with, where acting like a sleazy, arrogant, socially desperate pervert actually works enough to get them to leave with you, but I'm not one of them. I wouldn't step foot outside of work with you, even if you paid me to do it." Giving him a final look of distain, she pushed past Dalton and walked off, aiming for the refreshments table, when he caught up to her.

He was absolutely astonished and livid at how she had talked down to him in front of their colleagues, like she was Queen of the Nile or something. When he heard the other men snickering at his expense, it sent him over the edge. She obviously had no idea what he was capable of, or how far he was willing to go. She would learn soon enough. Reaching out, Dalton grabbed her arm and yanked her back to face him. She looked angry at first, demanding for him to let her go, asking how he dared to treat her in such a way. That is, until she saw how pissed off he was. Growling through gritted teeth, he could see the fury twisting the features on his face mirrored through her eyes. She fell quiet but lifted her chin in defiance.

Dalton made it perfectly clear that if she ever disrespected him like that again, she would suffer for it. Her family would suffer for it. He would use every resource, every connection available to ensure her father would never get a contracting job again. No matter where they moved, or how small the job was... He didn't care how long he had to follow them or how much it'd cost. In the blink of an eye, Dalton could have their whole world crushed and crumbling down around her.

So he mentioned that it would be in her and her father's best interest if she played nice around him. She wouldn't, after all, want to be the one responsible for ruining her father's career, or the lifestyle he worked so hard for, just because his spoiled brat of a daughter wouldn't go out with their new partner and head of the company who was responsible for hiring her father to begin with.

Dalton knew he had her right where he wanted her, when her eyes drifted downward and her shoulders slumped. The love she had for her father would keep her right where he wanted her. Fear and leverage were the most important tools in manipulation. This was how he ran his business and his personal life. It was the key to all his success. Finally letting go of her arm, he nodded toward the door and prompted, "So, how about that date?"

No, he wouldn't take things too fast with Ellora. He wanted to break her will, and that would take time. He *would* have her. *That* he promised himself. Dalton wouldn't stop until she submitted to him. He wanted her to belong to him, and him only! In the meantime, he would enjoy breaking her spirit piece by piece, until she was as dark on the inside as she was on the outside. Everyone knew that Dalton Ramsey Claiborne III *never* backed down from a challenge.

Ellora raced down the hallway as fast as her legs could carry her. Dread gripped her when she heard his heavy footsteps pounding on the hardwood floors behind her. His powerful presence echoed around the eerily empty house. It didn't matter how fast she ran; he was always right on her heels.

Ellora quaked violently when she made it to the stairs. If she couldn't make it out of there, she'd never survive. Reaching out, she gripped the railing with both hands and used the leverage to fly down the steps. She skipped so many at a time, it felt like she was flying. He thundered down the steps after her. The smell of his rancid panting snaked its way over her shoulder, the stench stung her nose. Ellora risked looking back, finding his large black eyes, vicious with a murderous rage she didn't understand, were only a few feet behind her. He was close enough to grab her.

Oh my God, this is it. *He reached out... and she lunged, taking a giant leap before she got to the last three steps. She successfully made it over the carpeted runner at the bottom. Her ankles stung as she landed hard on her bare feet. Easily ignoring the pain, Ellora sprinted to the front door. She heard him land on the runner and crash to the floor as the rug slipped out from under him.*

Shaking, she fumbled with clumsy fingers, trying to unlock the deadbolt and doorknob. After several slips from her bloodied hands, she finally heaved open the door. She skidded on her own blood, which was trickling down her legs and pooling onto the floor. The cool air rushed in, sobering her. Chills raised goosebumps on her skin as she dashed out the door.

Ellora looked back to make sure he wasn't behind her. This action caused her to lose her balance, tripping down the driveway and crashing right into the car. She remembered leaving it unlocked, so she wrenched the door open and jumped inside, immediately locking the doors in record speed. It took only a moment for her to get a grip on her debilitating panic. Frantically searching her pockets for the car keys, first the front then the back, Ellora froze.

A devastating hopelessness made her stomach drop when she realized that she'd left the keys in the house. She hung her head in defeat... BANG! BANG! BANG! The sudden violent pounding sent Ellora shooting out of her seat, frightened to death as he pulverized the glass window with his fists. He stopped his onslaught abruptly and pressed his face against the window. His disturbing eyes and malicious sneer held her captive as he lifted his hand, presenting her set of keys and shaking them. 'NO!'

"Noooooooo!"

Ellora shot upright in her bed. "Oh my God. Oh my God," she cried out, violently trembling as the all too real images continued to torment her. She weakly wiped at her tear-stained cheeks, using the back of her hand, and gripped the sheets tighter as the unspeakable memories still played out in her mind. She curled up into a ball and sobbed.

After what felt like an hour, Ellora finally stumbled out of bed on shaky legs. She noticed the comforter was lying in a twisted heap on the floor. "Geez, I must've been thrashing around all night," she mumbled to herself. Reluctantly, she sauntered over to the washroom. Exhausted from the lack of sleep, she leaned her elbows on either side of the sink, trying to remember the last time she slept soundly without any nightmares. It'd been too long because she couldn't even remember a time without them. Splashing cold water on her face helped to calm her. She pulled in a deep cleansing breath, steadying her weary nerves and hammering heart. Like every other night, her throat was hoarse and dry from screaming and crying. Grabbing a tiny paper cup next to the sink, Ellora gulped down the deliciously cold water, relieving some of the aching soreness.

"I might as well just stay up," she mumbled to herself. There was no point in even trying to go back to sleep with her heart pounding the way it was. Glancing out her open window, Ellora watched the sun as it came up, casting pink hues through her pale yellow curtains. The view drew her closer to the open window. She marveled at the breathtaking view along the harbor. The beauty didn't look real; like an artist's masterpiece, it was far too perfect. Ellora still didn't know how her mother let her father take her away from all this. She tore her eyes away from the dark blue waters, still cold looking from the long winter months. The frothy waves gently rolled to shore, the peaceful rhythmic motions calming her. The rising sun, a bright burnt orange, looked like it was climbing right out of the sea. Seeing movement out of the corner of her eye brought her out of her daze. She glanced down at the large man walking out of the pub one floor below her.

It was Behr. He stopped mid-stride on the sidewalk, deep in thought. After a few moments, he turned and looked up at her window. He looked shocked at first by her presence at the window, maybe even a little embarrassed. Was it because she was standing there looking down on him, *or* because she caught him looking up? His eyes warmed over, a big beautiful smile lighting up his features, which made his pale blue eyes sparkle. He lifted his hand in greeting and winked at her flirtatiously. Ellora felt brave enough to openly stare at him from the safety of the second story window. Whether she wanted to admit it to herself or not, Behr was an absolutely magnificent man to look at. That's when she realized that she was standing in a big open window wearing her tiny shorts and cami, for the whole world to see. Her face burned with embarrassment, and she quickly ran into the washroom. She figured she might as well shower and dress for the day because she had a long one ahead of her. Eight days of continuous rain had kept her indoors, so she'd used that time assessing the damage downstairs. She planned to make a supply run to the hardware store today, happy that she could finally get to work.

Grady finished mopping up the floors and continued pulling down all the chairs off the table tops. Others might think he was a joke for getting the place ready for all the people that clearly wouldn't show up, but he had a routine that kept him busy and there was no reason to stop now. Kristy cheerfully bounced in from next door.

"Grady, I 'ave some extra food left o'er from next door. Let me make you some breakfast."

"Aye, that's just what I need Kris. Thanks. An' where's Ger this morn'?" he asked over his shoulder.

"He's cleanin' up after the mornin' rush. He'll be by shortly after." She made her way around the bar and into the back, firing up the griddle.

Grady lifted his head up when he heard the door open. "Aaah, Behr, t'what do I owe..." he bellowed loudly, grinning as he patted him on the shoulder.

"Aye, Grady, g'mornin' to ya. I was just wonderin' if I could get some o' your excellent coffee to start m'day off right. I've a long one ahead of me. The *Sea Witch* is needin' a repair or two before I head out to the mainland today."

Grady shot Behr a knowing glance, and shook his head in disagreement. "Is it the coffee you're wantin'? Or is it for a peek at our new girl that's got you eagerly coming in at day break for the last eight mornins in a row?" He smirked at him and winked.

Behr chuckled back. "Just gimme the coffee, ya ol' goat, or I'll be takin' m'business elsewhere."

"It's love, brother. It bit him hard," Gerard yelled out, walking in behind Behr.

Kristy, amused by the taunting, leaned her head out, shouting," Stay a while. I'm makin' breakfast. If your day is goin' to be long, you'll need more than just coffee in ya."

"Aye, Kristy, that'll do the trick," Behr agreed happily. He sat himself down on the bar stool and grabbed the dark coffee Grady handed him.

"Soooo, how's Ellora settling in now?" Behr awkwardly brought up between sips of his coffee, trying hard not to look too interested.

Kristy came in from behind the kitchen with two plates of eggs, ham, and toast, glancing at Grady and Gerard as she set the plates down.

"This be the third night in a row that she woke up in a panic, screamin' and hollerin'. Aye, and I heard a bit o' sobbing coming from her room in the wee hours," Grady admitted, twisting the bar rag in his hand nervously.

Behr's eyes grew wide. "Is that right... again?"

"Aye, we heard her through the walls next door last night. It sounded like the devil was on her heels," Kristy declared, and Gerard added, "It must be the big change in her life, and the passing o' her ma and da."

Behr shook his head in disagreement. "Sobbing for your loved ones, aye. That I can believe. But screamin' the roof off your head... I've been thinking on it, n' I'd bet my *Sea Witch* that she's running from someone or something that's done her or maybe her parents harm."

"Aye." Grady nodded. "I saw the look o' her when Gavin grabbed her shoulders... nearly leapt outta her chair, she did. I thought that was odd."

"Should we ask her 'bout it?" Kristy asked, concerned for the girl she now cared so much about.

"Nae, we should let her be. She'll tell us when she's willin'," Behr commanded sternly, gobbling down the rest of his food. "Well, all, I must be off. The *Witch* awaits." Behr smiled and raised an arm, signaling his goodbyes, and marched out the door.

He was thinking about Ellora as he walked out of the bar and onto the sidewalk. He couldn't get the thought of her sobbing out of his head. His heart ached for her, and he wondered if there was some way he could help, or at least ease her fears. There was just something about the girl that made him act like a possessive caveman. An uncontrollable need to protect her from those who meant her harm grew inside of him. He knew she was stubborn, though, and wouldn't ever ask for help, even if she needed it.

Still deep in thought, he stopped mid-step down the walkway. He couldn't let a girl get to him like this. She had been the only thing in his head since the night she stumbled into Grady's pub. He turned, looking up at her window. For a second, he thought he was daydreaming when he saw her standing by the window. She was looking down on him, like a heavenly angel. His heart skipped a beat at her majestic beauty. The morning breeze gently blew her hair around her shoulders. His heart pounded erratically inside his chest.

This was the first time he'd gotten a good look at her since she showed up. For the last week, she'd been wearing all dark clothing -- navy blue or black V-neck t-shirts and dark jeans, hiding her body. He could still see that she had a body men would fight over, though, and Behr couldn't help stealing glimpses of her while she leaned over to help Grady wipe down the tables. Her low-cut shirts revealed her soft plump cleavage, while her tight jeans showed every curve, leaving little to the imagination, as she would bend over looking at small leaks in the corner floor.

But now, she was wearing hardly anything at all. Ellora's just outta bed hair cascaded down and rested just below her perfect round breasts, which were just short of being revealed through the thin material of her tight tank top. He lowered his gaze down to her soft tiny waist, her navel just barely peeking out of her extremely short shorts. Those slender, creamy thighs and curved tight backside...

Just as quickly, he brought his gaze back up to meet her exquisite emerald eyes, embarrassed at where he was letting his mind wander. Pausing for a moment to get his head right, he smiled and waved. He better get outta there; he couldn't stand there staring at her all day on the street, or people would think he'd gone mad.

Giving her a wink, he strolled off. Ellora Belle Sutherland was trying to make off with his heart. *But it's too soon*, he thought to himself. He'd given his heart to another, and she'd made off with it, breaking it in two. He couldn't go throwing it away again so soon, not after only a month of healing.

Ellora skipped her way down the stairs to the intoxicating smell of coffee and eggs. She made a short list of repairs throughout the week that this place needed done the most, which wasn't as bad as she originally thought. Some small cracks in the foundation outside had led to a little bit of water leakage inside, which is what caused mold to appear on the walls inside. A few missing shingles and a damaged downspout caused the leaks that trickled down from the ceiling. There was nothing that needed to be completely gutted or replaced, though, which was a plus. The rest was cosmetic -- fresh paint, a new sign, sanding down and resealing the hardwoods. Nothing she couldn't handle. She'd make her way into town to the hardware store today to finally start the project. Since it had finally stopped raining, the walk should be a nice one.

Ellora walked through the hall and into the bar area, giving Grady a quick kiss on the cheek. He was starting to feel like an adopted father to her, and he, in-turn treated Ellora like his very own daughter. They both had an unspoken *need* for one another's company, empathizing with the loss of the other's loved ones. They recognized when the other was suffering with their grief, and helped to ease the heavy burden of their loneliness. With just one look into one another's mournful eyes, they could identify with what the other was feeling that day. Ellora walked behind the bar to the back counter to grab a mug, filling it to the brim with coffee. The first few days here, she was grateful for the coffee maker Behr gave her. She still used it in the evenings, but she didn't mind sharing breakfast with the kind, lonely old man who'd opened up his home to her.

"Kristy, that smells to die for!" Ellora gushed as her mouth watered at the deliciously intoxicating smell wafting out of the kitchen.

"'Ave some, sweeting. There's more than enough", Kristy hollered back.

"I've some good news," Grady announced with a cheerful smile and a matching shuffle. "My God-daughter, Adelle, has accepted a position as a teacher over at the Portree Primary School on Blaven Road. She starts in September, so she'll be looking for a permanent place to stay. In the meantime, I've offered her the other flat upstairs for as long as she needs it." Grady tossed a relaxed gesture at Ellora. "She's about your age, Lor."

Ellora couldn't help but smile at him. It meant a lot to Grady to fill this place up around him with people he cared about. She was also looking forward to meeting someone her own age to hang out with. It'd been awhile since she'd had any friends.

"How wonderful, Grady. She's such a smart girl. I just love it when she comes to visit. Now, you can have an extra pair of hands to help you out over the summer with your repairs, Lor. Ah, heaven help this town. With two beautiful women walkin' into the hardware store, men will be following you both home." Kristy wrinkled her nose and wiggled her eyebrows. "Aye, that's a good way to get s'more folks around here. Send out the two beauties you've got here."

"That's not a bad idea, Kris," Grady agreed, chuckling.

After finishing her breakfast, Ellora grabbed her supply list along with directions to the hardware store. "I'll see you later, guys. I'm heading out," she shouted out as she headed toward the door. Ellora was offered a ride in, but being such a gorgeous day out, adamantly declined. She wanted to soak in the sun and check out her new town, not to mention, she'd been cooped up here for a week and needed to stretch her legs. She knew it rained a lot here in Portree, so she might as well get full use of a clear sunny day. As she stepped outside, she drew in a deep cleansing breath. The air was so fresh; she could smell the cold salty sea and the lush green vegetation that surrounded the town.

Starting out on Wentworth and heading toward Main Street, Ellora took her time looking at all the buildings and shops. Just like the houses on the pier, these buildings were were all connected in rows. Each one had its own character and color; some were made of brick, some stone, and others stucco. She passed an ice cream parlor, a pharmacy, Jackson's Wholefoods, and Vibe -- a music, movies, and video game store. Ellora was extremely excited to spot Vital Signs, a sign making shop. That's where she'd look into getting Grady a brand new sign; he'd love that.

This town had everything one would need. She passed a clothing boutique, Matheson's shoes, a jewelry store, and a hairdressers on her way. Ellora was in awe of the town's beauty and the artful streets she was walking on. It was the type of town she'd seen in movies, and it was just so perfect. The sidewalks were clean and neat, made of stone pavers. Lamp posts stood proudly at the end of every block. Ellora couldn't stop smiling as she adoringly took in the colorfully charming buildings. They looked like they were straight out of the pages of a comic.

Walking through Somerled Square, Ellora observed that the buildings on this side of town were newer and separated. There were several more restaurants, The Skye Museum of Island Life, the town's Post Office, Skye Property Centre (estate Agent), the Police Station, and the Scottish Court Service. Making it past the center of town, and at the end of a long, winding Dunvegan Road, she ended up in the Industrial Estate complex. Finally, she reached her destination -- Jan's Hardware store.

By the time Ellora made it to her destination, she was pretty worn out. She rubbed the cramp forming in her leg, now realizing that the time it took to get up here was grossly under-exaggerated, and she was in no mood to wander around trying to find what she needed. So she handed her list to the overly helpful and eager to please sales clerk, who went about finding everything for her. As Ellora stood at the counter, she heard heavy footsteps approach behind her. A deep rumbling voice followed before she began to panic.

"Enjoying the sunshine, love?"

Turning on her heel, Ellora rested her eyes on Behr, who stood directly behind her. Casually, he moved up beside her to lean on the counter. Ellora nervously looked up at him, her skin tingling at his closeness. He looked genuinely surprised to see her standing there as he looked down on her and smiled. His expression was warm and adoring, a change from his usual broody look. One corner of his mouth turned up in a half smile, his eyebrows lifting curiously. That's when she realized that she was just staring at him like an idiot and never answered his question.

"It's breathtaking," she finally answered. Ellora realized in that moment that her comment was meant for his smile, *not* his question. She smiled back at him and watched as his eyes fell to her lips.

"Aye, it is. I'm glad I saw you 'ere." He lifted his gaze directly to her eyes, holding her captive. The passion that came through them froze Ellora on the spot. The air crackled intensely around them as time seemed to stand still, and this made Ellora incredibly nervous.

She quickly broke the spell, asking, "Aren't you

supposed to be on the ferry?"

Behr nodded non-committedly, a ghost of a smile playing on his lips, like he knew something she didn't. "Aye, she's an old wench that needs a freshenin' up every now n' again. I've got to take special care o' her, or she gets temperamental on me, so I stopped by to grab a few things. Do you need any help, love? You're gathering things to fix up Grady's, no?"

"Oh, yes, the guy's getting them for me. I'm still not familiar with this place yet, so I didn't want to waste a lot of time wandering around." This all came out in a rush, embarrassed that she might come across looking like a spoiled bimbo in distress.

"You could've asked me to come 'ere with ya Lor. I could've helped you out, you know."

Just then, the clerk came back with a flatbed cart stacked high with all the items on her list. He was a tall skinny boy, not more than eighteen, with sandy brown hair and freckles on his nose. He looked at Ellora and smiled, trying to be smooth and laying it on pretty thick. On his name tag, it read Isaac. "So you're that American girl from New York the whole town's talking 'bout, right? You're staying over at Grady's?"

"The whole town is talking about *me*? Oh, great," she grumbled.

Behr looked at Ellora, amused. "It's a tight knit town, love. Better get used to people nosing their way into your business."

"I could have all this stuff delivered over there for you, if you want. I could *personally* take it over, you know, to make sure it isn't damaged." Isaac crossed his arms over his chest and widened his stance in confidence.

Shocked, Ellora looked up at Behr, who was snickering at her, amused at the young man's pass. Running his big hands through his thick hair and down the back of his neck, Behr nodded at the clerk. His eyes never left hers. "Not 'ere but eight days, and already, you've got the boys drooling at your feet, eh, love?" Before Ellora could protest to either of them that she could handle it, Behr donned the serious brooding look that she'd come to know and glared down at the clerk, who noticeably flinched and gulped hard.

"I can take it from 'ere, Boyle. What Miss Sutherland needs is the help of a man." His tone was deep and abrasive. After a brief standoff, Behr released the clerk from the prison of his glare. His demeanor softened when he turned back to Ellora. "I've got m'truck outside. I can give ya a ride back, if you'd like?"

Her heart fluttered at his kind offer. She felt the pit of her stomach twisting and bubbling with nerves, hating how he had this strong of an effect on her. Whether it was like a teenage crush, or possibly a reaction from her worst fear, Ellora's body was confused on which. For crying out loud, the man didn't even talk that much, but just the way he looked at her had her whole body reacting. It was as though he could see right to her soul. It was both flattering and unsettling.

Knock it off! She mentally shook her head. Crossing her arms over her chest, Ellora nodded her head in approval, trying to look like it wasn't that big a deal. "Thanks, Behr. That would help me out a lot."

"How didja get up here, love?" Behr inquired curiously, grabbing the heavy cart for her, as Ellora took out her credit card to pay the clerk. "Did someone drop you off?"

"No. I walked up here." The look on his face told her he thought she was crazy. "I wanted to check out the neighborhood and get the most out of this beautiful spring day. What? No one walks around here?" she commented sarcastically. He just shook his head and gave her a lopsided smirk.

"You're too pretty to be such a smart-ass. You must get that from your father. I was just wondering how you were planning to get all this back there. Unless you've got a donkey parked out front I didn't see?"

"Well," Ellora said with a playful tone. "I guess I would've just had to take Isaac up on his kind offer then, huh!" She batted her eyes at him.

Behr bellowed out a hearty laugh, tilted his head, and brought both his hands to his chest, mocking a broken heart. "And break the young lad's heart when you refuse him later. You're a cold-hearted lass, you are, Ellora Belle." She jabbed him in the arm as hard as she could, hurting her own hand instead, laughing along with him.

They stopped at his truck, and as he loaded up the bed with her items, she took the dolly back to the cart return. When she returned, Behr was holding the door of his truck open for her. She hated to admit it, but his kind gestures melted some more ice around her heart. He was starting to get to her. Ellora smiled, thanking him as he reached out and gently grasped her hand. He helped her step up into the cabin and shut the door carefully behind her. The attentiveness he always seemed to show her made her cheeks turn as red as a tomato.

Behr jumped into the driver's side and looked over at her, hesitating for a moment before starting the engine. "We don't 'ave to go back straight away, do we, love? How 'bout a bite?"

"That'd be perfect. I'm starving. Where'd you have in mind?"

"I'll take you to one of my favorite places, aye, and I 'ave something to show you as well that I think you'll enjoy," he uttered with a low soothing tone, just above a whisper. He gazed at her, his eyes searching over her face intimately, then looked back at the road.

ehr took Ellora to the Cafe' Arriba Bistro, on the north end of Bank Street. It was on the upper level of the *Over the Rainbow* gift shop, and had spectacular views of the Harbor. Behr picked a table located in the corner next to the windows and pulled out her chair for her. She'd already scanned the funky, chalk menu board when they first walked in and knew exactly what she wanted.

When the waitress came around to ask what they wanted to drink, Ellora quickly listed her full order. "Yes, I'll have a Coke and the Spicy Tomato, Olive, and Mozzarella Flatbread Melt with the Meatball soup." She was definitely starving.

Behr shook his head and smiled. Without even looking at the waitress, he raised his voice, "I'll 'ave a Black Cuillin Beer and the spiced beef Burger on a toasted bagel, with salsa, garlic, and mayo, and chips as well. Thank you." When she left, he leaned in closer. "I like that you've a good appetite on ya. There's nothin' sexier than seein' a beautiful woman order something other than a salad."

He was doing it again, gazing at her with those beautiful blue eyes and crooked smirk. It was like he enjoyed watching her squirm and blush under the heavy weight of his stare. As if reading her mind, he snapped himself out of it and started a conversation. "So, Lor, are you quite comfortable and settled in at Grady's yet."

"Yes, he's such a kind, sweet man. They are all very generous and welcoming. It is such a beautiful town, too. I'm looking forward to making this my home."

Behr looked happy with that answer. "I just hope I can fix up the pub for Grady in enough time for him to get a good enough crowd this summer. Kristy told me about his wife..." Ellora paused for a moment, remembering how heartbroken it made everyone talking about it. She'd finally passed after a long-suffering battle with breast cancer. "And how his place suffered afterward," she continued woefully.

"Aye, he was in a bad way for a while. She was everything to him. I envy them for having that." He mumbled that last part in such a hushed whisper she almost didn't hear him make the comment.

"We all want to see the pub hopping like she used to. I will be proud to help in any way I can, love."

The waitress came around with their drinks, and let them know their food would be right out. She gave Ellora another glance, adding, "Ah, you're Ellora, right? BB's girl? Kristy told us about ya, aye, and we are glad a Sutherland found their way back to the Isle. You look just like your mother, dear."

Ellora thanked her, and the waitress looked at Behr,

patting him on the shoulder. "You'd better snatch her up, Behr, before all the other lads 'round this town see what a beauty she is and steal her away." With that, she strutted off. Behr looked dumb-founded. His face reddened pretty quickly, which made Ellora snicker a little. It was good to see that he could get just as uncomfortable as she so often was.

"So, Behr, you're a bachelor, huh?" Ellora couldn't even believe that came flying out of her mouth unfiltered, and she couldn't even stop herself.

His demeanor changed almost immediately, turning icy and guarded. "Aye," was all he replied curtly, and without elaborating any further, which had her curious.

"No girls catch your eye, or you're just not the kind of guy who likes to be in a relationship?" Ellora did her best to copy the same intimidatingly penetrating stare that he usually gave her.

"Neither. I want nothin' more than to settle down and 'ave a family of my own. It's just that..." Behr started to shift uncomfortably in his seat, his jaw muscle flexing as he ran his hands threw his hair in frustration. Ellora raised her eyebrows, waiting for him to continue, because he left that sentence hanging in the air, just building up the suspense and her curiosity. He glanced up at her and let out a long winded breath.

"I might as well tell ya. You'll only find out 'round town eventually, or irritate me to death 'til you find out, stubborn as you are." He lifted the corner of his mouth in a crooked smile to let her know he wasn't really annoyed.

"I dated a girl named Shannon since we were in high school. All we'd ever talked 'bout was getting out o' 'ere and traveling the world together. Well, that's all she ever talked 'bout anyway. Aye, n' I would've followed that lass anywhere, too, I thought at that time. We graduated, and I was offered the Ferry Boat for practically crumbs from Gavin's dad. He knew how much I loved being on the water. I fixed her up, n' she wound up bein' one o' *the* main boats used to transport people. Aye, and that angered Shannon like nothin' else, knowin' that the more I was depended on 'ere, the less likely it was that I was gonna leave."

Behr drank some of his beer, deep in thought for a moment. "We dated on and off for a few years now. She managed to sweeten her way back into my heart, just to try a new scheme to get me to leave. When I refused, she left me behind." He held the neck of his bottle, swirling it around in a circle, with a far off look in his eyes and continued. "Aye, just a month past, I found out she was with another man while still with me, all along trying to get me to sell the ferry boat. Her goal was to get her greedy hands on the money and leave with *him*. So I found out I've been wasting all these years with the woman. She dinnae love me, *never* had. She was just looking for a ticket out o' this town." Behr squeezed his eyes shut, like he was trying to squeeze Shannon out of his memory. When he opened them, Ellora was hit with the full force of his sapphire gaze. After a few breathless moments, he looked down. Ellora's heart broke for him. She could feel his heartache over it, even though he tried hard to hide it.

"There now, love, did that satisfy your curiosity for a bit?" He wasn't making eye contact with her anymore when he said that, and she was struck with the realization that she'd started to like their eye contact. If the saying, *eyes are the window to the soul,* was true, his soul was beautiful. But now, she felt awful for even asking. Her stomach tied itself in knots at the thought of his heartbreak and the betrayal he encountered.

"Well, I told you m'story. Now, it's your turn. How many hearts has ElloraBelle Sutherland broken, leaving so suddenly like ya did?" He glanced up slowly, and what she saw was a burning curiosity laced with concern. He wanted answers, but she couldn't give them to him. She froze on the spot. She should've seen this coming. Of *course* he'd ask her about her personal life after his open and honest confession. *Idiot!* She mentally cursed herself. Ellora's eyes roamed the room frantically. She wasn't sure if she should lie, change the subject, or give him a sugar-coated version?

Behr reached across the tiny round table and placed his hand on hers, which were cold and clammy in contrast to his strong, warm ones. "You dinnae 'ave to be afraid, love. It's just a question. But, you dinnae 'ave to answer if you're not ready. I want you to trust me. I want you to trust that, if or whenever you decide to confide in me, it will *remain* between you and me."

Ellora gulped down her Coke. She didn't stop for air until it was gone, her mouth suddenly extremely parched. She decided to take her time and choose her words wisely when answering his questions. So badly, she wanted to tell someone, just blurt it out and get this enormous weight off her shoulders. "I... I don't have a boyfriend. I never had one..."

"*Never?*" Behr raised his eyebrows in disbelieving shock.

"No, my father wanted me to wait until I was out of high school. He wanted me focused on my future. So, I never dated anyone, before..." Ellora's mouth fell open then snapped shut again like a fish out of water, as she tried hard to think of what she *could* say next.

"Has nae man ever done right by your father and asked him if they could take you out?"

"There are *no* real men over there, at least none I've ever encountered." Bristled in anger, she shook as the memories crept into her head. The reality of what she'd left behind was still too much for her to think about, especially right there at a crowded restaurant and sitting in front of a magnificently intimidating man.

"They are too vain to think about what a woman wants, too selfish to treat her how she deserves, too arrogant. Their only goal is getting into a girl's pants to boost their own egos... or, or..." Ellora's voice turned quiet, fear making her sound childlike as the blood drained from her face. "Or a *monster*!"

She shook uncontrollably, tearing her hand away from Behr's before he noticed how much. "But, to answer your question, there was one man who sort of asked. Actually, he demanded a date. He was my father's business partner. My father despised this man and flat out refused him." She wanted to tell him more but didn't dare go any farther, so she just left it like that.

The waitress came around to finally hand them their steaming plates. *Thank God! Saved by the food.* The waitress shifted her eyes between Behr and Ellora. "For heaven's sake, it looks like someone just slapped you both in the face. Lighten up, kids. It's a beautiful day. These kids today, always so broody," she grumbled to no one in particular as she walked away. Ellora's eyes scrunched together at her bluntness and smirked. The spunky waitress, in her forties and with too much eye make-up, instantly pulled her out of her reverie and into a much better mood. *She's right. I'm here now. I've got to let the past stay in the past and try to make a fresh new start.*

Ellora let out a long breath. "Wow, that was a little heavy for a lunch conversation, huh?"

"Aye, love, at least we got our skeletons out early then." He picked up his burger and shoved half of it in his mouth in one bite.

Following his lead, Ellora gobbled down her melt and

slurped up her soup. The rest of lunch went by smoothly with pleasant conversation. She mentioned to him about Adelle arriving. He told her all about Adelle. She had always been the 'smart one' in school, always had her head on straight. She was a sweet person who used to volunteer at the animal clinic, or helped waitress at Grady's, back when it was a full house every night.

He also told Ellora some gossip on how Gavin had *always* had a thing for Adelle but never wanted to admit it in school. Gavin feared his reputation as a 'lady's man' would be tarnished by falling for the 'smart girl', but all that changed when they graduated. He started to fall harder for her and grew out of the 'I can get all the women I want' stage. But before he could make a move, she went away to college and hadn't been back for a while.

"I just love that. We should play matchmaker and get them together," Ellora said, laughing and wiggling her eyebrows excitedly.

"Aaah, nae, lass, I cannae even play the matchmaker in my own life without screwin' it up. Who am I to fix anyone else up?" He said this in a playful manner, but Ellora couldn't help but see that he meant it. It made her heart ache for him. Instantly, she hated Shannon for doing this to him.

"Well, we can make some popcorn and sit back to watch the show then!" she offered, winking at him.

"Aye, that I can do. Save me a front seat at the bar tonight, love. I wouldnae miss it!"

The waitress came around to hand them the bill and they both reached for it.

"Ellora, I'll take it from 'ere. We are not in Syracuse, love. We *real* men pay the bill when taking a girl out, so dunnae be taking my dignity away from me." His tone was so hot and passionate, it scorched her to the bone. Ellora nodded and let him take it. He paid the waitress, who then told her to let everyone at Grady's know that Moira 'sends her hellos'. She smiled and assured her that she definitely would. Behr stood, pulling out her chair for her. She didn't know why it felt unsettling to her to have someone be so gentlemanly and polite. It must be because she wasn't used to it.

"All right, you ready to leave then, love? I've got somethin' I wanna show ya." She slowly nodded her head, unsure about where they were going or what it was that he planned to show her.

They walked out of the restaurant. Ellora was turning toward his truck when Behr reached out, gently grasping her hand, and laced his fingers with hers. Ellora whipped her head around in shock, looking down at their joined hands.

"We can walk from 'ere, Lor, that is, if you dinnae mind it?" He flashed her a pleading look, silently begging for her trust...

"Umm, okay." Ellora gulped nervously, hesitating for just a moment. "Yeah, sure, Behr, no problem. Where are we going anyway?"

He just smiled. "You'll see. You'll love it!" He led the way down Bank Street, and as they walked down the paved sidewalk, Behr lifted their *still* entwined hands and pointed up at the tall lamp posts. "Your da wanted to spend all his time with your ma. He loved her so much. They just couldn't get enough o' each other's company." Ellora nodded. Even after years of marriage, they still loved one another in that way.

"All our parents had the *street light* rule. We had to be home by the time the street lights came on. Well, your da was never ready to let your ma go. One night, he went about throwing rocks up at these lamp posts. He went all the way up one side of the street and down the other, busting all of the lights out, so he could 'ave the excuse that the street lights never came on when asked." Behr looked down at Ellora, her rush of emotions making her tremble like a leaf. This was the first time she'd heard that story. "Kristy told me that story once," Behr mentioned thoughtfully.

They came to a stop in front of a smaller row building, only two stories tall and made of brown stucco.

Behr was excited when he glanced down at her. Ellora's curiosity peaked. He nodded his head toward it. "This is called the Armadale House. It was built in the 1880's, and has been *the* hardware store in Portree for well over one hundred years." He squeezed her hand and flashed her a heart-stopping smile. "This is the ol' hardware store your father worked at as a lad, and ran it for a while when he grew a bit. This is where he met your mother for the first time, before they started dating in high school. She came into the hardware store to pick up some items for her father's B&B. It was told 'round town that your father fell in love with her at that moment... right then and there. Once their eyes met, they knew that they would marry." Behr watched Ellora intently, adoration showing in his eyes. This surprise was the most thoughtful gift anyone could've given to her. Ellora became overwhelmed with the sudden rush of emotions.

Her eyes filled to the brim with fresh tears. Ellora placed a shaky hand over her mouth in astonishment, blinking once before the tears came spilling out. She gazed at the run-down building, imagining the loving encounter. She could clearly picture the very first time her parents locked eyes and fell in love. Ellora's whole body was filled with their love and warmth. The familiarity of that feeling gripped her broken heart, drawing out a grief-stricken sob from the very depth of her soul.

Instantly, Behr bent over and wrapped his strong arms around her in a warm embrace. Memories flooded her system of all the precious moments her parents shared a kiss or an embrace. Ellora was distracted by her daydream, imagining a happier moment in time, enough so that his closeness didn't bother her so much anymore. She actually needed the comfort, and Behr's embrace was trusting and genuine. It was just what she needed in that very moment. Ellora shamelessly inhaled his scent as it washed over her, invading all her senses. She breathed him in deeply as he held her tight. He smelled of some dark earthy cologne mixed with after shave, fresh soap, and ocean air. It was intoxicating. "Sorry, love, I dinnae mean for you to cry. I thought this would make you happy, seeing where they first met..."

"I am happy, Behr. I am," Ellora quickly interrupted. She closed her eyes. "I can almost *feel* them here with me." She opened her eyes again and looked up at Behr. "Thank you for bringing me here. You don't know what this means to me." Her ever guarded mind wanted to let go of him quickly and take a step back, but she found herself raised up on tip-toes to hold him tighter. Ellora nuzzled her face in his strong, muscled chest. It was so comforting, and somehow familiar. She didn't want to let go.

He brought his hand up and ran it gently down the length of her hair. "It's my pleasure, o' course, love." He breathed, pressing his lips into her hair. Slowly, Ellora came back to herself and reluctantly pulled away from the comfort of his arms. Turning her head around, she once again looked at the location where her parents fell in love. Behr reached out and wiped a stray tear away with the pad of his thumb. "It has long since been abandoned. A few shops came and went, but it's been empty since 2007. It hasn't been the same since they left, or so I've been told."

Instantly, Ellora's mind started to wander in the direction of maybe someday taking it over and turning it into her office, for a contractor-for-hire site. But, just as quickly, she pushed the thought out of her head. She would never be as successful as her father was.

"You ready to head back now, love?" Behr softly ran his hand down the length of her arm and once again laced their fingers together, holding her hand. This time, the gesture had her heart accelerating. Her body grew warm, and goose bumps spread across her sensitive skin. She was surprised that she didn't flinch or feel the need to pull away this time. Behr's tender touch didn't bother her so much anymore. She guessed that too much had happened in such a short period of time.

With a voice that was much too deep, she gave a low, "Yes," in response to his previous question.

At hearing Ellora's husky response, Behr's expression changed. His eyes darkened, slightly smoldering, as if her answer was one of desire – which, at that moment, it was, if she was being completely honest with herself. Ellora wanted to *want* him. She just wasn't sure if she was ready to take the next step beyond whatever step they were in at that moment. They just stood there, Ellora's hand protected in his. Some time passed, but it wasn't awkward or tense. Their eyes were having a deep conversation of their own. This time, Ellora didn't feel the need to turn away first. But she swore, if he kept looking down on her with *that* lustful, powerful look filled with an unspoken promise, her body was going to burst into flames.

"Behr... BEHR!" Their moment was broken when somebody shouted after them. A scruffy bearded, tall, lanky man wearing a brown turtle neck and wild lion-like hair came bounding over to them, thankfully breaking the spell.

"Aaaah, Behr, Moira done told me I'd find you walkin' this way with the pretty American lass. Gavin has got his undergarments in a twist over you nae showing up all day. He's had to cancel some tourist trips for the day on account o' the *Sea Witch* being out o' commission. I thought you were supposed to be gettin' her fixed up today," he blurted out in one long heavy breath, eyeballing Ellora jerkily from top to bottom. She nervously dropped Behr's hand.

"I decided to take the day off. I've nae had one since... oooh, forever." Behr looked down at Ellora and gave her a big smile, watching as she broke their point of contact. "I'll go deal with Gavin right now. Ellora, I'll drop off all your supplies tonight when I come by Grady's for a drink. Will that be all right?"

"Of course, I'm only a block down anyways, and I don't mind walking." *Right about now, I need the fresh air anyways,* she thought to herself. She had so many confusing emotions from the days' events that she wanted to sift through. "See you later, Behr. Oh, and thank you... for everything! I had a lot of fun today, and I'll never forget it." She smiled, turned, and reluctantly started making her way down the street. She didn't know what was going on with her, but she had this overwhelming feeling growing inside of her. There was a powerful pull between them that made it harder and harder to walk away from him. The more time they spent together, the harder it was for her to keep her guard up and stay away. That was dangerous.

Ellora heard a long whistle as the bearded man revealed to Behr, "Aye, lad, I'd never go back to work again, had that lass wanted to spend time with me, eh!" Her stomach twisted like a pretzel at the thought of people noticing her. As she made her way down the street, she noticed others smiling at her, so she made a pointed look back at Behr.

"Yes, Lor, other people can see what you're doing, you know. You're not invisible." She scolded herself. Well, she probably just loaded the town with fresh new ammunition for gossip. Oh well, she better get used to being watched, gossiped about, and being the center of attention for a while. Deep down, though, she feared the attention; after all, she'd come here to hide. On the other hand, these people felt like family to her, and the thought of not being truly alone anymore was comforting.

Walking into Grady's, Ellora heard a loud commotion that caught her attention. Taunts, chatter, and loud laughter echoed around the pub. She hollered her hellos, and everyone turned at the sound of her voice.

"Hey, there she is!" shouted Patrick.

All of a sudden, there was a squeal coming from behind the group of guys. A tall strawberry blonde came bouncing over to her, giggling, and threw her arms around Ellora's neck. She gasped, shocked by the girl's unabashed boldness.

"I've heard so much about you. I feel as though I know you already, like a sister. It's about time you got back. I've been surrounded by all these ol' goats over 'ere." She motioned with her thumb over to the guys sitting on the stools, and winked.

Ellora couldn't help but smile. This girl's positive attitude, stunning face, and bubbly personality was infectious. She liked her already.

She was striking. Her wavy, strawberry blonde hair fell down around her shoulders. Light pink cheeks, pouty lips, and big chocolate-brown doe eyes accentuated her clear porcelain skin that most women would die for. She was taller than Ellora, and carried a toned, athletic body, with a thin narrow waist and a slight curve to her hips. Instantly, this girl reminded her of an old Hollywood actress from the 50's.

"You're right, Kristy. She is a gorgeous one! Her eyes are greener than emeralds!" Adelle linked her arm with Ellora's and led her over to the bar. Lachlan, ever the polite gentleman, rose and waved a hand at his chair along with the chair next to his.

"'Ave a seat, Miss Ellora, Miss Adelle." Chivalry

definitely wasn't dead in this town.

"Aye, lass, the whole town's in an up-roar 'bout you and Behr holdin' hands 'round town today... I thought you had errands to run, ah?" Patrick wiggled his eyebrows at Ellora, lifted his drink up, and saluted, obviously taunting her.

"I did," Ellora tried to defend herself. "Behr has the supplies all in his truck. He was helping me bring it all back."

"Moira already phoned over and told us you two were on some kind o' a date." Ellora could see Patrick was just loving this.

"Well, I guess I don't have to relay to you all that Moira says hi," Ellora remarked sarcastically.

"I hear he brought you to your da's ol' hardware store, where your parents first met. Is that right, m'sweet? How romantic." Kristy tilted her head and looked off in the distance, like someone just told her a fairytale... Ellora wanted to barf. These people were testing the boundaries of her comfort zone, but that's what families do, right? They tease each other. She let them taunt her for a while because she knew it was coming; she just didn't know they'd find out within the same hour. Ellora just shook her head and chuckled at her own expense.

Gerard came up from behind the kitchen, stating, "It's good to see Behr interested in the ladies again. Aye, it's good for him. He's been with that awful wench o' a sea dog for far too long. Devil take 'er! He is the best man I know, and he deserves a good woman." Ellora blushed for the umpteenth time that day, shifting uncomfortably in her seat, as the whole bar seemed to be hell bent on setting her and Behr up. "You ladies want somethin' to eat?" Gerard asked, thankfully changing the subject.

"I've been dreaming of your corned beef and cabbage soup. Got any o' that back there, Ger?" Adelle clapped her hands excitedly. "I've been travelling up here all day. I'm starved."

"Nothing for me, Ger. As Patrick pointed out, I've already had plenty to eat." Ellora turned to Patty and stuck out her tongue playfully.

Behr met up with Gavin right outside the bar. He felt guilty about abandoning his work responsibilities and not informing his friend. But, he definitely didn't regret a single moment of the time he spent alone with Ellora. He only wished they hadn't been interrupted when they were. He craved more time with her, and already had an undeniable need to get back to her. Behr ran his hands through his hair. "My apologies, ol' friend. I just lost the hour. Ellora needed me. Er... I mean, uh, she needed m'help bringing back her supplies for the pub is all, n' I was starving for some lunch. It's just been so long since I've taken a day for myself. After Shannon..."

"Enough, ya ol' grizzly, I'm fine with that. No one deserves a vacation more n' you, my friend, but this isnae the Dark Ages. Ya should've called me on the cell n' let me know is all." Gavin squinted his eyes and turned his lips up in a cocky smirk. "Whole town's been talkin' about the two of you holdin' hands n' gazing into each other's eyes... Are you fallin'' for this lass already?"

"I don't know, brother. There's just something 'bout her. She intrigues me, n' the more she tries to keep to herself, the more I find myself being drawn in. I want to know her."

"You want to know her, or *know* her?" Gavin winked and nudged Behr with his elbow.

"Aye, she is exquisite. That much is plain, but it's more than that. She stole my breath away the moment I laid eyes on her. You should've seen her, Gavin. When I showed her the spot her ma n' da met, she lit up and let all her guards down. All her emotions came forward, and I could finally *see* her. There was nothing more beautiful than watching her today."

"Aye, Behr, if it's *not* love you're feeling when you look into those bright green gems, then you better step aside n' let me have a go, before the whole town comes sniffin' her way!" Gavin chuckled when Behr lifted his head with a menacing sneer and gritted his teeth. Gavin raised both hands in surrender. "That's the test, lad. Aye, it's love you feel when you can't bear the thought o' her with another." Gavin patted Behr on the shoulder. "Dinnae worry, my friend. I will head into town n' get all the repairs the *Sea Witch* will b'needin'. I 'ave a feeling you'd be more useful helpin' her out at Grady's, eh, lad? Now, let's get ourselves a drink."

Ellora watched Behr and Gavin walk in smiling, so she guessed all was well. She didn't want to get Behr in any trouble. They walked up to the bar and stopped short when Adelle came bounding up to them. "Hey, it's the two brothers I've never wanted." Laughing, she gave them both a squeeze and stepped back. "Didja hear the good news, boys?"

"Aye, I have. Ellora told me. Congratulations, Ellie." Behr gave Adelle a quick kiss on the cheek then made his way around her, leaving Gavin standing there with her. Behr walked over to where Ellora sat. "This seat taken, love?" Behr smiled brilliantly at her and gestured his hand up. "Hey, Grady, get us a pitcher o' the goods, ol' man."

"So I guess I didn't get you fired then, did I?" Ellora hoped.

Behr shook his head and laughed dryly. "It's my boat, love. Only I can fire me."

Ellora nodded. "Good, I'd hate to have that on my conscience." Grady brought the pitcher along with some mugs, wearing an ecstatic look on his face. Grady loved having so many people around. The pure joy that clearly shone, pouring out of his spirit, uplifted the formerly depressing atmosphere. "And some popcorn!" Ellora shouted to him over her shoulder. She looked up at Behr and winked, whispering, "For the show." She laughed and pointed over to Gavin and Adelle. He nodded, too, and laughed along with her.

Ellora carefully watched Gavin interact with Adelle, while he looked her over from head to toe. By the look on his face, she could tell that he still liked her. She wrapped her arms around his neck and gave him a big squeeze, but quickly let go. "It's so good to see you Gav. I heard you're runnin' the Ferry Terminal now. I'm proud of you."

"Aye, Ellie, that I am. N' what's this good news I've been hearin' about?"

Adelle gave him a swift kiss on the cheek. "I've been offered a teaching position at the primary school. I've accepted and will start in September, so I'm moving back here permanently. Lor will be giving me some company 'til I find my own place."

Gavin donned an amazingly bright smile, the first genuine smile Ellora had seen from him since coming here. He brought Adelle in for another hug and let his arms rest on her hips. "That's great news, Ellie! We missed ya 'round here. You look beautiful."

Adelle jabbed him in the arm. "You're not gettin' soft on me now, are ya, pretty boy?" Gavin flexed his muscle, playing around, trying his best to impersonate Arnold Schwarzenegger's voice. "Actually, I've gotten harder with all this work I've been doing. Check out all my muscles."

"Aye, answering phones is the new workout craze, eh, Gavin," Behr shouted at him.

Adelle just shook her head and giggled at them both. "I've missed this place. I'm so glad to be home! Now, let's have a drink and celebrate new beginnings!"

7

Dominick Antonelli walked through the terminal at Hancock Airport with his fists clenched, frustrated with the lack of cooperation. He would have received even less information had he not been a former crime scene investigator for the Syracuse Police department. He still would be, if Dalton hadn't offered him so much more money to be his private investigator. Dominick definitely missed the action and excitement from his former job, but the money he earned working for Dalton was so much better.

All the airline could give him was a receipt for a one-way ticket paid for with cash. He wanted to get his hands on the video surveillance, but without the proper warrant, or pressure from the SPD to help him out, a receipt was the best they could do. It didn't even specify where she was going. So, his next stop would be to go to her house and see if he could find any leads as to where she was going. He hoped he would get lucky once inside her home. Maybe he would find something she would've left behind that could help locate her -- a note reminding her of the departure time, her date book, a diary... whatever.

Pulling up to the address, Dominick noticed the home

was an impressively sized center-stair colonial. He looked inside the mail box to find it was packed with mail. "Wherever she left to, she never bothered to leave a forwarding address," he voiced to himself. Seizing it all, he flung it into the open window of his car and continued up the driveway. As he walked up the wide steps and onto the massive porch, he spotted something. "Is that blood?" Kneeling down, he studied the dried up drip spots, noticing that they originated from inside, then continued down the steps and stopped halfway down the driveway. "Must've been where the subject got into the car. Hmmm... Wonder if whoever left this trail of blood went straight to the hospital, or the airport, from here?" Dominick mentally cataloged everything he had seen so far, worried what he would see once finally inside the house. He didn't like what he'd seen so far.

He got to the front door and realized that it was slightly ajar. Unclasping his holster, he removed his standard issue Glock 22 and raised it. Carefully, he pushed open the door. Dominick took a step back, then using the 'slicing the pie' technique, scanned 180 degrees of the room. Walking from one side of the door, he methodically arched his steps to the other. Dominick cleared as much of the room as he could from outside, then picked up the pace, passing through the *fatal funnel* at a diagonal. He glanced over his shoulder at the corner, for any possible hidden threats behind him as he stepped through the door. Adrenaline heightened his senses, helping him focus.

Clearing each room on the first floor was done in much the same way. When he was positive there was no one in the house, he came back to the front entrance, finally noticing the dried up pools of blood and the skidded smear marks left behind. "Holy shit! What the Hell did Dominick get me involved in?" He let out a nervous breath and holstered his weapon. An unsettling feeling grew inside of him, making his gut twist. He wondered what had happened in here, and what was really going on with the young girl he was ordered to locate. There was definitely more to the story than a run-away investment. Dominick couldn't help it; the CSI in him switched on, and immediately, he wanted to solve this obviously violent crime he'd literally walked into.

Following the blood droplets up the stairs, he observed the trail as it continued to the left. Once again, he took out his gun and kept to the right side of the hall, heading toward the last room. The door was wide open. As he scanned and cleared the room, he was amazed at how trashed it was. Tables were knocked over, lamps were broken, and rugs had been pushed aside, all telling an unspoken story of an incredible struggle for one's life. Dominick spotted a straight line of sprayed blood on the wall, the spray pattern giving the impression that someone had been stabbed. This was obviously where the attack started, but there didn't seem to be any signs of a break-in that he could see at the front entrance. The attacker must have gotten in another way, he noted thoughtfully. He was going to have to come back when it was light out so he could inspect all doors and windows.

After some looking around, he saw a busted picture frame on the floor and picked it up. It was the girl, Ellora, and her father, with his arm around her. They were both smiling. His stomach started to churn. "I hope you're safe, sweetheart," he declared out loud. Placing the cracked frame back on the desk, he took in the gruesome scene and cursed to himself, "What kind of fucked up situation have you gotten me involved in, Dalton?" And he *was* involved now. There was no way he could ignore *this.* He had to investigate this creeped out scene further, job be damned!

After closing the front door on his way out, he sat heavily in his car, the weight of the world weighing heavily on his shoulders. He let out a frustrated breath, pinching the bridge of his nose. Looking over to her mail lying haphazardly on his passenger-side seat, he flipped through it. Most was junk mail, but a bill from Saint Joseph's Hospital caught his attention. He quickly ripped it open. It appeared like, a week before she bought her one-way ticket, the girl had left the hospital after a week's stay. "Hmm, I'm definitely heading over there. "I wonder if I'll have better luck getting info now, rather than in the morning..." Dominick mused to himself, and figured he might as well give it a shot. The sooner the better. His adrenaline was in high gear from the scene inside that house, so he might as well put it to good use. "Show me what you're running from, Ellora," Dominick exclaimed out-loud, as he sped down 81 South.

Dominick pulled up to the emergency entrance, took the keys out of the ignition, and sat there thinking.

"I could be wrong..." He spoke his thoughts aloud, trying to make sense of the situation. "That blood could be someone else's, and she could be the cause behind it. That would explain her wanting to disappear. But, my gut is telling me that there is more behind this attack. Is Dalton behind it? Money is *always* a good motive, but I don't think my boss would hire a former CSI detective to investigate the whereabouts of a girl he attacked himself. Nah, he'd hire someone, I suppose. He wouldn't want to get his rich hands dirty."

He took a deep breath and marched through the automatic doors. Once inside, he noticed a familiar face behind the reception desk. He couldn't remember her name yet, but she was what all the guys at the station would call a 'badge bunny.' Whenever they were interviewing a victim here, she would always hit on all the uniforms, offering up her 'services'. This was his in!

Dominick strolled up to the desk with his best GQ gait, and when the young lady looked up, he smiled and winked at her. By the look on her ecstatic face, she remembered him, and when he was close enough, he quickly glanced at her nametag before she noticed, her own eyes busy checking him out. "Vicky, didja miss me, sweetheart?" Oh yeah, he was going to lay on the flattery pretty thick tonight.

"Oh my God, Dominick! I haven't seen you around in a long time. You're never with your guys anymore. What happened? I missed seeing that handsome face around here," she gushed, batting her eyes at him.

"Yeah, my superior detective work landed me a gig with some rich corporate developer. I'm a private investigator now. I missed seeing that beautiful face of yours, too. In fact, I was supposed to come by in the morning to ask the day man some questions, but I thought I'd come by tonight n' ask you instead."

"*Me?* Why me, Dom?"

"Just an excuse to see you again, darlin'." He leaned on the desk and winked at her. Dominick took in her deep blush, while her eyes expressed the lust she so obviously felt. He was thrilled knowing that his game was working on her. It was good to know he still had it. He was no male model, after all, but his peak physical condition was top notch. He was pretty tall and his dominating, authoritative attitude always won over the ladies.

"Wait, how did you know I was working tonight? I switched with Eva at the last minute?"

Dominick leaned farther over the desk, stopping inches from her face, and stared deep into her eyes then dragged his gaze down to her lips. His voice lowered to a husky tone." Vicky, what kind of detective would I be if I didn't even know when my favorite girl was working?" *Shit. Nice save*, he appraised himself.

Vicky took in a sharp breath, and when she let it out slowly, her voice was just above a whisper, "Ooh, Dom, what I wouldn't do..."

He noticed her then for the first time. She was on the short side, probably five-foot four, with darker blonde hair up in a high ponytail, and dark brown eyes. On top of being large-chested, she'd been graced with a tiny waist, curvy lush hips, and a tight round ass. That was why she always got so much attention from the other badges. If she hadn't always been so eager to be with *any* and *every* cop, he would definitely have asked her to dinner. She was an attractive woman.

Dalton Ramsey's financial bullshit took up so much of his time, it had been a while since he'd felt the warmth of a woman's body next to him. If Vicky kept looking at him the way she was, he was going take her home and fulfill all of her cop fantasies by cuffing her to his bed. That was just his need talking, though. He wouldn't want to hurt her by rejecting her in the morning.

"So, what did you want to know, Dom? I'll try and help the best I can," she finally asked after their lustful showdown.

"Well, you had an Ellora Belle Sutherland stay for about a week here, after coming in with injuries. She was a partner with Dalton Ramsey Claiborne, and they need her records so they can comp the bill she received."

"Well, why didn't he come down himself to pay or fill out the necessary paperwork, for permission to obtain her records?" She lifted a suspicious eyebrow at him.

Dominick let out an obnoxious laugh and snorted. "Honey, you know the rich. They never show up in person for anything! That's why he hired me... to do all the grunt work. Luckily, it pays better than a detective's salary. Don't worry, darlin'. I'll sign the paperwork if you need me to. I'm a lawman. You can trust me. How many times have you seen me in here saving a life, or protecting it?"

"I know, Dom. It's just that... well, she has to sign off on them, too. It's a privacy clause."

Shit, she's going to make me work hard for it, Dominick thought. "You see, honey," he said, leaning in close, easily towering over her, hoping his size and authority would intimidate her enough to get the answers he wanted. "She was actually reported as missing. I'm trying to keep her and her partners safe. We believe whoever hurt her is coming after her to finish the job. She hasn't been to her house or gotten her mail in over two weeks. If this hospital ever wants to get paid, then they should be lenient with the rules and let Dalton help. Ellora is probably too scared to surface." Boy, was that some incredible bullshit. Dominick did a pretty good job of pulling that explanation out of his ass on the spot.

Vicky nervously bit her lip, unconsciously fidgeting

with her fingers. "I did notice some strange things one night when she was here, but I didn't think to say anything."

"What? What *things*? Tell me."

Her eyes got wide, and she shook her head. "Not here. I get off in a few minutes. Do you want to go and get something to eat? I will explain there."

Dominick tilted his head to the side, narrowing his eyes in suspicion. He gave Vicky a questioning stare. Was she just trying to get him out on a date, or was she worried about the cameras catching her handing over paperwork to him?

Vicky let out a huff of breath at his expression, and quietly explained, "I'll give you what you asked for, but not here, okay?"

"We'll take my car. I'll wait for you outside, sweetheart." At that, Dominick walked out.

He definitely wanted to take his car; that way, he would be in control of the situation. As he sat in the car waiting, he was curious as to her statement about noticing *strange things*. Had Ellora said something that might give away who'd done this and why? Did she know the attacker? Did she get any visitors or a call?

"I'm going to have to call my old partner and see if Ellora or anyone else filed a report on this attack." Out loud to himself, Dominick ticked off the list of things he'd need to accomplish.

They headed out to Dinosaur BBQ on West Willow Street. This was the only place open until one in the morning, and it was Dominick's favorite place. He led Vicky in, opening the door for her, and they were quickly seated in a booth near the back corner. It was dimly lit, and the rowdy patrons took the edge off of their first dinner out together. Professional or not, there was less pressure for polite conversation.

Vicky looked over the menu, but Dominick had no need. He already knew what he wanted. The waitress came around and asked for their order.

"What'll it be, darlin'?" Dom directed for her to go first.

"I'm not that hungry. I'll just have the small order of fried green tomatoes and a salad with the Bar B Blues house dressing, please," Vicky ordered self-consciously.

"What would you like to drink, miss?" the waitress asked, scribbling on her note pad.

"A Coke with no ice, please."

"And for our regular?" The waitress winked at Dominick. He was there every weekend like clockwork.

Dominick chuckled. "I'll have the Cuban pulled pork sandwich with black beans and rice, and I think I'll try your house lager tonight," he ordered confidently.

"All right, one Ape Hanger and a coke, coming right

up."

With their orders out of the way, Dominick focused his attention on Vicky. He wanted to see what she knew. "So, Ellora Belle Sutherland was admitted to the hospital. What injuries did she sustain?"

Vicky let out a breath, and Dominick noticed that she carried a lot of tension in her shoulders. "She was treated for a pretty bad laceration wound to her back. It started at her upper right shoulder and went down her back to her left hip. It took a lot of stitches to close her up, and she lost a lot of blood."

Well, that would explain the dried blood all over her house, Dominick concluded. "She drove herself there?" He really wanted to look over the interior of her car. There might still be physical evidence that had been left behind, which could lead him to where she was hiding.

"No, she was brought in by an ambulance. She was in and out of consciousness."

Where the hell was her car, he wondered, confusion still apparent on his face. Deciding to move on to the next question, he asked, "Did she tell anyone at the hospital what happened?"

"The staff called the police, and a few of your friends came in to speak to her. I'm not sure what she told them, though," Vicky stated.

"Oh, that's good. I can give them a call and see if there's a report I can look over. What are the *strange things* you mentioned before?" Dominick was curious about this uttered statement.

Vicky took a few moments to collect her thoughts, then started. "Well, the night before she left, I was working my rounds. It was insane there. We had a bunch of gunshot victims from the West side of Syracuse come in from some kind of fight. I didn't think about it at the time, but I did notice that there was a tall man slowly walking down the hallway toward Ellora's room. The man had a doctor's white coat on, a stethoscope and gloves... you know, the normal uniform. I only noticed him because, in a sea of rushing doctors, nurses and emergency personnel, he was the only one striding calmly down the hall without a care in the world." Vicky shuttered at the memory.

"A while later, Ellora's heart rate monitor alarm sounded off at the nurse's station. Her heart rate had spiked so high, it scared everyone. I was the first to rush down the hall toward her room, and that same man or doctor... whoever he was, came out of the room right before I got there. His head was turned away from me, so I couldn't see his face. When I walked into her room, she was ashen grey. Her eyes were wide and frantic with fear. She was sweating and hyperventilating." Vicky continued to shake as she retold the story she obviously couldn't forget from that night. That man had left a lasting impression on her, and Dominick was glad she'd told him. This may not have been the best of leads, but it was something.

"Holy shit." Dominick leaned forward, listening intently to her story, his knuckles whitened from clenching his fists. "Who was it?"

"That's the thing. I never found out. She told me she just woke up from a nightmare. Later on that night, Eva, another nurse working with me, said that a man claiming to be a cop demanded all her files and past medical records. When she refused to hand them over, he threatened her and left quickly. Well, I photocopied everything without letting anyone know, because that man from the hallway gave me a strange feeling. Sure enough, the next day, *everything* about Ellora Sutherland we had on file was wiped out, and Ellora Had left before my shift."

"Son of a bitch! At what time did she check out?" Dominick questioned anxiously.

"She never did. She wasn't scheduled to leave for three more days. Her doctor wanted to make sure she wasn't going to develop an infection. They wanted to instruct her on how to dress and clean the wounds properly before she was discharged. She disappeared from her room without a word to anyone." Vicky twisted the thick cloth napkin in her hand over and over. That encounter obviously weighed heavily on her mind since it happened. She looked relieved to finally recount the odd events.

Just then, the waitress came around with their food. "Enjoy, guys. Holler if you need anything else."

With rattled nerves, Dominick dug into his meal with

purpose instead of pleasure. He was on edge and hardly tasted the food, which was a shame because he knew it was amazing.

Vicky moved her food around her plate with her fork for a while, then reached into her deep canvas bag and took out a white envelope. "Here are her copied files. It's not all of the stuff that was wiped out, but at least it's something, I guess." She handed it to him across the table, with a look in her eye that said she wished she could've done more.

"Thank you, Vicky. I'm sure this will help in some way. I've just got to get to the bottom of this somehow, and if not for your smart thinking, I wouldn't even have this." He waved the envelope in his hand and gave her a genuine smile, meaning what he'd said. At least he had a story to go on and a possible lead. He just had to make a trip to his old station to find out who the lead investigator was that night, and see if they'd tell him anything they may have found out.

"You didn't come down just to pay the bill, did you, Detective Antonelli?" She arched an eyebrow at him.

"Actually, darlin', I'm doing my own detective work. I'm doing more than what I was asked to do." Dominick chuckled dryly.

"Since when have you *ever*?" Vicky shot back.

On the drive back to the hospital to drop Vicky back off, they were both silent, lost in their own thoughts. Dominick pulled up to where her car was and walked her to the driver's door. "Thanks for all your help, darlin'. I might be able to locate this girl because of your quick thinking." He wasn't sure that was true, but he might need her help again, so he threw it out there.

"I hope you find her safe, and maybe we could go out again. You know... when it doesn't involve a case." She fidgeted with her hands nervously. Dominick entertained the idea of going out with her again. He had seen a different side to her personality tonight. But now wasn't the right time to pursue it.

"Here's my number, just in case." Vicky slipped him a piece of folded paper.

Plastering on a sideways grin, he kissed her forehead. "You got it, sweetheart!" With that, he hopped in his car and sped off.

While sitting at his desk in his small apartment, he looked through the contents of the envelope. Mostly, it was just medical jibber jabber but, he found more sheets with billing info on it. There were bank account numbers and credit card numbers she had used in the past for payment. Using his police credentials, Dominick set up a monitoring site. If she used her credit cards or withdrew any money from her bank account, it would notify him, which would help him determine her current location.

Exhaustion set in, and Dominick gave in to it. Kicking off his boots and stripping to his boxers, he crashed in his bed.

There was a steady high-pitched sound relentlessly beeping in the background, which got louder as she slowly came back to consciousness. Ellora's eyelids were still heavy from sleep, but still she tried opening them. She squinted when a bright overhead light shined painfully in her eyes. After blinking several times, they were finally able to adjust. Ellora took a ragged breath in, as she was becoming more aware of a throbbing pain in her back, her head… Everywhere seemed to hurt.

She tried lifting her hand to shield the brilliant florescent light with it. Her head ached even more with the cursed light pointing right in her face. A pinch in her arm stopped her from stretching it out all the way, something tugging it back. Turning her head lazily to the side, she saw tubes taped to her arm, delivering liquid to her veins.

With a groggy look around her, Ellora observed that she was, in fact, lying in a hospital bed. Her eyes were fully adjusted now, so she looked around the room, trying to figure out what had happened and how she wound up there. Standing quietly in the corner shadows, a tall figure in a white doctor's coat looked over her chart. His back was to her.

Ellora pulled in a weak, shaky breath like it was her very first one. His back straightened at hearing her, and the man stopped what he had been doing and slowly turned. Ellora closed her eyes and let out the breath slowly, relieved that she was out of that house and finally safe. A heavy hand smacked down hard over her mouth… Her eyes snapped open at the abrupt assault, revealing those vicious black eyes that must've climbed right out of her nightmare to get to her.

His fingers dug painfully into the flesh of her cheeks. His weight crushed her as he climbed closer, stopping a mere inches from her face. Ellora's heart hammered through her weak chest. That beeping from the machine raced, setting off some sort of an alarm. He squeezed her mouth impossibly tighter, the pressure pulsing painfully in her jaw. The other hand held a curved blade, and he skimmed it down the side of her face.

Leaning in closer, he whispered, "It doesn't matter where you are in this world, Ellora, or how many people are around… I will always find you." With the sharp point of the blade pressed under her chin, he painful forced her head up so that she was looking directly into his eyes. He seemed to relish watching as her fear paralyzed her. Ellora quaked helplessly in his grasp as tears streamed down her paling cheeks. "You can't hide from me… I'll always get to you."

"ELLORA! ELLORA, wake UP!"

She was jostled awake by someone aggressively shaking her shoulders. Only then did Ellora realize that *she* was the one thrashing around and screaming. She stopped once she noticed that it wasn't her monster. Cold sweat dripped down her temple. Adelle was hovering over her with a panicked look on her face. Once she let go of Ellora's shoulders, she began running her hands down the side of her face, trying to soothe her. Ellora didn't know who looked more scared... her or Adelle.

"Thank the Lord! Ellora, honey, are you all right? You scared the life outta me!"

Ellora sat up, but tears continued to roll down her flushed face. "I'm sorry... I... I didn't mean to scare you. Umm, how did you get in here?" Ellora was suddenly embarrassed. Her nightmares were too personal, and she was used to suffering through them in silence. Having someone right there witnessing it made her feel ashamed.

"It sounded like you were fighting it out with the devil himself in 'ere! I 'ave a spare key from when I used to stay 'ere. I jumped outta bed and outta my skin when I heard you screamin', and rushed over here to help you. For the love o' God, that was some nightmare you were 'avin'."

Ellora took in Adelle's appearance. Her usually neat, wavy strawberry hair was now a mess, and her face was without any makeup. She wore a sleeveless silky night top and matching shorts. Adelle sat bare foot and Indian style on Ellora's bed, with a wooden bat lying next to her. Ellora laughed breathlessly, having no more voice for the action. The thought amused her. She nodded her head in the bat's direction. "You were going to best the devil with a bat?" She smirked, lifting up one eyebrow.

"Shut it, witch. I improvised." She pushed at her shoulder lightly, laughing. Adelle leaned over her, reaching for the bedside lamp, and turned it on. She looked at Ellora's face, which knew must've looked like a hot mess -- blotchy, red, and puffy. She could just feel the disaster that marked up her face. Worry creased Adelle's brow, proving her previous thought. She lifted both hands, thumbing away the tears that trickled down her new neighbor's face. "Lor, tell me why you 'ave these terrible nightmares almost every night. Tell me what's got you so scared." Her eyes were serious now; they narrowed in intensity and bore right through her.

Ellora's gut was telling her that she could trust Adelle, and she needed to unload some of the weight that rested on her shoulders. She decided to confide in her, only she just wouldn't give *all* the details.

"A man broke into my house about a month ago. He waited for me in the dark and attacked me when I got home. I just barely got away and was taken to the hospital. He was never caught." She paused for a moment, mentally skipping over a lot of the details. "Without my parents, or any other family members, there to help me through it or to comfort me, I was horrified out of my mind, thinking about how he could be right around the corner ready to strike, or waiting for me at my parents' home to finish the job. The home I grew up in, with all the loving memories I had of my parents, was no longer my safe-haven. There was no peace of mind as long as he was out there, roaming free. I always felt unsafe and paranoid, like I was a sitting duck, just waiting to be struck down... *again*. So, I decided to pick up and leave, and got as far away as possible."

Adelle wrapped her arms around her softly, and Ellora rested her head on Adelle's shoulder, giving up on trying to push her away -- or push anyone here away anymore. At that moment, she was extremely exhausted and defeated. Ellora was, to the depths of her soul, tired of going through it all alone. Adelle embraced her, giving a supportive squeeze. "I thought as much. Oh, Lor, I'm so sorry! He hurt you bad, did he?"

"Yes, a little. He had a knife, but I'm okay now." There, she'd said it. Even though it was just a little tidbit of what went on, she felt so much better having said *something*. She could tell by all the looks she got each morning, that everyone heard her nightmares. It felt good to confess a small portion of her fears out loud to someone, and she was glad it was Adelle.

"Well, we are your new family now. I'm 'ere for ya, however you need me. I've always wanted a sister." Adelle let go and leaned back, looking at Ellora with those big honest brown eyes, and smiled.

Yup. Ellora liked Adelle so much already. She had an adoringly kind and caring personality. Ellora smiled back. "I am too... Umm... Please don't tell anyone what I told you. I'm just not ready for the whole town to know." Ellora was a little nervous that she might be as gossipy as the others. She didn't want her telling anyone anything personal. Especially Behr.

"Aaah, Lor, dinnae you say another word. I willnae be telling a soul. Mark my words. I'm different than all the others 'ere. Aye, n' I've never been one to gossip, not even in high school. What ye say to me dies with me. Understood?" Adelle donned a serious, stern expression, and it reminded Ellora of a look her mother would've given when scolding her.

She nodded, deciding to switch gears and change the subject. "So, sis," she said, winking. "Speaking of gossip and high school... A little birdie told me that Gavin has a thing for you." Geez, now she was acting like a sixteen-year old girl at a slumber party. She giggled at the thought. Oh well, anything was better than going back to sleep.

"Aye, Ellora Belle, you're a slippery witch you are, changing the subject on me." Adelle squealed out a high-pitched laugh and slapped Ellora's leg. "I dinnae know who your speakin' with, but Gavin's never had his eye on me. He had 'em on every other skirt in town. I was of an awkward shape, younger, and several grades under him and Behr. I was into the books more than the boys, which didn't win me any friends. Behr and Gavin treated me more like their irritating kid sister."

Adelle started studying her hands as she fidgeted

with her fingers. Her eyes showed evidence of the past coming back to her. "I did think he was a beautiful sight to see and followed him around like a puppy," she admitted.

"You're crazy if you don't notice the way he looks at you, Elle, and why wouldn't he? You look like the epitome of Hollywood glamour! You are Regal. I wasn't there to see how he behaved then, but I have been around long enough to see how he feels for you now. It's as plain as the nose on my face. I think he just doesn't know how to ask you. After all, those other girls you mentioned didn't mean anything to him, and that's why he didn't care whether they said yes or no. You, on the other hand, he does care what your answer is. So, maybe that's why he's stalling. Well, that's what I think anyway."

It looked like Adelle was thinking about what she'd said for a minute, then all of a sudden, a glimmer flashed through her eyes. She cocked her head to the side just a little and smirked. "I also heard from a wee birdie that Behr is taken with you, as well." She puckered her lips at Ellora, looking smug.

"Boy, that birdie certainly gets around, doesn't he?" she huffed out.

"Do you like him all the same?" Adelle's eyebrows shot up in question.

Ellora paused, thinking about that question. Behr was definitely a handsome man, with a fierce body to match. He was thoughtful, kind, attentive, and a true gentleman. The memory of him helping her out with all her purchases, taking her out to lunch, then showing the spot where her parents first met and fell in love flashed at Ellora. But, there seemed to be a roughness about him. He was a large muscled man who could be dangerous if provoked. His eyes hid a sadness, though, one that made Ellora want to comfort him. He was also sharp witted. She thought back at how he saw right through her story when no one else had, smirking at the thought, which encouraged Adelle.

She clapped her hands excitedly and giggled. "I knew it! I knew it! Maybe he'll ask ya to marry him, and you can have a whole clan o' babies!" Adelle obviously enjoyed taunting her.

"No, no, no, I'm... I don't think…" she stuttered. "I'm not ready for that... not yet. I've never had a boyfriend before. I don't know if I am capable of fully letting my guard down and trusting someone with my heart. It still feels shattered after my parents' deaths, and I'm still trying to pick up the pieces. But, to be honest, I am curious about Behr. He definitely has captured my attention. I am interested, but I'm afraid that I'm too much of a tomboy. I don't know how to do the dating thing."

"Well," Adelle interrupted. "I'll help you. If you were ever to hand your trust or your heart over to anyone, Behr is the very best man for the job. I've known him my whole life. He'll keep your heart safe and protected. He would go to the ends o' the earth for those he holds dear. And, Ellora, you are now one o' those people.

"And as for the tomboy issue... Well, first, I can take you to town and help you pick out a few flattering dresses. Aye, you can be a tomboy handyman if you want, but that doesn't mean you 'ave to dress like one! I had my roommate in college help me out. She transformed me from an awkward bookworm to a classy lady with wit. So I guess it's time to return the favor n' pay it forward." She winked at Ellora playfully. "You're gorgeous and petite, so you'll be makin' my job easy. We'll 'ave him droolin' at your feet for sure." Adelle crossed her arms over her chest as she had already set her mind on the decision.

"Well, first things first, I have to fix a few things for Grady tomorrow..."

Adelle gave Ellora a warning glance, not to side step her plan, but Ellora put her hand up to let her know she wasn't finished. "If you help me out a little, I will go shopping with you. Deal?"

She smiled and nodded. "Aye, it's a deal." She reached out and softly grabbed Ellora's hand in both of hers and rubbed it softly like a loving mother would. The gesture warmed her broken heart.

Ellora took in the moment they both shared, appreciating the talk they'd just had. It'd been so long since she'd talked to someone about *anything*. Sitting on her bed, talking about hot unattainable men, felt to Ellora like they really were sisters. The thought made her heart swell. She reached out and drew Adelle in for a hug. "Thank you, Adelle. You have no idea how much this has meant to me."

Adelle hugged her back hard. "Now, let me go get a few hours o' beauty sleep." She stood, pushing her hair back over her shoulder, and grabbed her bat. With a wink, she walked out. Ellora already loved the girl.

Walking down the narrow steps to the first floor, Ellora felt better than she had in a very long time. After the talk with Adelle, she actually got a few hours of uninterrupted sleep. And without another nightmare. A first. She was up earlier because of it. Her body wasn't used to that amount of sleep, so she had a hot refreshing shower, donned her favorite heather grey V-neck and dark skinny jeans, and headed down for some breakfast.

She rounded the corner with a wide goofy smile on her face. Grady was pulling down chairs, like he did every morning. Kristy was cooking bacon, eggs, and sausage in the back. Adelle was making coffee behind the front counter. Behr and Gavin sat on stools at the bar, annihilating their plates. Ellora's grin widened when she caught Gavin checking out Ellie's backside. *Ugh, he's got it bad.*

"Good morning, guys! How's everyone doing this morning?" Ellora passed Grady, giving him a quick hug and a kiss on the cheek, then skipped behind the bar, aiming for the mugs.

"Aye, Ellora, m'sweeting, would you like a bite this morn'? Eggs, bacon?" Kristy shouted, waving the spatula as she spoke.

"Definitely, Kris, thank you. Hey, sis." Ellora nudged Adelle's arm and winked. "Fill 'em up."

Adelle laughed, the sound light and airy. She poured them both some coffee, then noticeably pointed her eyes in Gavin and Behr's direction, snickering. Her vibrant expression had Ellora struggling to hold in her giggle. She looked *amazing* this morning. Even after little sleep, every strawberry wave was neat and looked like rolling hills, and her makeup was fresh and soft. She wore an empire waist dress with small ruffled cap sleeves, the royal blue color making her hair look like a siren. Ellora admired her elegance. "Playing it up for your number one fan...?" Ellora whispered, enjoying the blush that crept up, staining Adelle's cheeks in response to her teasing.

She mouthed the words -- *shut up, heifer.* An un-ladylike snort escaped, and Ellora almost choked on her hot coffee. Adelle eyeballed Ellora's plain outfit, and wrinkled her nose. She lifted her perfectly manicured eyebrow, obviously disapproving of her outfit choice. Sticking out her tongue, Ellora walked back to the kitchen to grab her plate, and kissed Kristy's cheek.

"My, my, you look like you just had a stroll through the heavens! Good to see you're in bright spirits, m'dear."

When Ellora reappeared with her plate and coffee, she caught Behr staring right at her with a brilliant grin. How was it possible that he seemed to get better looking every day? He was wearing a much too tight, dark hunter green t-shirt. The cut muscles in his shoulders, arms, and chest stretched out the material. She let herself admire him for a moment.

Choosing the stool next to him, she plopped down. She was in such a pleasant mood that instead of avoiding Behr's scalding hot gaze, which always gave her goose bumps and made her blush, she decided to just grow a pair and acknowledge it. Turning to him, Ellora looked right into his blue eyes. "Good morning, Behr. How are you feeling this morning?" Ellora shoveled a fork full of eggs in her mouth. Hey, she was starving. Manners suck anyways. His eyes twinkled as he appraised her mood.

"Aye, it's better now that you're here, love. Now, I get to see that breathtaking smile you're wearing... Is that for me?" His voice was a sensually deep baritone. He tilted his head, amazed by her upbeat attitude.

Ellora blushed at his attention. He continued to look down on her longingly, and she felt warmth at the pit of her stomach. Once again, he won the intense staring contest. She smiled deeper, then turned and changed the subject. "Grady, don't bother with those chairs. I have to move them anyway. I'm going to get started sealing those cracks, cleaning up the mold, and paint on the Armor concrete protectant. It'll have to dry through tomorrow. Then, I'll head outside and seal the walkway cracks that lead to the foundation. I also plan on adjusting the down spout so it leads all this rain you get, out and away from the building."

"I thank you, Ellora, m'sweet. You're just as amazin' as your father was." Grady wasn't a handy man at all. He literally used duct tape for *everything*! The evidence of that was the now peeling piece pathetically placed across the ugly cracks on the wall.

"I'll stay and give you a hand today, love." Behr stood, towering over Ellora. He made it perfectly clear that it wasn't an offer, but a statement of fact. In that moment of realization, she grew a little timid and nervous at the thought of working alone with Behr -- all day, side by muscular side. Oh boy. She was in trouble. Ellora nervously tried to come up with an excuse.

"Well... umm... Actually, Adelle was going to be my helping hand today," she rushed out, suddenly remembering their deal.

Gavin laughed, nodding his head in Adelle's direction. "Aye, by the way she's dressed, she is going to get her hands real dirty, *eagerly* helping ya out!" Ellora couldn't help but smirk at him. He spoke sarcasm well.

Adelle scowled at him, slapping his forearm teasingly. "Aye, Lor, I hate to say it, but Gavin's right. I'm nae properly dressed for that kind o' work. I've got errands of my own to run in town today. I've got to get myself properly settled in. Take Behr up on his offer. He is far better help than me." She quickly glanced over at Gavin out of the corner of her eyes. He met hers with a knowing smug grin. At that moment,

Ellora couldn't help but feel like this had been their plan all along. Brat!

"Thank you, Behr. The job would run a lot quicker with *competent* help." She stressed the word while pointing a stern glare at Adelle. "I appreciate it." She snickered at Adelle, who placed her hands on her hips and grunted in mock offense. "Maybe Gavin can go with you to town?" Adelle took in a sharp breath. She looked like she was going to get her later for that, and it would be so worth it. Two could play at that game.

"Aye, I would love to, Ellie. That is certain. But, I've got to head out to work this morn'. If this grizzly bear is lending a hand 'ere, I 'ave to direct people to other ferry boats today." Gavin looked elated for the invitation, and frustrated that he couldn't spend the day with her. Adelle had a moment of disappointment flash across her face. "But, I'd be more than happy to meet you for lunch, darlin'. Anywhere you want." He grabbed her hand and kissed her knuckles. "I'll call ya when I'm on m'lunch." He got up then and dropped some bills on the counter, lifted his arm, and saluted goodbyes to everyone.

"How does he know my cell number? I gave that to him before I left for college," she whispered to herself.

"Ellie, he's never forgotten." Behr leaned in, confirming to Adelle what everyone else already knew. She really was blind to his affections. Grinning from ear to ear, she continued to sip her coffee.

Behr leaned in closer to Ellora. "What say you, love... ready to get started?" He ran his imposing hand down the length of her cheek, and tucked a stray tendril of hair behind her ear.

Ellora's heart thrummed inside her chest at his tender touch. She wasn't sure she could concentrate on her work with this magnificent creature standing so close... all day. She tried one more time to give him a pass to opt out of the project. Though she hoped he'd say he would, she prayed he'd stay at the same time. "You don't have to skip your responsibilities to help me, Behr."

"Dinnae you worry 'bout me, love. I've wanted to help this ol' goat for a long while. Now is the best time for that. I've already brought your supplies out back, so we can start when you're finished if you'd like." Behr looked down and carefully grasped Ellora's hand, softly rubbing circles on the back of it with his thumb. His gaze showed a hungry desire as he slowly looked up at her with longing through the cover of his dark lashes. This moment stole the breath from Ellora. She had no words. She had completely forgotten how to talk or think.

Adelle broke up their private moment. "Don't worry, Lor. I will keep my eyes open for some hot numbers for you in town today. I get the feeling you don't like shopping anyways, so I will save you the trouble." Adelle smiled wickedly, dabbed her mouth with her napkin, and rose gracefully from her seat. "I look forward to seeing all the progress you make today. Can't wait to talk about it tonight when I get back." Ellora knew she was referring to Behr. Little she-devil! She sashayed out the door with an elegance Ellora admired. Her mother would've absolutely adored her.

Ellora took a deep breath and let it out slowly. "Alrighty, it looks like it's you and me today, Behr. Why don't you go grab the supplies, and I'll clear out the rest of these chairs."

Behr saluted her like a dutiful soldier. "Aye, lass, as you wish." Smiling ruefully, he marched out back.

This was definitely going to be an interesting day, to say the least. *Well, here goes nothing.*

Behr and Ellora got started with the mold on the wall first. It needed to be thoroughly removed from the wall before they could start filling the cracks. First, they washed the walls with a mild detergent solution her father showed her, and allowed it to dry.

"Okay, Behr, hand me the other bucket. We need to wipe the walls with a mix of a quarter-cup of bleach for every gallon of water."

Behr grabbed the bucket with water, the bleach, and some heavy duty yellow plastic gloves. He spanked Ellora with the gloves playfully, looking pleased when she let out a squeal. "Safety first, love. I wouldn't want you to burn those lovely hands of yours." He reached out, clutching her hand, and rubbed the back of her palm with his thumb. Ellora's heart skipped a beat at the skin to skin contact. Her body used to feel fearful and anxious at another's touch, but now, her body seemed to anticipate it, crave it even. He took care in placing her gloves on each hand, his all-consuming sapphire eyes never leaving hers during the task. Ellora still didn't know how to act around him when he turned up his intensity. She became jittery and nervous, but deep down, she had an aching desire for him to touch her again.

Ellora's skin was heating up from the hungry look in his eyes, and all she could say was "Th... thank you." How could his ex, Shannon, *ever* have left him, when she had this irresistibly sexy man all to herself? Geez, he just had to look at her and Ellora's temperature rose, heating her to the core. She stared suggestively at his mouth and wondered what it would be like to kiss him. Were his lips strong, passionate, and dominating? Unknowingly, she licked her lips at the pleasant daydream.

Behr zeroed in on her, his eyes narrowing on her wetted lips. His eyes darkened with desire to a deep ocean blue. He blinked once and sucked in a quick breath. Running his hand through his thick hair, he let the breath out slowly then bent over and grabbed his gloves.

Ellora wondered if he was as affected by the sexual tension between them as she was. "Right, well, let's get scrubbing. This bleach is making me dizzy." Ellora stretched to grab the sponge. She knelt down and started scrubbing in quick circles. Geez, what was going on with her today? She must be going crazy.

Finally, they were on the last step to removing the mold on the old walls. She used her dad's secret weapon, a quarter-cup of laundry detergent to a gallon of water. Worked every time!

Ellora was working up a pretty good sweat; cleaning away the mold had become quite a workout. Either that or she was really out of shape. The temperature felt like it had risen, and the smell of the chemicals was starting to make her lightheaded. Her V-neck was damp with sweat, sticking to her skin. If she wasn't so busy, she would've been embarrassed. Behr was working just as hard beside her, except he looked as fresh as he had that morning. Unfair!

As they worked their way down the wall, Ellora caught glimpses of Behr watching her from the corner of her eye. He looked like he really wanted to ask her something. Whatever it was, it looked like it bothered him.

Finally, he opened his mouth to ask, "So, love, 'ave you been sleeping better at nights yet?"

Ellora's hand froze on the spot. Oh my God. She so did *not* want to talk about this. Especially *not* with him. Did Adelle tell them this morning, after she had promised not to? Her mouth dropped open. "Did Adelle tell you all I was having nightmares?"

"Nae, no one had to tell a soul. We can hear you at night." His expression turned to pained sympathy, and she didn't like it. Ellora was utterly mortified. "I'm worried 'bout you. That's all, love." Behr stuttered his answer when he saw her reaction.

She vigorously scrubbed the walls as anger took over. She was furious at herself. Upset that everyone *could* in fact hear her at night.

"Look at me, Ellora." Behr laid his hand on hers to stop the scrubbing. She turned her head slowly, staring at her feet. "What happened back there? Tell me why you scream in your sleep all night. Tell me why you came here. I want to help. I worry about you." He reached out, cupping her chin, and lifted her head up to look at him. His face was full of concern. She wanted to be mad. She wanted to tell him that it was none of his business, that he shouldn't bother being worried. But, she just couldn't.

His honest concern touched her. Ellora thought about telling him what she told Adelle. It was a pretty safe story, and if he hadn't said anything to anyone so far, she doubted he ever would. But she bit her lip to keep her mouth shut, and gulped hard. Behr saw her hesitation. His eyes bore into hers, which had her resolve faltering. Her stomach twisted itself into knots as she thought about what had truly happened. She felt faint as visions of the vicious attack flashed through her mind.

Half daydreaming, Ellora's eyes were unfocused and stared at the nightmare only she could see. She ripped her gloves off and stood on shaky legs. "I need some fresh air." With that, she hurried out the door.

Cool salty sea air blew instant relief in her face when

she yanked open the door. The cool breeze was refreshing, instantly calming her frazzled nerves. She walked to the edge of the pier and leaned on the railing with her elbows. She still felt dizzy, like she just got off a spinning carnival ride. Ellora took slow deep breaths, trying to quell her nausea. Heavy footsteps approached, crunching the gravel behind her, and she knew it was Behr. Her body could feel him when he got close, as if there was a pull between them. He stopped right behind Ellora, paused, and let out a deep rumbling breath. Leaning down, he grabbed the railing right beside her. He clenched it tight, his knuckles turning white with the force.

"Sorry for prying, Ellora. It wasnae m'place to go nosin' about." Behr stood up straight, letting go of the railing and turned toward her. He let his eyes roam all over Ellora's face. The look he gave her was so smoldering it burned through her stomach.

She smirked at him weekly. "No need for apologies, Behr. I'm just not ready to talk about... that. Yet."

Behr considered that answer for a moment, and nodded. He reached out and brushed the hair out of her face, tucking it behind her ear. "Well, I'm 'ere for you, whenever you are ready, love." His concern grew as he took in her change in appearance. "You look pale, love. Are you feeling sick at all?"

Ellora nodded. "I feel dizzy. I think it's the bleach. Let's get to work out here for a while, okay?"

Behr ran his thumb softly back and forth across her cheek. "Whatever you need me to do, love… I'll do for you."

They went to work on the outside cracks in the foundation, sealing them with an extra strength epoxy. Now Behr was sweating. She had him grading the mud that was under the stone walkway, away from the foundation. All the digging, lifting, and grading had his shirt deliciously sticking to his skin. He made sweat look sexy as it glistened under the bright sun. She caught glimpses of his roped muscles, twitching, working, and flexing under the thin material. She was shamelessly drooling, imagining him as a powerful gladiator. He was exactly the reason why sculptors carved out magnificent statues. He was an Adonis. Luckily, he took over most of the work, because she was struggling to pay attention to the job at hand.

When the stone pavers were all back in place, Ellora caulked the seams that were flush to the foundation. They both stopped when they heard the sirens blaring in the distance, the noise getting louder as it came nearer. A fire truck came barreling down Bank Street, turning onto Quay. It slowed down as it came their way, and Ellora saw Patrick standing on the platform near the truck door, holding onto the hand rail. He leaned out and smiled at them.

"Is that *MY* pink tool belt you're wearing, lass?" The other guys whooped n hollered at Ellora from the truck.

"It looks better on me anyway!" she shouted, turning in a slow circle with her hands on her hips, showing off the famous belt.

They began whistling and cat calling, which was all in good fun. Ellora winked and blew them all a kiss. She curtsied, playing along. Patrick threw his head back and laughed heartily.

"This be the lass I was tellin' you all 'bout. She's gonna fix up Grady's place like a shiny new penny, she is!" Grady bellowed, proud of her teasing attitude.

One of the firefighters shouted out, "Aye, if that be the girl, then you'll find us coming 'round more often."

"Where you off to, Patty?" Behr hollered at him over the sirens.

"Steven McGuiness almost lit his ass on fire, trying to fry a turkey on his balcony over at the Quayside Apartments. Giant ass that he is!" And with that, they sped off.

They were both thankful for that encounter because it lightened the mood immensely. Behr and Ellora looked at each other for a long moment. He smiled as she continued to laugh at Patrick's eccentric behavior.

"I was told Patty almost set the whole town on fire once." Ellora's eyebrows shot up at the confession. "He was setting off homemade bottle rockets, and they landed in some bushy tree tops, catching them on fire." Behr's chest vibrated as he tried hard to hold in his laughter at the story.

Ellora let out a loud cackling laugh. "Are you kidding me? And he became a fire fighter? That is too funny!" They laughed together.

Then their eyes met again, and the whole world stood still. They held on to each other's gaze for what felt like an unending moment. The moment turned sultry as their eyes penetrated one another. Her breathing hitched and her blood heated. Behr's eyes roamed suggestively from her eyes, her lips, and slowly down her body, until they came to rest on her hips where the belt hung. His erotic gaze stimulated something deep down inside of her. She blushed scarlet.

"I will render a guess that your tool belt *does* look better on you, than it would on Patty." Behr looked back up into her eyes and winked. He took a step closer, running his finger along the compartments on the belt. Ellora shivered as his fingers grazed the sensitive skin along the small section of exposed skin on her stomach. "What next, boss lady?"

Across the street, Shannon stood on the sidewalk with her group of friends, engrossed in the scene between Behr and Ellora. "Who is that plain looking heifer flirting with *my* Behr?" Shannon hissed with her fists clenched, her voice dripping with jealousy.

The much too bony brunette to her left responded, "Aye, that must be the American staying at Grady's. The whole town is talking about her. Aye, people 'ave seen the two of them holding hands 'round town. Isaac told my sister that she was at Jan's hardware getting supplies to fix up

Grady's Pub... for *FREE!*"

Shannon's eyes narrowed into slits, glaring at them. "Who does she think she is? Holy Mary, mother of God? Behr n' I share a history. Try as he might... he just cannae resist me. I will win back what's mine."

Shannon's other friend standing behind her decided to weigh in. "Shannon, you're bad. 'Aven't you played his heart enough? Behr is a *really* good guy."

"I was just teaching him a lesson is all. If he doesnae go along with my plans, then he doesnae get me." Her anger elevated the pitch in her voice, rising higher after every word. Shannon's obvious jealousy had her acting like a vengeful vindictive child. But no one had ever gone up against her like this. No one but Shannon had ever dared to make a pass at Behr. All the women in this town knew better. Shannon fought dirty.

"Well, I think ye pushed him into the arms o' that American. I dinnae think he got your *lesson*, Shan. They look like they are just moments away from a very public and sexually erotic encounter." The boney brunette giggled, provoking her.

Jealousy burned like hot coals in the pit of Shannon's stomach. She couldn't bear the thought of another woman wrapped up in his big, powerful arms. Even though she had been caught cheating, she still loved him in her own way. She wouldn't have done it had he ran away with her. Is that selfish? Yes. Did she give a shit? Nope. Now, she had no golden ticket to the States, and no man by her side. That just wouldn't do. Aye, the moment her new boy-toy, Chris, took one look at a very angry Behr, he dumped her immediately and high-tailed it back to the States as fast as was humanly possible. Behr always had that effect on people. Shannon remembered the night she met Chris at a pub in town. She was out partying it up with her girlfriends and having a good time. She flirted with the tourists and gained a few numbers, and a few free drinks as well. She didn't worry about Behr seeing her, because he only ever frequented that shitty hole in the wall he called a pub. It was pathetic, really, how he cared for all of them. Lot of good it'd do. They were just dragging him down further. Well, she did think Chris was kind of cute, so she thought she'd play the part of an innocent small-town local and see where it'd take her. Shannon went back to his hotel room and successfully charmed the pants off of him… literally! After one week, he promised to take her back to the U.S. with him. She'd scored big-time with that one. That was exactly what she tried to get Behr to do. Shannon always thought that she was meant for bigger and better things than this ancient town, and she would stop at nothing to get it.

Now left with no man and no ticket to a better future, she was back to square one… *again*. Shannon switched her focus back on Behr. Her territorial and prideful personality wouldn't allow her to just let this new skirt move in here, become a popular legend overnight, and steal Behr away with her do-good attitude. He'd play right into her hands with that act, too. Behr was a sucker for girls like her.

A terrible thought burst into her head, like a bull on a rage. If Behr bought into her act, then she decided to move back to the U.S... where she belonged... would Behr want to follow her there? Anger heated her flesh, the thought causing her to break out into a sweat. There was no way in Hell she would let that happen. He was a homebody, after all. That was the reason he had always given her for why he wouldn't leave. He didn't even like America.

But there was no denying the smoldering passion that lay hidden under the surface between the two of them. Anyone on the street could see the irresistibly hungry desire in their eyes. Even a blind man would feel it, just as Shannon could from where she stood. This revelation had Shannon's previous certainty of gaining him back faltering. If Behr wouldn't go with her... then she sure as Hell wouldn't let him go with this bitch either! She decided right then and there that she would break them up. She didn't care how she had to do it. It was already over between them. They just didn't know it yet.

"We'll just see about that now, won't we?" Shannon growled, gritting her teeth. "C'mon, girls, let's pick out something hot for me to wear tonight. Shannon's going hunting!" she announced with conviction. She forced herself to drag her eyes away from them. She would put the girl in her place soon enough.

"Ooooh, NO! I don't think so! Will that even fit?" Ellora stared in horror at the colorful array of dresses, skirts, blouses, and accessories lain out on her bed.

"They will fit, as they should, and you're welcome!" Adelle gracefully waved her hand at the items like a Scottish Vanna White.

"Go ahead, Lor, try this one on. It's my favorite. Aye, n' it will make your green eyes pop." She held up an emerald green jersey wrap dress. Ellora didn't want to admit to her that she was in love with the style and color; she thought it was best *not* to encourage her. "Now, get your round ass in that wash room and try it on, or off to my room I go to grab m'bat. I shopped all day with you in mind, so go and pretend that you love it for my benefit." Adelle shoved the dress in her arms and pushed her toward the washroom.

Ellora stuck her tongue out playfully as she marched into the bathroom. She flinched when easing the dress on, careful not to drag it down her sensitive back.

It was gorgeous and fit her shape perfectly, like it had been sewn specifically for her body. The soft cotton fabric made it move and flow delicately. It had a plunging vneckline, which made Ellora a tad nervous because it was extremely low and extremely sexy. Although it was beautiful, they were two things on an outfit she'd never before thought she'd ever be caught wearing... *ever.* The covetous dress wrapped around, barely covering all the appropriate areas, and tied at the side of her waste. A small knot kept it all together as it cascaded down to her thigh. The dress came to rest a few inches above her knees. Ellora walked out with her arms out and strutted her stuff toward Adelle. "You likes?"

"I'm pretty good at this. I should get paid," Adelle gloated. "You should wear it downstairs and show everyone. Maybe *somebody* will enjoy the view." She wiggled her eyebrows scandalously. "Ellora, you look so sexy, the path you walk will surely melt behind you."

She plopped down on the bed. "So how was your lunch with Gavin?" she probed, changing the subject.

"Well, I umm... I told him I was too busy, n' aye, that I was. I shopped all day for you, and nearly forgot about my own needs. So when he called, I told him I was swamped with errands and that I would see him later." She nibbled on her bottom lip, unsure.

"Chicken!" Ellora shouted, shoving her shoulder lightly. The look on Adelle's face said it all. Under all her confident and beautiful façade was an incredibly self-conscious girl, who when close to her crush, becomes the insecure girl from high school all over again. Ellora leaned in closer and asked softly, "What's wrong? What happened, sweetie?"

"I want to *believe* that he likes me. I really do. I'm just nae ready to accept it yet, I guess. He has to prove to me that I'm nae just another notch on his belt." She fidgeted, shifting in her seat as she twisted her fingers in her lap. "Aye, it's hard to forget the past."

Ellora nodded in agreement. That was something she totally understood. "No need to rush, sweetie. Get reacquainted with each other and let whatever happens between you two grow at its own pace."

Adelle smiled at her. Her eyes glistened with the threat of fresh tears. "Aye, sis. Lets' go downstairs and 'ave ourselves a drink."

They got up, and Ellora followed her down the stairs, their arms linked together. She forgot all about wearing the dress, blaming the comfy fabric.

"Gerard! Where are my Haggis Puffs?" Kristy shouted out back. "Grady, we are going to need a few more souls in 'ere to lend a helping hand, we are. This place is swamped!"

Grady rubbed his salt and copper bristly beard, his eyes wide with disbelief. "Aye, that we are."

He looked out at the bar as Patrick walked in with his crew from the firehouse, finding stools next to Behr, Gavin, and his staff at the terminal. He scanned the rest of the pub. Moira and some folks from the diner showed up, along with some of the older local high schoolers, all sitting at the tables to the left and right of the bar. Loud chatter and light laughter filled the place. Grady teared up. It had been a long time since this many people were in his pub like this.

Behr listened as Patrick expressed animatedly with his hands about saving the Quayside Apartments from the volcanic flames, singlehandedly of course.

Kristy, Gerard, and Gavin had spread the word about Behr and Ellora renovating his place, getting it ready for the upcoming season. Even though repairs had just begun, that didn't stop the curious spectators from stopping by, not only to see Grady's place but to take a curious look at Ellora, as well.

As conversations filled the lively pub, Behr looked up and saw Adelle and Ellora walking arm in arm around the corner. His jaw dropped. Behr's eyes widened as his heart accelerated, pounding erratically inside his chest. "Beautiful," he whispered under his breath.

"Aye, brother, they both are an incredible sight to be seen. That's for certain," Gavin acknowledged, slapping Behr on his back.

Behr chugged down the warm liquid in one gulp. "I'm gonna need another round. This is going to be a rough night. I can see that."

Behr couldn't take his eyes off her. That dress... It was stunning, and it was dangerous. It hugged every delicious curve. His eyes roamed over her like a desperate man needing water. That sinfully sweet, mouthwatering dress showed off her soft slender legs, showing a sneak peek at her curvy thighs. Her perfect breasts almost spilled out of the revealing dress. The knot holding it all together seemed to be begging him to unravel the tie. Behr's hands grew clammy with the animalistic need to slowly unwrap her, like his very own gift. His fingers twitched at the thought of undressing her. The color of the dress made her green eyes stand out like emeralds, and her hair like black silk. He'd never in his life felt this strongly about wanting to wrap his arms around a woman and get lost in her. Behr *needed* to taste her lips.

"Easy, Boyle, your look will scare that lass away. Just tone down your intensity, brother. Play it cool," Gavin murmured, low enough for Behr's ears alone. He let out a ragged breath, realizing that he had been holding it in. It dawned on him, as he watched her greet everyone with a smile, how much he *wanted* her. The feeling was overwhelming. The power of the pull he felt toward her made it impossible to think of anything else... She was becoming his entire world. He had no choice but to make her his. Behr knew he had to be patient, though. She was holding back a terrifying secret, so he'd have to wait until she was ready for him to protect her, to love her, and possess her the way he wanted to. She didn't know it yet, but she was already *his*.

Ellora walked into the main pub area with Adelle, and immediately heard a bustling chaotic noise. "I can't believe it! There's a crowd!" Ellie and Ellora looked at one another with delighted surprise.

Then Ellora's eyes found Behr in the crowd. He was pretty hard to miss; he was looking at her with such appraising, lustful intensity that her whole body scorched from it. Tingling shot through her, raising goose bumps on her arms. His eyes seemed darker somehow. She felt like he could see right through her, straight to her soul. The whole world seemed to fall away. In that moment, it was just Behr and Ellora in the room. His eyes were alight with passion. Ellora could feel the heat from them from where she stood. He almost looked like a predator, his gaze unwavering. Her core could almost feel his desire for her. This feeling struck her like lightning, sending an electric shock through her system. Blushing, she looked down and realized too late that she was still wearing the dress. She wanted to turn around and run back upstairs to change. She was just about to do just that when Grady and Kristy ran up to them.

"Thanks to you pretty ladies the whole pier is buzzin' 'bout what's going on here. We need some help. Start takin' orders, ladies! We 'ave some thirsty folks waitin' for some of our brew, n' just maybe they'll have a bite as well."

"Oh, how exciting. Come, Lor. I will get you a pad n'

pen and show you where our drinks n' trays are. This will be fun." She grabbed Ellora's arm, but she yanked back.

"Wait, let me go change first. This won't work! I've never bartended before. I can't do this."

"Don't be stubborn, you mule! You'll get better tips with that dress. You look like a goddess." Her smile was infectious, and Ellora took a look around. Everyone was in good spirits, laughing, smiling, and telling wild stories. She once again felt at peace here. This felt like home. Grady was on the verge of tears with happiness. She couldn't let him down. She wouldn't. Ellora needed to get over herself and help him out.

Adelle added quickly, not fully convinced that Ellora would help, "I will show you all you need to know. I used to help out 'ere every summer before I went off to college. This will be more fun with a partner in crime, though." She scrunched her nose, stuck out her tongue, and gave her signature wink.

Making up her mind, Ellora walked behind the bar and grabbed a pen and pad. "Who's next?"

She hadn't laughed this hard in forever! Ellora couldn't even remember when the last time was. Her legendary taunting with Patrick had been so over-told and exaggerated that she was belly laughing so hard, she thought she should have ripped abs by now. Her cheeks hurt from smiling all night. Ellora had gotten offers from several people who wanted to donate their time, money, or products to help get Grady's back to its original charming character. And, of course, she accepted. Grady deserved it.

Feeling stoic and confident, she decided to put that feeling to good use, and awoke her inner runway model as she strutted toward Behr. He had been nursing his mug for a while now, refusing Adelle when she offered him a refill. Ellora wasn't sure if that was a hint, but hey, why not take a chance. This was the best she'd looked since arriving here. Who was she kidding... she was a tomboy. She *never* dressed like this. It couldn't hurt to flirt just a little, right? After the way their chemistry sizzled while working together earlier that day, and the way he seemed to feast his eyes on her from across the room, he probably felt it too. Right? Ellora decided to take a chance and find out.

"Hey, Behr, how about a refill? That must taste warm and flat by now." Ellora leaned her back on the bar, facing him, until she felt a sharp sting and jerked back up before he noticed. When he looked up at her, she smiled.

His jaw muscle clenched then twitched. He looked down at her mouth, then back up into her waiting eyes. At first, it looked like he was angry and trying to hold it back, but then one corner of his mouth curled up. "I will take anything you want to give me, love." His voice was warm and soothing.

Smirking, Ellora lifted up one eyebrow. "Why, Mr. Buchanan, is that innuendo pouring out of your mouth? Tsk, let me get that." She snatched her bar rag that was draped over her shoulder and made it look like she was going to dab his mouth with it, when he took hold of her hand. Stealing the towel out of her hand, Behr tossed it on his lap and gave her a devilish grin. He pulled her hand into his and brought it up to his mouth, kissing each fingertip. Behr's eyes were trained on Ellora's, holding her captive with his all-consuming gaze. He turned her palm face up, giving it a little peck. The sensation made Ellora weak in the knees. She wasn't sure what to do… so she just let him continue. His pecks turned into playful nibbles. It looked as though he was trying to elicit a reaction out of her, but she was stuck on the spot. Frozen.

Ellora's heart thumped inside her chest in an erratic rhythm as she trembled. Desire coursed through her veins. Ellora longed for him to continue this wonderful torture. She imagined him kissing her lips in the same way, nibbling his way down her neck. In the midst of her daydream, she heard whistling and cat calling. They broke loose from their personal trance and deep connection to look around the room. Everyone was watching them, amused at the entertainment they'd unknowingly provided.

"To young love and lust," Patrick shouted, raising his mug high in the air. He laughed and patted his buddy's back.

The bar shouted out a thunderous, "AYE!"

Behr picked up the bar rag from his lap and snapped it at Ellora's behind. "Where's my brew, woman?"

Letting out a nervous giggle, Ellora relented. "I'm

going, I'm going. Geez, hold your horses."

The door swung open, and Ellora watched a tall bleached-blonde woman walk in with a *look-at-me* attitude. She had hazel cat eyes and a roundish face with freckles. She was taller than Ellora and extremely skinny. Immediately, the woman zeroed in on Behr. Ellora instantly knew that it was Shannon, Behr's ex. She marched in with determination, wearing a short black skirt and halter top. Boy, she was over the top. She was trying way too hard. At first, she sat at a table out of his line of sight and just watched him. Ellora wondered what her game plan was. What was she doing here?

Ellora walked over to where he sat, hell bent on keeping his eyes away from her. She had hurt him. Bad. More than once. She hoped she wasn't here to rub his nose in it. "Here you go, Behr." Ellora handed him a full mug. "Are you hungry for something? Can I get you anything?"

He eyed Ellora while taking a large gulp, his Adam's apple bobbing with each pull. "I'm starving for something, love, but food, it is not!" He grinned wickedly and slid his thumb down Ellora's cheek. He lowered his hand and laced his fingers through hers.

Wow, Ellora thought. She needed air. She feel dizzy and feverish all of a sudden. The pub was crowded, and the stale air was thick with the chemical smell from earlier. It started to feel suffocating to her.

Ellora heard the woman's shrilly voice coming up

from behind her, and cringed. The moment, *their* moment, was over. "Beeeehr, aren't you going to introduce me to the new help?" *Ugh. She is such a bitch already*, Ellora thought.

Behr froze on the spot, turning pale. His eyes iced over, turning glacial. He slowly turned toward her and just stared. Ellora's heart dropped to the pit of her stomach. She wished that she could shield him from her. He had been so happy over the last week. He looked less broody and more at ease. That is, until *she* walked in. Ellora decided to jump in when he hadn't made a move to answer.

"I'm Ellora Belle Sutherland. And you are?" She didn't want to look jealous in front of Behr or anyone else there. She figured they all knew what kind of person she was, so Ellora decided to kill her with kindness. That always irritated girls like this even more, when they couldn't get a rise out of others the way they wanted to.

"How rude, Behr. 'Aven't you told her about your girlfriend?"

Ellora forced a smile. "That's funny. Behr NEVER mentioned you. Do you have a name?"

Her eyes narrowed into slits. "My name is Shannon. Now, how 'bout makin' yourself useful and skirtin' back where you belong to fix me a drink, m'kay!" She wrapped her arms around Behr's neck and leaned in to kiss him. He finally snapped back to reality, jerking away, and pried her arms off him.

"*GIRLFRIEND!*" he shouted loudly. The look of disgust

marred his beautiful face. "'Ave you forgotten that you tossed me aside for another?" His voice thundered like a sub-woofer, and Shannon flinched. "You *cheated* on me, woman!" He couldn't look at her anymore. He looked down, scraping his hands through his hair repeatedly. The betrayal and hurt he tried so hard to hide was overwhelmingly palpable. Ellora's heart broke for him. "You tried to take what was mine and give it to another! You just used me..." His voice was just above a whisper. He paused, then slammed his fist on the bar top, shouting, "*USED ME*! To get what you wanted, or 'ave you forgotten already?" Behr gritted his teeth and hissed out, "You are nothing but a lying, cheating, and selfish waste o' human flesh." Ellora smirked. *Go Behr! Get her!* "I've wasted all these years with you, all this time that I could've been spending with another. Someone who would *want* to share a life with me and stand by my side, no matter what!" His voice sounded like he was standing his ground, but his eyes, they told a different story, and Ellora could see it. He looked furious, crushed, and vulnerable. Ellora hated it. She wanted to put a stop to it, but what could she do? It was a personal history between the two of them and obviously none of her business. But still, if given the chance, Ellora was going to jump in.

Everyone in the bar went quiet and just watched them -- Shannon, Behr, and Ellora. They were just watching to see what would happen next. Tension was mounting in the now cramped space. The air was thick with the unmistakable feelings of hate, regret, bitterness, and jealousy. One could almost taste it.

Shannon's eyes flashed like liquid fire. "I was your first and only love. I loved you the way no other woman could."

Behr roared out, "Impossible! You dinnae know the first thing about love."

Shannon was getting desperate to get through to him. This was obviously not the outcome she was hoping for when she walked in tonight. She yelled back, matching his tone, "But I still love you, Behr. Despite everything, I still want you back."

Behr grabbed her elbow and led her toward the door, while glancing back at Ellora. Several emotions passed over his face, like he was sorry that she had to see this. Sorrow passed through her, and his brows dipped at the sight of her pity. His forehead creased as anger set in. "Keep your voice *DOWN*" he growled as he yanked his hand back, as if he'd be burned just by touching her.

Behr's continuous rejections and rough handling sent Shannon down a destructive path, hell bent on embarrassing him. She was going to go for a cheap shot, the easy kill. She continued, her voice still loud enough for the whole bar to hear. "You had a chance to leave with me, but you werenae man enough to make a difference with your life. Like a coward, you chose to stay in this shyte o' a town! You are such a disappointment. That's why *they* picked up and left you behind without even a second glance."

Ellora wondered whom Shannon was speaking of when she said 'they' left.

Behr was shaking, trying hard not to lose control. "I said, *NAE ANOTHER WORD!*" His voice was deep and scratchy. It vibrated through his chest and echoed around the too quiet bar.

Kristy, obviously hearing enough, came barreling up from out back, outraged by what was said. "Mind your tongue, witch, or I will scratch your eyes out!"

Gerard grabbed her arm, stopping her from moving any farther. He whispered to her, "This needs to happen. Let it play out. This is between them." Ellora only heard because she was standing next to them both. Kristy barely held herself back. She looked like a wild panther ready to sink her claws into her prey.

"Now, I'm willing to forgive you, and I will take you back..." Shannon continued without pause, undeterred by Kristy's threat. "All I ask is for an apology from you for making me do that."

Behr was breathing deeply, almost hyperventilating. He was livid. You could feel the anger as it rolled off of him, pulsating in rhythm with his erratic heart. "It's over, Shannon! There's nothing between us, nae anymore! I could *never* again be with the likes o' you. Nae after all you've done. I'm disgusted by you!"

Shannon's mouth hung wide open. She slapped him

right in the face. Hard. Heading toward the door, Shannon suddenly turned on her heel, staring daggers at Ellora. "Even if you weasel your way into Behr's arms, which is so obvious -- you look like a cat in heat -- he'll just drag you down. In the back o' his mind, he will always think of me because I will always be better than you in every way!" She lifted her chin up in triumph.

Ellora quaked with an anger she'd never felt before. Shannon didn't even know her. How could she have so much venom for a stranger? She couldn't stand the way she spoke about Behr, or the way she'd just ripped into her. Ellora developed an idea and decided to act on it now, while she had the guts and adrenaline swimming around inside her. The dress she was wearing also helped to boost her confidence. This was it. This was her chance. She gathered up all her courage and took it.

Lifting one eyebrow, Ellora smiled devilishly at her. Shannon looked confused by her reaction. Slowly, Ellora glided her way toward Behr, swaying her hips seductively as she made her way over to him. She bumped Shannon with her hip, effectively moving her out of the way, then captured Behr with her eyes and held him there. She gave him her raciest smoldering expression. Bringing herself within inches of his face, she reached up and slowly ran her hands up his defined chest, gliding them over his shoulders and up his neck. She cupped his cheek with one hand and ran her fingers through his hair, fisting it with the other. He drew in a sharp breath, surprised. Instinctively, he placed his hands on her waist. She could feel the heat of his hands burning through the thin material of her dress. He squeezed with just enough pressure to elicit a tingling shockwave that travelled through her body.

"Let's just see about that, shall we!" Ellora challenged, dragging his head down to hers. Ellora tenderly touched her lips to his, and immediately, she felt a white-hot electric shock burst within her. It spread through her lower belly, burning its way outward. Behr must've felt the connection as well, because at her touch, he hissed in appreciation. Their lips moved together softly at first, but gained in intensity as Ellora nipped at his lower lip playfully, trying to get Behr to react. She must've really shocked him at first because he stood as still as a statue. She lightly glided her tongue along the seam of his lips. Growling deep in his chest, he wrapped his arms tightly around her. Ellora winced in pain for a moment, but relaxed into his arms as it subsided. He opened his mouth to her. Ellora took his invitation and invaded his mouth with her tongue. They tangled and coiled together, exploring as they took their time tasting one another. He must've come to his senses, because he brought his hands up, cupping her face, and took over the kiss. She could feel his need. The dominating way he kissed was exactly as she dreamed it would be. Her very core melted like a pool of fire. The heat that came off of them was enough to set the pub on fire. Behr glided one hand up slowly, tangling his fingers into her hair. Ellora pressed her body in tighter. A quiet little moan escaped her lips. She had never experienced a kiss like this. Ever. Every sweep of his probing tongue, every pull and nip of her lip, had Ellora melting into him. Her knees went weak from his touch and buckled. Behr easily held her in place in the safety of his arms. Behr's corded muscles twitched and flexed, as if he tried very hard to hold himself back. At hearing her response, Behr's kiss grew in intensity. It escalated a little rougher, as if he needed to have her -- all of her, right then. He pressed his body hard against hers. Panic crept its way inside her at his needy forcefulness. That act snapped Ellora back to reality. *What am I doing?* She knew she better stop their kiss before it went any further. It couldn't go any further. Ellora was sure she'd made her point.

She placed her hands on his chest and slowly pushed him away, stopping the kiss. Behr stopped reluctantly, groaning his disapproval at the separation. Ellora looked him square in the eyes, and what she saw there both scared and excited her. She took a few more steadying breaths, using the time to compose herself. That life-altering kiss affected Ellora in a way she wasn't sure she was ready to explore yet. Behr just looked over her face with an awed, adoring expression that melted the ice off her heart and cracked the wall protecting it. Ellora gave him a soft peck on the nose. Smiling brightly at him, she turned back to Shannon, who, like everyone else, had her mouth hanging wide open. Her confidence was shattered.

"Oh. You're still here? I think he has already forgotten *all* about you, sweetheart! On behalf of Behr and Grady, you're not welcome in this pub anymore!" Ellora grabbed her arm and pushed her roughly out the door. "You are a dime a dozen, honey, replaceable and easily forgotten." She slammed the door in her face. Ellora staggered a little but regained her composure after a moment. A satisfied, Cheshire grin grew on her face. *That* felt awesome!

When she turned back around, the pub erupted with applause, cheers, and hysterical laughter. The noise was so deafening, Ellora feared the roof would collapse. Patrick called her the Quay Street Legend, and Gerard proclaimed that she got that fighting attitude from her dad.

Ellora wasn't sure if it was all the excitement whirling around her, but her head started to spin. She felt very *strange,* and it wasn't from the kiss. She didn't know what was wrong with her, but the walls felt like they were closing in. Stumbling over her feet, she clutched the door jam, trying to right herself. She desperately needed some fresh air. Ellora wasn't sure if it was just the flood of adrenaline in her system, or if she was coming down with something. To her, it felt like the temperature rose a few degrees higher. Beads of sweat formed on her temple. Maybe she was coming down with the flu or something. She didn't know whether it was from the overwhelmingly crowded pub, or the fact that she was burning up, but it was extremely hot in there to her. Oddly enough, she had chills, too.

Everyone else was cheering and reliving what happened, all except for Behr. He was weaving his way through the crowd toward Ellora. His eyes narrowed, focusing intently on her, obviously aware that something wasn't right. Ellora's vision blurred. She started breathing harder, and blinked her eyes several times trying to get them to focus. She had to look down at the floor, which felt like it was moving out from under her. As she rocked side to side, a throbbing pain, like sharp glass, rained down on her back. Sweat was freely dripping down her face, getting cold as it settled into her brow and hair line. An overwhelming nausea bubbled up inside as her system was attacked by a violent sensation of vertigo, so she closed her eyes.

"Ellora!" Strong arms caught her before she fell. She heard Behr asking if she was all right, before her ears started buzzing and everything slowly faded to black.

All the laughter and celebration ceased when Behr called out to Ellora. His tone was laced thick with panic. "Ellora Belle? What's wrong, love? Oh, God, she's burnin' up. Kristy, call ahead, let Lachlan know we're coming straight away. Patrick, here's my keys. Bring my truck 'round." Behr tossed his keys across the room to a very concerned Patrick. All humor had dissipated. Kristy frantically pulled out her cell and punched in the needed numbers. Behr lifted Ellora carefully and cradled her in his arms. He felt hot wetness dampen his arm. What he thought was just sweat at first accumulated and dripped down his arm. Behr lifted her up slightly and saw blood seeping through the back of her dress. His panic grew as he rushed her out of the door. Behr carefully placed Ellora in the passenger side of his truck. When *the fuck did this happen?* He thought to himself. He buckled her up best he could then hopped in the front seat.

Behr's speed increased dangerously, as did his worry for the girl who'd captured his heart and moved right into his soul... who now lay bleeding and feverish in the front seat beside him. How had this happened? When had this happened? Guilt hit Behr hard. He let her work herself sick today. Of course. He remembered her comments about feeling dizzy, and her complexion had paled as she worked hard by his side. Behr's grip on the steering wheel tightened, turning his knuckles white. Guilt flooded his system, overwhelming him with regret. He should've done more to help. She overdid it... and he'd let her. Gritting his teeth, Behr tried hard to concentrate on the road instead of punching the steering wheel. He looked down on her still form and zeroed in on the dark blood stain marring that beautiful dress. How had she hurt herself? And when? Was this one of the many secrets she was hiding? No matter. All he cared about was this precious gift that tripped into his life captured his heart. Behr fell hard and fast for Ellora. He was helpless against it. He pressed the gas pedal to the floor, as precious minutes felt like hours. Behr refused to ignore the world around him anymore. *Nothing will hurt her again*, he swore to himself as he came to a halt at the hospital's entrance.

11

ominick made his way up to the Syracuse Police Station, jogging up the wide steps. He strolled through the double doors, past the lobby, and down the long hall. Hoping to catch his old partner, he got there pretty early. He needed to talk to him and maybe enlist his help. Passing the arched doorway, Dominick rounded the corner into an open room with high ceilings and fluorescent lighting hanging from the rafters. Moving past several rows of desks, he made his way to the familiar person in the back.

Anthony Stevens was leaning far back in his desk chair, pinching the bridge of his nose, deep in conversation with someone over the phone. He looked frustrated, taking it out on the pen he was grinding between his teeth.

Dominick walked up behind him and slapped his shoulder as a sign of 'hey buddy, how ya doin' and nodded at him.

Anthony nodded back, smirking at him, and held up his hand, signaling him to hold on. "Yes, I'm on top of it. I always am! I can handle him. NO! I will contact you when I have something to report! Piece of cake. I'll be in touch." He slammed the phone on the receiver, cursing.

"Hey, partner, how've you been, you lil' son o' bitch?" Dominick slapped his hand in Anthony's and gave a quick one-armed hug.

"Not as good as you, lil' prick! How's that gig of yours? Sitting pretty with that rich ass boss of yours, huh?" He shoved him, laughing. "Have a seat, Dom. What brings you down here?" Anthony rolled up the sleeves of his buttoned up uniform, and loosened up his already loosened tie.

Dominick sat down, all humor gone. He donned a serious look. "Toni, man, I'm on a case right now, trying to locate a girl. She disappeared over a month ago. She was last seen at Saint Joseph's Hospital, where she stayed for about a week after sustaining a serious injury from an attack inside her home. I was told by the front desk that this unit was called to file a report. Does an Ellora Belle Sutherland ring any bells?"

"Yeah, the daughter of the top corporate rehab developer in Syracuse. Why? Was that her at the hospital?"

Dominick nodded. "Did she tell you who or why she was attacked?"

Anthony shook his head. "We were called out there by the hospital staff, but when we got there, the meds the doctor had her on made the girl pretty out of it. When she was coherent enough, she just wouldn't cooperate with us. There was no trust there. She seemed to be scared of everyone around her, and she refused to answer any of our questions when we tried to get her to tell us what had happened. She was heavily sedated and had no identification on her person.

"We decided to let her rest, and came back a while later when she was awake. She was too frightened to utter a word to anyone. Whoever did this to her wanted to make sure she wasn't going to talk. We tried one more time, going down there near the end of the week to see if she would offer up anything useful, but she had disappeared. No one has reported her missing."

"Yeah, I guess no one would, since her parents are dead. It doesn't appear she has anyone."

Anthony nodded his head in agreement, his eyes widened and frantically looking around. He caught a glimpse of Dominick staring at him. He hesitated then said, "Yeah, it's too bad what happened to them. Stupid fucking car!"

The tone in his voice caught Dominick's attention. It was as though he was talking about something else entirely. He was acting strangely. His suspicious behavior sounded alarms inside of Dominick's head. "Hey, man, you all right?"

"Yeah, yeah, just a huge work load with time lines ticking away is all." *Yeah right*, Dominick thought. He was going to have to keep a close eye on him. Something just didn't feel right.

"Hey, Tony, now that you mentioned cars, it reminded me of something. Did Ellora's car get impounded here?"

Anthony's head snapped up. "I don't know. Why do you ask?"

"I have reason to believe she jumped into her car, trying to get away from her attacker, but the staff at Saint Joe's said she came by way of ambulance. So I would like to search through the contents of that car to see if I can find something, anything that might lead me in another direction."

"Sure, man, I can have someone search the lot and get back to you…"

"No, no, no, man," Dominick interrupted. "I can look myself. Just lead the way. This is my *only* case, so I've got nothing but time. But, here's the thing… I don't think she does. I'd like to check *now!*"

"Dom, man, I've got a lot of shit on my plate right now."

"You owe me, Stevens. If you can't do it, then just give me the access key," Dominick requested while leaning forward, glaring at Toni and giving him the *'DON'T FUCK WITH ME'* look.

"Relax, Dom, she probably just ran away with her boyfriend or something. Why would she want to stay here anyway? If she was attacked, she probably just got in his car and drove away. Ever think of that? No skin off my sack, though. Here, take it." He tossed the key card on the desk.

"Thanks, partner. Now, get back to work, ya bastard, and stop chewing on those fucking pens. You'll get a snaggle tooth, then no one will date your ugly ass!" Dominick punched him, faking a hit to the face, taunting his old partner. "I'll see you a little later, all right?!"

"Fuck you! You coming back later? I'll be around." Dominick snatched the key card and headed down to the lot.

Symphony Place Hotel and Condominiums Downtown Syracuse
7:56 am

"Mr. Claiborne, sir?" Her voice came through the speaker.

"Yes, Susan, what is it?" Dalton snapped, letting his foul mood show.

"I've gotten a hold of Mr. Antonelli like you asked, sir. He is on line one."

"Thank you, Susan." Dalton ran both hands over the sides of his head, slicking back his hair. "Put him on hold. He can wait."

"Yes, of course, sir," Susan answered hesitantly. He'd kept Dalton waiting for information for a few weeks without any word. *Just who does he think he's dealing with?* Dalton thought, slamming his fist down on his mahogany desk. He ground his teeth in frustration.

After the first week with no word, he had his man shadow Dominick to see if he was sitting on his ass or actually looking for her. He was *NOT* pleased with what he heard back.

Dominick was seen at Ellora's house, then at the hospital asking questions. He went as far as taking the receptionist out for what looked like an information exchange. Where he was headed now was unacceptable! He was *NOT* hired to solve the crime, just to locate a small girl. How hard was that?

Not knowing where Ellora was, who she was with, or how she was doing had him on edge. He was also getting a lot of pressure from his investors on the lack of progress. His time was running out. He didn't give a shit about what they wanted, though. He always had another investor waiting in line to replace the other. But he couldn't bear the thought of Ellora out there, possibly with someone else. He had to find her, *now!*

Dalton took a couple deep breaths to calm is irritated nerves. He let his mind wander to Ellora, to how she had tried to evade him then, just as she was doing now.

Dalton stalked up behind her. She couldn't hear him approach with the noise protectors in her ears. She was bending over with the nail gun, securing the subfloor as a base. He enjoyed seeing her like this, and envisioned her in this same position in his bed. Dalton unplugged the extension cord and tossed it aside. Ellora turned around with annoyed confusion. When her eyes meet Dalton's, a panicked look of dread washed over her as she realized that she was alone with him.

She had successfully avoided Dalton at all costs after the Christmas party, clinging to her father like a freighted toddler, afraid of finding herself alone with this creepy pervert. Like she now found herself. His obsession was growing more and more intense. The more she rejected him, the more unstable he became. The more she ran from him, the angrier he became. As far as Ellora knew, her father didn't know about his partner's unhinged obsession with his only daughter, and she wanted to keep it that way. Her father loved his career. He worked very hard to get it, having picked up and moved his family for this opportunity, and she didn't want to be the reason it was all taken away. But there was something terrifyingly off about Dalton. He wasn't just some rich creep... He was dangerous, and she believed his threat. Based on the manic look in his eyes, Ellora knew he would follow her family to the ends of the world. He'd go out of his way to make sure that the rest of their lives were a living hell. There would be no expense spared when it came down to exacting his revenge.

Ellora watched in horror as he slithered over to her. He took his time, enjoying watching the despair work its way through her. She backed up in response as he got much too close. The cold lifeless look in his eyes frightened her to the depths of her soul. And he loved every moment of it. When her back hit the wall, she scanned around the tight space, trying to find a way to get out. He kept moving forward until he was within inches of her. The smell of his cologne was overbearing and overpowering, making her nauseated. Dalton lifted his arm up over her head, and leaned on the wall casually.

She was trapped. Enraged, she demanded, "What the hell do you want from me, Dalton? Let me get back to work or NO ONE will get paid." She stressed her words with a forced calm she didn't really feel. "Besides, my father should be back any moment." Ellora added that last sentence hoping to deter him, but she was learning pretty quickly that nothing seemed to deter him from what he wanted. Dalton leaned in closer to her. He sniffed in heavily, like a dog sniffing his mate's scent. He ran his nose down the side of her face, and when he blew out the breath, Ellora had to hold back a whimper. His rancid breath and threatening stance made her quake uncontrollably. "Dalton... I've got to get back to work. This isn't a pick up bar." She pushed on his chest, trying to get him to step back and away from her.

"There's always time to play." He reached up to touch her cheek, and she flinched away from him.

"Don't. Touch. Me." she ordered as threateningly as she could with her shaky voice.

Dalton grabbed her shoulders and slammed her into the wall. Ellora's head hit the cracked concrete wall hard. The impact shocked her, stilling her struggles. He grabbed both of her wrists and pulled them up over her head, holding them in place, while his other hand roamed up the inside of her thigh. Ellora tried kicking him between his legs when his hand went up her stomach and groped her breasts.

She cried out in panic, "Stop this! Get the fuck off me!

NO!" Ellora freaked out when he continued to maul her, completely unfazed by her struggles or screams. In fact, her struggles seemed to encourage him farther. He was enjoying this. Ellora feared what would happen if she couldn't stop him. How far would he take this? Dreadfulness gripped her when he wrapped his fingers around her neck. She immediately kicked, kneed, and thrashed, trying everything to shake his hand off her neck and to wrench her arms free from his unbreakable grip.

"Don't fight me, Ellora. I will just fight harder." He squeezed her neck hard enough so that she gasped for air, proving his point.

Her eyes grew wide as the realization of his very real threat washed over her. Goose bumps rose on her skin, but Ellora tried to keep her calm. She planned on staying pliant until an opening presented itself to her, then she'd run and keep running. He crushed his lips to hers, and she immediately forgot about her plan as panic set in. She pinched her lips shut, trying to keep him out of her mouth. Bile started to rise up her throat as he drenched her with his saliva. Ellora couldn't keep her calm with Dalton assaulting her this way. He moaned, her struggles obviously just turning him on even more. Dropping her arms, he kept his other hand firmly around her throat. Ellora rained down punches against his chest. Hot tears ran down her face as her struggles grew more desperate. Dalton just smiled after every strike. He loved it. Finally, he broke away from her. With a satisfied grin on his face, Dalton took a step back.

"See, now that wasn't so bad, was it, sweetheart? Yeah, I

think you kind of enjoyed that, too. Didn't you?" He sleeked his hair back into place and straightened his tie.

Ellora shook uncontrollably. "FUCK YOU!" she ground out through gritted teeth.

Dalton smiled at Ellora like she'd praised him instead of cursing at him. "I want to spend the evening with you, and maybe if you're a good girl, I'll let you fuck me. I will pick you up tonight for dinner." He reached out to thumb away a stray tear, just as Ellora's father walked in.

She jerked her head away from his touch and spit in his face. "I'm not going anywhere with you!" She shoved through his stance, and ran past her father and through the exit.

"Just what is going on here, Dalton? Why are you up here alone with my daughter?" Joseph walked right up to Dalton with an angry, protective look on his face. "What was done to have my daughter running out of here like her heels were aflame, crying like she was?" He got right up into Dalton's face, both hands on his hips in an offensive stance.

"I was just asking your daughter out to dinner with me tonight. That's not going to be a problem with you, is it?" Dalton stated with a stern commanding voice.

Joseph's face turned red. Anger shook his usually controlled resolve. "I believe she gave you her answer when she ran out of here like she did, and let me tell you, Boyle, it did not look good for you. So, yes, it will be a problem for me. You do not have permission to take my daughter anywhere with you! Stay away from her! Understand? Now, why don't you go back to work in your ivory tower, my friend."

Dalton leaned in closer. Now nose to nose with Joseph, his eyes were void of all emotion. "I do not tolerate rejection well. I warn you, Joseph, I will NOT be ordered around, and doing so will NOT end well for you. My FRIEND, remember that. Do not get in the way of my affairs or you'll regret it for the rest of your life. I'll make sure of it."

"Is that a threat, Mr. Claiborne? I am not afraid of you or your connections. If you want a piece of me, you better step up and take me on yourself! Or are you too afraid of getting your hands dirty? Go near my daughter again... I'll coat this building with your blood."

Dalton lifted one corner of his mouth in a spine-chilling sneer. He tilted his head to the side, almost amused with Joseph's challenge. "I hope you don't mean that, Joseph. Nothing gets in the way of what I want." Dalton lifted up one eyebrow, walked passed Joseph, and turned slightly on his way out. "Just remember, Joseph, I warned you! I know how far I'm willing to go... Do you?"

Dalton shook his head at the memory, as the buzzer sounded in the background.

"Excuse me for interrupting, Mr. Claiborne, but Mr. Antonelli is still holding on line one. Do you want me to have him call another time, sir?"

"That won't be necessary, Susan. I've got it."

"Yes, of course, sir."

Dominick made his way down to the garage to the impound lot, using the key card to get past the secured door. He held his cell to his ear, waiting for Dalton to pick up the line. He had been on hold for a while now, and knew he was going to get chewed out for not contacting him sooner.

He sauntered over to the counter, nodding at the very bored looking man.

"What can I do for you, detective?"

Handing a piece of paper over, with the make, model, color, and license plate number of Ellora's car, Dominick told him, "I need this car located."

The man read the paper, grunted, then looked at Dominick, eyeing him briefly. "It'll be a minute. Hang tight."

He switched his cell on the other ear, pacing back and forth across the old linoleum floor. Now, he was waiting on two men. Patience was *not* one of his strong suits. The phone clicked over, and he heard the sound of a man clearing his throat. *Here we go...*

"Dominick Antonelli, I know I don't have to express my extreme dissatisfaction at the amount of time you've kept me waiting for information. I've had to take time out of my *VERY* busy schedule to call you. What information have you collected thus far? Where is Ellora?"

"Mr. Claiborne, Dalton, sir... Yes, I have been meaning to get a hold of you, but kept getting sidetracked with all the dead ends. I didn't want to bother you with something that wasn't concrete."

"My man has informed me that you have been to the airport, her house, and the hospital, and you're telling me that you still don't have anything to tell me yet?"

"You're having me followed, sir?" *Well, this is bullshit,* Dominic thought.

"I always keep a close eye on my investments, Mr. Antonelli. Since I *AM* paying you a hefty salary, you WILL have eyes on you at all times. Now, what have you found out?"

"Well," Dominick hesitated, "I set up an account to monitor her bank transactions. She apparently booked a one-way flight out of Hancock and paid in cash. I found a statement on her account that showed she used her credit card a few weeks ago, somewhere in the U.K., but it will take a bit longer to pinpoint where, sir. I'm not sure if she is still there."

Shit! Dominick really didn't want to tell him that, but he knew he had to give him something. Too much time had passed, and he wasn't a stupid man. He didn't want to get thrown aside on this one. If Dalton fired him, he'd never figure out exactly what the fuck was going on! He couldn't walk away now. Something very wrong was going on, and he needed to find out what.

"The U.K.? Are you sure it was her card? Was it credit card fraud?"

"I'm looking into that, sir. I'll find out soon enough."

"If this rings true, I want you there on the first available flight. I will arrange everything for you. Just let me know. Oh, and Detective, don't go sticking your nose in, playing the detective. That's NOT what I'm paying you for! Let someone else do that. It's not your concern anymore. Understood?"

LIKE HELL IT ISN'T! Dominick screamed inside his head. "Of course, sir, I will let you know if I'm heading there, so you can make arrangements for me."

Dominick heard Dalton's conniving snicker on the other line. "Of course you will. You couldn't afford the trip." Then Dalton hung up the phone.

Bastard! Dominick had to figure out where the girl was and head out there ASAP!

He wanted the chance to question her before Dalton got to her. If his intuition was correct, she needed to be warned. He'd have to cover his ass, too, now that he was being followed.

Looking past the counter, he saw the man a few car rows down, talking frantically in the phone, sweat beading on his temples and glaring at him.

Dominick grunted in aggravation, "I don't have time for this bullshit!" Hopping the counter, he walked straight for the man. "Where's my car, son?"

"You can't come back here... Yes, sir, I will give you an update after I'm through here," he spoke into the phone.

"You need clearance to come back here." The man almost stumbled over his words, obviously nervous.

Dangling his key card in the guy's face, he said, "I have all the clearance I need. Now, *WHERE'S* my car?"

The man looked around. "I... I... I... its right, right over here, this way." The man walked a few car lengths down and a few more rows back, constantly looking back at Dominick. "It's right here. What do you need it for? I need to know, for... the uh ... paperwork I have to fill out."

"Fuck off!" Dominick barked at him. "I will fill out the paperwork myself. Now, get the fuck out of here. Leave." Dominick shooed him away with his hand.

The man shuffled off, muttering under his breath.

After pulling out some rubber gloves and putting them on, he circled around the car. He stared with a hawk eye, concentrating on every detail. He could see lots of smudge marks on the window, but knew that dusting for prints and searching the national database for a possible match would take up time he didn't have. Carefully, he opened the door and pulled out a small palm-sized flash light. He inspected the floor, the dash, and the passenger side. He observed some dried up smeared blood on the driver seat back.

In the distance, Dominick heard heavy uneven footsteps echoing on the concrete. It was coming closer, so he stepped out of the car to see who it was.

"Holy shit, Dom, is that you? Yeah, I thought that was

you! What're you doing here, bro?" A heavyset man with cropped hair and a wide smile strode toward him.

"Anderson! What's it been, man? How're you doing?" Dominick clapped him on the shoulder. "They got you working down here now?"

"Yeah, I'm the only one here who knows shit about cars. Dumb ass pansies. I head up crime scene investigations, but mostly when it comes to crimes involving motor vehicles. I can tear them apart and put them back together with my eyes closed," Andy announced with pride.

"You always could, brother, no doubt about it." Dom gave his old friend a wide grin.

"So watch ya looking at this one for? They got you on the Sutherland case now or what? I thought you left."

Dominick nodded. "I did, but yes, I've got someone trying to locate her. The whole thing looks shady to me, so I'm looking a little closer. How'd you remember this was her car? Were you here when it was impounded?"

Anderson shook his head no. "It wasn't impounded. It was dropped off. Yeah, man, I was down here when they brought it. When I opened the driver's side door, I noticed blood in it, so I took a closer look, just in case it ended up being classified as a homicide case. I wanted to go through it thoroughly while it was fresh on the scene, you know?"

He leaned in closer to his friend. "And what did you find, Andy?"

"Besides the blood, nothing. That is, until I got it on the lift. Come here." Anderson brought the car back on to the lift, raising it up about six feet. He came back around to Dominick, waving him over, and then pointed at a certain spot under the car. "Take a look, Dom. Do you know what that is?"

Dominick lifted a questioning brow. "Just looks like a bunch of pipes to me, man."

"Look closer," Anderson urged. "Do you see that hole there?" He pointed again.

"What is that, Andy? The brakes?"

"When you press on the brake pedals, you're pushing on a piston. That piston pushes on brake fluid in the master cylinder, pressurizing the brake fluid. It flows through thin pipes, brake lines," Anderson pointed at the lines, "to pistons at each wheel. Those pistons apply pressure to the brake pads, and they squeeze against the disk or drum to stop the car. If you have a loss of fluid going to each wheel, nothing would happen when you pressed on the brake."

"Did the lines burst?" The detective scratched his scalp as he ran his hands through his hair roughly.

"If that was the case, it would be from normal wear and tear, but look..." Anderson pointed at small pinholes on the lines leading to both the front and rear brakes. "Normal wear would not happen on all four lines, with the same sized hole, in the same area. These were cut! And whoever did it knew what they were doing."

Frustration washed over Dominick, because he was no closer to finding out what was going on. "Well, after she was attacked, it looked as though she got in her car first, but records show that she was taken to the hospital in an ambulance. I guess that explains why."

"Yeah, I've only seen precise work like this on one other car. It was a year or so before this one, and it just so happens to have been her parents' car!"

"WHAT DID YOU SAY? Did you say her *parents'* car? Is that car in this lot as well?"

"No, some badge came in a week after we got it and removed it, their reasons being it was an on-going investigation that they were now handling. It bothered me when I saw this car come in with the exact same cuts, in the same place as her parents' car."

"The report just showed that they were in a car accident," Dominick whispered, still in shock at hearing that news.

"Yeah, I'm sure they were... when their car didn't stop when they expected it to." Anderson gave Dominick a sideways glance, showing him that he had the same suspicions as his friend.

"So, whoever did this either wanted to shut them up or... get them out of the picture?" Dominick mused, staring at the underside of the car deep in thought.

"Or both," Anderson added. "Be careful with this one, Dom. The Sutherlands were honest people, working with big-time sharks on this project downtown. They are well known for getting what they want, or so I've heard. If you need me for anything, I'm here, man." Anderson reached his hand out and shook Dom's, patting him on the shoulder.

"Will do, man, and thank you for your help. Watch your six. I don't want you getting into some shit for helping me."

Dominick jogged out of the garage and up the stairs. He made his way down the hall and out the doors, heading to his car. He had to find out the location of the store she made her purchase at, and make his way there before Dalton found out.

Two days later
Portree Medical Center
Room 8

"Lachlan, tell me all you know, brother. What happened with Ellora? I need to know what's going on with her." Behr anxiously paced the length of the room, running his hands through his hair over and over.

After Ellora's collapse, Behr carried her out of Grady's and settled her into his truck to take her to the Medical Center. Kristy called ahead to warn Dr. Lachlan Sinclair of their emergency. All he knew was that when he lifted her and carried her in, she was burning up and blood was seeping through the back of her dress.

He'd driven himself crazy for the last two days, trying to figure out when her injury had happened. He had worked with her all that morning. She'd complained about feeling dizzy, sure, but when had she been hurt? Behr stopped pacing and turned to face Lachlan, letting out a worried breath. He glared at him, unblinking, and waited for an answer.

"Behr, you know I shouldn't discuss her medical case with anyone but immediate family." Behr gritted his teeth, his jaw muscles clenching tight, and walked menacingly toward him. Lachlan held up his hand, giving him a stern look of caution.

"But, seeing as she has no immediate family, I will discuss my findings and concerns with you, knowing you will keep this to yourself and respect her privacy."

"Privacy! The bar was packed that night. Everyone saw what happened, and I'm sure there are about ten different accounts on what happened!" Behr lost his cool, shouting at his friend as he thought about the rumors that must be running rampant.

Lachlan stared stone-faced, motionless, and dead serious. Behr knew he wouldn't go on if he didn't agree to keep this between them, so he finally nodded and relaxed his defensive stance. "I will."

"Well, when you brought her in to us, she was suffering from a dangerously high fever. When we got her in a room and removed her clothing, to put a hospital gown on, we were shocked at what we found... There's a substantially large wound on her back, running from her shoulder down to her hip."

"Are you shyting me, Doc?" Behr shouted, interrupting. "When did this happen? She never mentioned she hurt herself."

"Behr, this was *nae* a new injury. It had been sewn up

properly by a medic. I'm sure of it. But, it's been poorly looked after. The wound was terribly infected, and her body was fighting it hard, causing her high fever. We had to remove the old stitches, clean out the infected area, and stitch her back up. We gave her a strong pain injectable and antibiotics to help with the infection."

Lachlan blew out a breath, his clinical, serious expression turning to concern. His eyebrows raised as he laid his hand on Behr's shoulder. "My concern is that the wound looked as though it was a laceration... from a serrated knife."

Behr's eyes grew wide as he shook his head in disbelief.

"I know it sounds crazy, but I think Miss Ellora was in some kind of danger over there. I'd bet my life on it. While out, she has suffered terrible nightmares."

"Aye, we know 'bout them. She's had them since the day she arrived here. I had my suspicions that she was running from something that very first night." Behr turned and looked down on her still form lying in the hospital bed. His heart constricted thinking about what might've happened to her, the worst scenarios making his imagination run wild.

"I'm in agreement with you, Behr. I also suspected as much. She was frightened enough to travel to the other side of the world and start over. She is a very brave lass, in need o' a new life and people to stand by her." He regarded Behr when saying the last part.

Behr's heart swelled when he realized that he would never leave her side now. He cared too much. "I will nae let anything happen to her, not while I live." Behr's face softened as he watched Ellora sleep. He walked over and sat in the chair next to the bed, then reached out and captured her hand, kissing every fingertip while stroking the back with his thumb.

"I know you willnae, and I suspect you're nae alone. I know that whatever has happened, she was obviously nae ready to talk 'bout it. Otherwise, she would've done so already. Dinnae press her when she awakes. She'll confide in someone when she is ready." Clutching his clipboard, he made his way to the door. "I've got to make my rounds. Holler if you need anything. I'll be back in a while to check on her again. I know Kristy will bring by food later. She is worried sick and hasn't stopped cooking."

"Thanks, Doc."

Ellora wrenched open her car door, jumping inside at lightning speed, and locked the doors immediately. It took only a moment for her to get a grip on her debilitating shock. She frantically searched her pockets for the car keys, panicking as she checked the front then the back. As despair washed through her, her body broke out into cold sweats. Her stomach bottomed out

when it dawned on her... that she'd left the keys in the house. Ellora was hyperventilating as she frantically tried to think of another way to escape. The fragrance of the pine air freshener seemed overpowering now that her senses were on high alert. The unpleasant smell assaulted her nose, making her feel nauseated. She hung her head in defeat...

BANG! BANG! BANG! Ellora leapt out of her seat as the monster nearly cracked the glass pounding on the window. She turned her head slowly, terrified at what would happen next. Her heart slammed hard inside her chest. His evil black eyes glared, unblinking, back at her. Pressing his face against the glass, he lifted his hand up and jingled the keys... Ellora's keys.

"Forget these?"

Time stood still. The jingling of the keys seemed to echo loudly on the quiet street. The sound grew louder and louder as Ellora's reality came crashing down around her.

She watched in horror as he lowered the hand that grasped the keys. Everything moved in slow motion as her brain tried to wrap itself around her predicament. She heard him push the key into the lock. Ellora lunged into the passenger seat, getting as far away from him as possible. She grabbed the door handle and waited for him to unlock the door. If she could make a run for it, she'd yell and scream down the street until someone helped her. Ellora pushed the door open the moment he unlocked it. Scrambling to get out, she slipped on the blood that coated her leather seats. Ellora was halfway out of the door when his hand came down hard, grabbing her ankle in a tight *vise like grip. She yelped in surprise. He yanked her leg back, almost pulling it right out of the socket. Ellora winced in pain as she fought against his powerful hold. He easily forced her back into the car.*

"Where do you think you're going, sweetheart?"

Ellora held on to the door handle with all her might, using it to pull herself away from him. Her muscles twitched and shook as she used every bit of strength she had left, hoping she could break free from his unbearable command. She stared at the opened door, focusing on her escape. Grabbing the door handle, she pulled harder. Ready to run.

"You will only get hurt worse if you try to fight me." His fist came down hard, pounding into the gaping wound in her back, disabling her efforts. Ellora's scream shook the windshield, and she didn't stop. Her forceful shriek grew hoarse and eventually became nothing more than a breathy whisper. Blood splattered all over the interior of the car and continued to ooze out onto the seats. Excruciating pressure exploded in her back, throbbing from the abuse. The sensation had her close to losing consciousness. She finally let go of the door handle. Her arms fell limply on the seat. The whole world was spinning as she felt him tugging her onto the driver's seat and flipping her on her back.

In the distance, sirens blared, announcing their arrival getting louder the closer they came. Ellora felt hopeful that they were coming their way. "Well, I can't have you talking, my sweet." He adjusted his body so that he was straddling her. He pinched her nose with one hand and covered her mouth with the other, effectively cutting off her air. He pressed all of his body weight onto Ellora's face. The punishing heaviness bore down on her, and she feared her front teeth would break under the pressure. She struggled weakly, trying to pry his hands off. If she could move just enough, she would be able to suck in a breath, but it was no use. Blood vessels broke in her eyes as the pressure built from the lack of oxygen. Her head felt like needles were piercing her from the inside.

"That a girl. Sshhhhhh, just shut your eyes. It will be over soon, honey," he whispered soothingly, which made it that much more disturbing. All her strength left her body. No longer able to fight him off, she stopped kicking and let her legs fall limp. Ellora's body finally gave up the fight. Her eyes blurred with the flood of tears. Her last thoughts were of her parents... She would finally get to see them on the other side. Everything got dark and cloudy as she slowly faded away into oblivion.

He rose up off her, grabbed the keys, and walked toward the ambulance that approached him. Waving his arms, he shouted, "Help! This girl needs help!"

Ellora awoke with a start, jerking her head up off the pillow, and gasping for air. She took a look around and felt the panic start to rise up as a dreadful sense of déjà vu crept inside her. She was in a hospital room, and she didn't remember how she got there. Ellora was clenching her bed sheets in tight balled-up fists. A giant hand came down on top of hers. She gasped, startled, when she realized she wasn't alone. She flinched and yanked her hand away. Breathing deeply, Ellora readied herself for an ear-piercing scream. She grabbed for the tubes in her arms to rip them out. That's when she heard the most divine voice she'd ever heard.

"Relax, love, it's all right. You're 'avin' a bad dream, but you're safe 'ere with me." He steadied her hands in his and rubbed them soothingly. "You gave us all a scare, Lor." His voice was warm, deep, and irresistible. It had her whole body humming like a bee to honey. Ellora closed her eyes listening to his breathing, letting it calm her.

"Oh my God, what happened?" She rubbed the restless sleep from her eyes, and pinched the bridge of her nose. That action made her cringe. Her head pounded at every small movement she made. Sitting up in the bed proved to be difficult as her back protested every move.

"You dinnae remember? You collapsed in Grady's pub. We brought you 'ere a few days ago. Lachlan's been caring after you. He got your fever down and patched you back up." Behr left that hanging in the air. Ellora looked up at him, straight in his eyes, and realized that he knew. She nodded, not knowing what else to say. What could she say?

They let the silence stretch out between them. It wasn't awkward or uncomfortable... just quiet. Behr was holding her hand, rubbing the back of it gently with his other hand. Ellora was happy that it was Behr who was there beside her when she woke up. She watched him caress her hand, enjoying the feeling of it. Surprisingly, his touch didn't bother her, not even after such a gut-wrenching nightmare.

Ellora took the time to get a good look at him. He was unshaven and disheveled, and he looked like he hadn't slept. It was only then that she realized Behr was in the same clothes that he had been wearing when they were working together. She'd always remember the amazing connection they shared that day. Then something he had said before finally sunk in...

"You said I've been here for how many days?"

Behr tilted his head to the side and nodded. "Aye, you've been here for two and a half days, love."

Ellora blew out a breath. "You've seen my back then." Her face flushed with humiliation.

"Nae, love, I wouldnae invade your privacy in that way. I do know about it, though. It was badly infected, Lor. Lachlan had to take out the old stitches and replace them. Ah, the pain you must have felt..." Behr shook his head as a pained look spread across his face. "You should've told someone, if not me, love."

Ellora just shrugged; it had always been hard for her to ask someone for help, or let them see her vulnerability. She didn't like feeling helpless. Plus, how would she bring up *that* subject? 'Hi, my name's Ellora. I'm homeless, I was almost killed, and oh yeah, check out this bodacious scar on my back. Isn't she a beaut?'

"I'm sorry I worried you all." She looked up at Behr, tears filling her eyes, and continued. "I should have been smarter about caring after myself. I... I should've told someone, I know, but I just wasn't..." She hesitated. Ellora was so bad at this, at explaining how she really felt. She'd gotten so used to hiding her real feelings. It was hard trying to talk about it, especially with this man.

"I just wasn't ready to tell anyone, or ask for help. I'm still not ready. I had just met you all. I... guess I'm having a hard time trusting again. I am absolutely petrified." Lowering her head, the tears streamed down her flushed cheeks.

"Well, love, you dinnae 'ave to ask a soul. You 'ave help now, whether you want it or not. You dinnae 'ave to go through this alone. We are 'ere for you... I am 'ere for you, and I won't let anything harm you. Not while I live." Ellora looked up at him through her wet lashes with disbelief. If only he knew. Before she could refute him, he went on. "Adelle will help you clean and dress the wound. She and I 'avenae told a soul what we now know." Behr reached out and tucked a stray hair behind her ear. His hand lingered there as he rubbed his thumb soothingly back and forth across her cheek. Gazing into Ellora's eyes, he added, "And it's going to stay that way, love."

Ellora placed her hand over Behr's, lacing their fingers

together. She placed his hand on her lap, holding it tight. "Thank you. I'm sure everyone at the bar has already told everyone in town by now, though." Her anxiety rose to new heights at the thought of everyone knowing her hidden secret. She wouldn't be able to stand the pitying looks. People would be undressing her with their eyes, imagining her grotesque scar.

Behr shook his head adamantly. This movement snapped Ellora out of her terrible thoughts. "All they know is that you had a bad fever. The whole lot of 'em think you caught the flu, love. Almost everyone has stopped by Grady's or 'ere to check up on you."

Looking around the room, she finally noticed that it was flooded with flowers and balloons. In the corner, on the counter, were empty food cartons, and the trash was full. Behr followed her gaze, and commented, as if reading her mind. "Kristy has been cooking non-stop since that very first night. She knows nae what to do with herself if she cannae help. She made sure I stayed well fed while I sat by your side. I 'ave but to say the word, and she will 'ave food brought down faster than the turn of the tide! Fattened up is what she'll 'ave ya by the end of the week, if she's got a say in it." Behr lifted his head, peaking at her through the curtain of his thick lashes. His mouth turned up in a crooked grin.

Ellora laughed weakly at his expression, but a sharp pain stopped her immediately. Wincing as she felt her stitches tighten with the slightest move in the wrong direction, she drew in a quick breath. She pinched her eyes closed and hissed, "Oh, ouch, don't make me laugh. It hurts."

When she blew the breath slowly back out and opened her eyes, Ellora saw the concern all over Behr's face. He looked exhausted. She felt awful that he must've felt obligated to stay there with her, since she had no family or friends to be there by her side instead. God, she must look so pathetic. This thought made her soul ache for her parents to be there, to hold her in the safety of their loving arms just one more time. Ellora wondered if she would always feel this empty -- this alone.

"Well, I'm okay now, Behr. You don't have to stay here any longer. I'm sure you have better things to do than sit here with me. I make poor company. I can't even laugh at any of your hilarious jokes." She scrunched her nose and smirked, trying her best to tease him. Raising her arm like a queen on a thrown, Ellora flicked her wrist. "I release you! You may go now."

Behr had his head down, looking at her delicate hand in his, and snickered lightly at her sad attempt at humor. Drawing imaginary figure eights on the back of her palm, he shook his head slowly then raised it, leveling her with his deep penetrating stare.

"Miss Ellora Belle Sutherland, trying to be rid o' me so soon, are ya? A hard job o' it you'd 'ave, too, if you knew me well enough." His crooked grin turned into an erotic smirk.

Looking at his sultry eyes and dangerous smile was like looking into an eclipse. You know you shouldn't stare, but the magnificent beauty of it drew you right in. Her stomach performed little flip-flops when his expression darkened. "I am nae the sort of man to back off so easily once I have something I want in my sights."

Ellora shook her head, ready to interrupt his banter with a witty comeback, when Behr reached up and cupped her chin. He lifted it so she was again looking him straight in the eyes, as his playful expression turned serious. "You 'ave people 'ere who care about you now. You'd best be used to it..." Behr hesitated for a moment, like he was debating on what he should say next.

"And I... I care about you, Ellora." He let that sink in and continued hesitantly. "I, or um, we will be by your side. Whatever is going on, you dinnae 'ave to endure it alone. Think on that."

But, she didn't want to. She didn't want to think about anything right then, but getting out of there. Being in a hospital bed so soon after the last incident made her want to run and hide. The longer she stayed, the more fearful she became. Each tick from the oversized clock above the door felt like a countdown to her inevitable capture. She felt like the longer she laid in bed, the better the chance that *he* would find her there.

"When can I check out of here? I want to get out of here, like now! I *DON'T* like hospitals!" Ellora felt the panic grow steadily inside of her. She could tell by the look on Behr's face that she wouldn't be able to get out of there as fast as she wanted. Cold sweats appeared on her forehead, and her palms grew clammy as she started to hyperventilate. The walls felt like they were closing in on her. Prickles of stress spread across her body, the sensation making her want to claw at her skin.

Thankfully, that's when Lachlan walked through the door with confidence in his step and a bright smile on his face. "As long as it's the facility that has you desperate to go, and not the doctor that's been caring for you. How is my most popular patient today?" Lachlan stopped at the foot of her bed, holding a clipboard and what she assumed was her chart in his hands.

"Hey Dr. Lach," Ellora called out. "It's not you. Hospitals are creepy. So Dr. L, when can I bust outta this joint? I've got things to do and people to see."

Behr let out another hearty laugh that sounded deep and soulful, which made her spine tingle. Ellora realized then just how little he laughed when she first met his broody self, and decided then how much she loved the sound. She would try to get him to laugh more often. For *both* of their benefits.

"Well, you've got the fire back in that spirit of yours! That's a good sign. Let me make a note of it in your chart." Lachlan mocked writing with an imaginary pen, verbalizing his pretend notations... "Resumed her normal smart ass comments." The two men laughed at the doctor's dig at Ellora. "In all seriousness, Miss Ellora, you will be well on your way tomorrow morn'. You will be heading home with an antibiotic, which you MUST keep taking until finished. It is strong on the stomach, so take it with food. I also put up something for the pain if you should need it."

Lachlan was silent for a moment, then he walked around the foot of the bed to her side. He finally donned a serious expression before continuing. "I printed out an instruction sheet on how to *properly* clean and dress the wound, which you *must* do in order to have it heal correctly. Miss Adelle demanded one as well, so I printed one out for her. You could use some help. It will be a difficult task for you alone."

Ellora looked down, feeling guilty for being a bad patient and not taking proper care of herself the first time. She just nodded, ashamed. Behr gently squeezed the hand he was still holding, and she liked the way hers felt in his strong, encouraging hold. She realized how she hadn't shied away like she usually did when he was this intimate and forward. Ellora was at ease with him. She didn't feel a need to yank her hand away either. Not only was his caress okay, she liked how it felt.

"I know. I'm realizing that I'm going to have to start asking for help when it's needed. There are some things I simply can't do on my own, no matter how uncomfortable and on edge it makes me feel. I get it, Doc. I will have Adelle help me. I'm sorry for all the trouble and worry I've caused you all."

Behr snapped his head up as though what Ellora had said had a different meaning to him. He searched her face, almost waiting for her to say more -- willing her to say more. She knew he was aware of her back, and had heard of the constant night terrors. It's an explanation he wanted, but one she couldn't give to him.

"Oh, and thank you, Lachlan, for everything."

Lachlan nodded his head. "You are nae trouble, Ellora. Dinnae worry yourself." He looked at her then to Behr. "All right, I will sign off on your discharge papers for tomorrow. Get some rest. I will see you a little later."

"Soooo... what will it be, love?" Behr lifted up one eyebrow, reached over to catch another stray hair, and curled it between his fingers before tucking it behind her ear. Ellora couldn't see what she looked like, but she was sure she had a severe case of bed-head. She must've looked like she stuck her finger in a light socket.

Her eyebrows knitted together in confusion, so Behr continued. "You must be starved with nothin' but this liquid drip in your veins. What would you like to eat, love? Just name it and it's yours."

With eyes as big as saucers, she realized just *how* hungry she was. "Oooooh, a double bacon cheeseburger, with everything on it, toasted buns, greasy fries, and a thick chocolate milkshake... for starters." She snickered with amusement at the shocked look on Behr's face. "Don't look all judgy. I'm hungry, okay," Ellora shot back, amused by his expression.

"What was it you were sayin' 'bout toasted buns now, love?" Behr lifted his eyebrows and gasped with mock horror.

"Speaking of which, you need to get your buns in there for a much needed shower." Pointing a weak finger at the washroom in the back, she cupped her hand around her mouth and whispered, "You kinda stink!"

Behr choked out another long laugh. "Aye, woman, is that your way o' trying to get me naked then?"

It was her turn to start choking and coughing her brains out. She had no response to that.

Behr leaned forward, putting his hands on either side of her head, caging her in his arms. She laid back from his close proximity.

"That's right, you best keep that mouth shut with those smart ass remarks of yours. Aye, you wag that tongue one more time, I might just give it a little bite." Behr wet his lips, looking long and hard at her mouth. Ellora's pulse quickened. She found herself breathing heavily, thinking about how much she wanted to feel his lips on hers in that very moment.

Then it all came rushing back to her. She'd kissed Behr... in the pub... before she collapsed. And it was AMAZING! A rush of emotions hit her all at once -- longing for him to kiss her in that moment and not stop, humiliation for her brazen kiss that night, and maybe a little bit of fear. Fear for liking him so much, so fast. Fear of never having had a boyfriend before. Fear that she might just be a rebound for him, so soon after his long relationship. Well, now maybe even a little awkward, because in this moment, she didn't know how to act or what to say.

In a nanosecond, Ellora's face switched from longing for a moment of passion, to awkward sideways glances. She looked anywhere but at him and started fiddling with her fingers. Behr dropped his hands and sat back down at her side, obviously feeling the arctic air change around them.

"Behr, about that night... I... I'm so sorry for... um... putting you on the spot like that. But I um... it's just that..." She left that pathetically unfinished statement hanging in the air, because all of her explanations sounded incredibly lame in her head. She scrambled to try to say something, but instead, she was babbling like an idiotic fool.

Behr bent his large frame down to her eye level. "Hey, hey, hey now, love. Whatcha' got to be so sorry about, eh? I'm not sorry *at* all. *THAT* was exactly what I've always wanted. That's how a *REAL* kiss is supposed to feel. The only thing you should be sorry about is not doing *that* sooner." He lifted one side of his mouth in a devilish grin, his eyes hitting her hard with an undeniable desire for her.

Gasping at his admission, Ellora couldn't help but smile at his cocky expression. He didn't mind telling her he desired her. He showed his feelings proudly.

"I guess that was just my way of shutting her mouth and making her feel insanely jealous and stupid," Ellora finally proclaimed, giving a naughty smile of her own. "It seemed to work pretty well."

Behr's eyes twinkled as he laughed, running his hands through his unruly hair. He got up and walked over to a duffel bag beside the bedside table. He continued to laugh, mumbling something to himself.

He pulled out some clothes and shouted out over his shoulder, "If that's what you do to get folks to shut their mouths, then I'm going to be *VERY* talkative from now on, eh, love."

Winking at Ellora, he made a kissing noise. Before he shut the bathroom door, he added, "Try not to dream about my hot toasted buns, will ya, lass. You need your rest, all right."

Ellora grabbed the plastic jug of hospital water on her bedside table and chucked a handful of ice at him. "Dream on, bigfoot. Go cool off!"

few days had gone by, and Behr had stayed right there with Ellora through the night, refusing to go home. She teased him, asking, "Aren't there visiting hours here? And aren't they over?"

Behr would just widen his stance and throw his arms off to the side with cocky confidence, and declare, "It is if the head doc isnae your friend and drinking pal, which he is, love. The rules dinnae apply to me."

Adelle showed up the next morning to help Behr get his patient home and into her room. Ellora's homecoming proved to be quite dramatic, to her dismay. Everyone in town seemed to know all about her 'flu' and knew when she would be discharged. They all showed up at Grady's to see how she was holding up. Many brought food; they wouldn't have to go grocery shopping for a decade with all the food they'd been brought.

She was relieved when Adelle went in the kitchen to gather the supplies needed to tend to her back. It left her and Behr alone together. Even though they did spend some time alone at the hospital, she never quite felt comfortable there. Now she was home. A feeling of contentment washed over her as Behr guided her over the threshold.

Behr bent down to her. His whisper felt rough as his voice rumbled against her ear. "Did you need me to carry you up the stairs, love?"

Turning her head into him, she leaned in to whisper back, "I think I should try to walk. I'm supposed to be recovering from the *flu*, remember? I don't want anyone any more concerned than they already have been."

He nodded, his face stubble abrading her cheek as he did. Ellora loved having him this close to her. She felt protected... safe. A feeling she hadn't had in a very long time.

Behr carefully wrapped his arm around her waist, and even though her feet were on the ground, he was basically holding her, taking on all her weight. Lifting her arm, Ellora wrapped it around his neck automatically. He guided her through the throng of people, obviously more patient than she was. Kristy, Grady, and Gerard hugged and kissed her, letting her know how worried they were and just how many heart attacks she'd caused that night.

Patrick announced to everyone that the points Ellora had gotten from kicking Shannon out of the pub had been taken off for 'fainting like a girl.' He would probably never let her live that down.

They made their way to the back narrow stairwell, where he scooped her up in his arms and skipped stairs like she weighed nothing more than a doll.

"You're such a caveman." Ellora giggled into the crook

of his neck.

Walking down the hall, Behr was opening the door to her room when he looked down on her with that big crooked grin that she had grown to love so much. His eyes were bright with amusement.

"Aye, that I am, and you like it. Don'tcha, woman. Dinnae be pretendin' that you don't." He gave a loud primitive grunt for emphasis, which had Ellora laughing again.

"OUCH! My stitches! Why do you all of a sudden become a comedian when it hurts to laugh at you?"

Behr let out a deep-throated laugh. "Because your pain amuses me, ya smart ass."

Huffing out a deep breath, and having no other way to get him back, she bit him on the neck, thinking, *ha! That'll show him.*

Behr stopped just inside her room. Slowly, he turned his head and looked down on her. He no longer had a twinkling look in his eye or a bright smile. His look darkened, becoming sultry, suggestive... heated. His eyes dipped low as he stared longingly at her mouth. Then he slowly dragged them back up to meet her eyes.

The energy crackled around them. Ellora could feel the heat of his body rise, as he continued to paralyze her with the powerful force his eyes always seemed to have over her. The intensity almost frightened her. No one had ever looked at her like *that* -- like at any moment, he would devour her, desperate to have her, to taste her. But it also excited Ellora, because she liked the thought of him kissing her with all the unbridled passion she'd read about in romance novels.

Behr placed Ellora on the bed before she even realized they were there. He gently guided her back, hovering over her. Running his nose across the length of her collarbone, he inhaled her scent deeply, then ran it up the sensitive skin of her neck. This action instantly made Ellora break out into goose bumps. She shuddered in anticipation for his next move.

As he nipped and bit a path along her neck, a guttural groan came from deep inside his chest. "Dinnae go startin' something you might not want me to finish, love. My restraint can only go so far before you push me right off the edge."

She believed him. His stern warning had her stomach flipping around and heating up like an old fashioned pizza oven. In that moment, she *wanted* him to kiss her. She was ready. Ellora's breath increased rapidly as she watched him watching her. His eyes raked over her body, as if he warred with himself about his next move. Should he make the move, or should he back off? Ellora wet her lips, hoping he would pick up on her invitation and her need for him. He leaned in, and his warm masculine scent washed over her. Closing her eyes in anticipation, she waited. His hot breath tickled her face as he leaned in...

That's when Adelle came bounding in with all her bubbly cuteness, breaking the spell. She stopped short, gasping at the scene laid out in front of her, and whistled. "Ooooooh, lock the door if you plan on ravishing her in broad daylight. Aye, get a room, you two!"

"I'm in my room, cow!" Ellora shouted with pent up frustration. Her body still hummed, wanting him to finish what he'd started. She attempted to toss a pillow at Adelle's head, but her shot came up short and embarrassingly to the left of her.

Behr let out a frustrated growl, baring his teeth. He leaned in and bit Ellora's earlobe, whispering, "We will continue this later, love. That is a promise, one I intend to keep." He gave the tip of her nose a quick kiss then slowly raised up off her, before pinning Adelle with a demoralizing glare.

"Oh, dinnae look at me like that, ya big baby. You knew I was coming up straightaway with her medical cleaning kit. Lachlan said I had to check her bandages and make sure they weren't seeping through yet, anyway, and I intend to see the task through." She strutted across the room, her long skirt swaying with her, to set the supplies on her kitchenette table.

Ellora's eyes followed her, and that's when she noticed the thirty-inch flat-screen TV for the first time. It stood on a tall, mocha-stained, wooden stand across the room, right in front of her bed and in between the two large windows.

She knew her eyes must've bugged out of her head, because Behr and Adelle's faces lit up. They looked at each other then back at her. Ellora could feel a cool draft, and realized that her mouth was hanging open like a fish out of water. She was stunned. Several minutes ticked by before she realized that she could speak.

"Oh my God, who...? When...? And why?" Was all she could manage to say. Definitely not her most eloquent moment ever.

Adelle came barreling at Ellora, jumping on her bed, giddy like a little kid on Christmas morning. "Do you like it? The three o' us thought you'd like it, we did! There is only so much o' that beautiful view a person could take, being stuck up here for as long as you'll be, before going mad, eh?" She turned up her lip and stuck out her tongue, mocking a disgusted gag, obviously kidding around with her. Ellora could *never* get sick of that view.

"The three of you?" she pressed, with one raised eyebrow.

"Yes, Behr, Gavin, and yours truly figured you needed to get yourself acquainted with Scottish pop culture so you would quit embarrassing us all the time. Consider this like an intervention, Ellora." She couldn't quite get the last part out without bursting out in laughter. "Now, we can watch girly movies, or... you can use it as background noise as you two eat each other's faces off!" Adelle snickered when she caught sight of Ellora's deep scarlet blush.

"You shouldn't have done this. It's just too much. I mean, usually, people just give flowers or get well soon cards. People just don't buy other people TVs. They just don't," Ellora argued. She was terrible at this. She'd much rather do kind things for others. She wasn't good at being on the receiving end of it.

Behr cleared his throat and walked back over to the object of his desire. He sat down beside her on the bed, his weight making the mattress dip down low. "We are *nae* just some people. We are your family, *AND* the people who care 'bout you. You dinnae have much in the way of possessions, so we thought this would be nice to help you feel settled… you know, so you'll feel more at home here."

Ellora considered his words as she fumbled with her yellow bedspread, looking from her fingers to the dip Behr made. She couldn't help the smile that spread across her face at the contrast between the very dated, pale yellow bed spread with the delicate little daisies on them… to this very LARGE, rugged, and muscular alpha male that sat on it. It was a very contradictory combination.

If only he knew that she felt more at home here than she ever had back in the States. Ellora opened her mouth to refuse again but thought better of it. She saw how happy it made them both to do this for her. She needed to stop being so stubborn.

"Thank you. I love it! I will start doing extensive

homework right away, Miss Adelle," she answered in her best childish, perfect little student voice. "I definitely don't want to *embarrass* anyone," Ellora stressed, teasing her friend right back.

"Well, I will see about getting you a... what was it again? Oh yeah, a double bacon cheeseburger and a chocolate shake." Behr winked at Ellora, cupping his hand on the side of her face. He kissed her on the cheek tenderly as he got up and back pedaled out of the room. His eyes never left hers as he did.

"Don't forget the greasy fries!" Ellora shouted out to him when she remembered to breathe.

Ellora had gotten some much needed rest in the following days, and she'd hate to admit it, but she *was* thankful for her new TV. She could kill Adelle for getting her addicted to her favorite daytime soaps, *Coronation Street* and *Emmerdale*, though. She never would have thought they would have equally dramatic soaps here as they did in the States. Ellora loved hearing the thick accents shouting dramatically in heated confrontations!

Adelle helped clean her wounds and redress the bandages. Sometimes, Ellora would just cling to her sheets, leaving her back bare so she could get some air to it. She knew it was healing well because it started to itch as it scabbed over. Adelle kept her company throughout the day, painting her nails and practicing applying a smoky-eye look with her new makeup. Apparently, Ellora had become her real life doll to play with, and she took full advantage of this, too, knowing full well she couldn't escape her.

Adelle let Ellora borrow her laptop so she could continue to work on Grady's renovation project. She checked out shops in the area, which she could enlist to help paint the outside of Grady's bar. Plus, she pre-ordered him a brand new sign. Ellora was disappointed that she had to find help, because she wanted to do this all on her own, but asking for help seemed to be the theme lately. She was, however, extremely excited to see how everything was coming together.

You'd think Ellora was an amputee by the way she had been confined to her room, or her bed more like it. Every time she wandered down the stairs to get something to eat or drink, stretch out her legs, and change the view, she was stopped. Behr would use his body as a barrier, holding out both hands like a street cop directing traffic.

"Nope! Think again. Turn 'round and get that cute butt back up those stairs, young lady. You are supposed to be in bed with the flu. Kristy will 'ave me stoned to death if I let you walk 'bout."

Trying her best at a pretty pouty-lipped look, Ellora batted her eyes at him and groaned, "Uuuugh, Behr, pretty, pretty, please with chocolate syrup on top! I am going stir crazy up there. I need to stretch my legs."

He would cross his arms over his tight chiseled chest and flex his biceps. He shot Ellora a determined glare, definitely *not* willing to let her pass. With a matching stern voice, he stated flatly, "You've got to let your back heal this time 'round. Dinnae make me tie you to the bed posts, you stubborn woman." He stressed each word carefully, which made her feel all the guiltier for doing such a terrible job the first time around.

Defeated, Ellora flung her arms out to the sides. "All right, all right, turn down the dramatics. I'm going, ya big bully."

"I'll be up straight away with your coffee and breakfast, love." His voice changed its tone to soothing and caring once again. *Oh my, Behr*, she thought.

When he came up with the loot, Ellora panicked at the thought of him leaving her there. It was going to be a few hours before Adelle came up, and the constant solitude had her feeling anxious, like the walls were closing in. Definitely a case of cabin fever. Reaching up, Ellora gripped his thick wrists, halting him. "Behr, please don't leave me. I don't want to be here all alone. Please sit here with me for a while."

Behr's expression softened. She could've sworn she saw a look of devotion and determination ripple through his expression as she studied him. A warm smile showed in his eyes, even though his lips wouldn't mimic the emotion. He closed his eyes for the briefest moment, a ghost of a smile tugging at his mouth. Tilting his head, he opened his eyes and looked down at her. "Aye, love, I will always be 'ere for you." Cupping Ellora's chin, he lifted it up. "Just ask and I'm 'ere."

Behr scooped her up, careful not to touch the bandages. He moved her over easily, so that he could sit right beside her. Ellora handed him the remote as he handed her the tray of food. Finding nothing else, Behr left it on *Britain's Got Talent*. Looking her way, he shrugged. "Gotta love Simon Cowell."

Ellora could say this about Behr: he was a *terrible* singer! He sounded like a dying cat in heat that had been hit by a pellet gun. And that was her being nice. He couldn't hit a high note to save his life. His deep voice wouldn't allow the foreign note. And Ellora loved every moment of it, bleeding ears and all. He was so funny like this, and the more she laughed, the worse he bellowed the tune.

Thankfully, he stopped when the commercials came on, because her cheeks and abs burned from laughing so hard. Ellora leaned her head on his large defined shoulder and draped one arm over his stomach. Their legs were touching side by side, but it just wasn't close enough for her. Breathing out a contented sigh, Ellora curled her legs up with his. Leaning down, he kissed the top of her head, breathing in deeply. She could feel his breath in her hair as he spoke softly. "Comfortable, Lor?"

Just like that, an overwhelming sense of déjà vu

struck her. A forgotten memory flashed back to the time Ellora got pneumonia.

When she was eight, her dad had to rush her to urgent care. While they waited in the tiny room with the flickering fluorescent light, Ellora's father looked helpless, out-of-control, wondering how he could fix this. He never knew what to do when she was sick like this. Ellora had a terribly high fever, and she was very weak and lethargic. Fat tears rolled down her red cheeks continuously. So her dad did the only thing he could do in that moment -- resort to humor.

The weak little girl watched as her dad opened drawers, removing gloves, Q-tips, gauze, and bandages. With his hands full, he moved them to the upper cabinet in the corner, carelessly shoving them in. He then grabbed the hospital gowns, booties, paper hats, and masks that were in that cabinet, and hid them in the other cabinet under the stainless steel cart at the center of the room. She looked on, laughing weakly, her body shaking with the effort. "Daddy, what are you doing?"

"Idle minds are the devil's playground. Serves them right for making my baby girl wait so long! The doctor will think he's gone mad." He sounded devilish as he laughed at his own joke. "Jack Pot." He pulled out the stethoscope, thermometer, and the blood pressure cuff, then threw them under the sink cabinet as they heard footsteps approaching their room outside. Dad quickly skipped across the room and sat on the bench next to his daughter, his poker face firmly in place. Ellora struggled to wipe the smile off hers as the doctor walked in.

It was hilarious watching the doctor fumble around, confused and flustered, as he went about opening and closing the drawers and cabinets, trying to find all his equipment, and shocked when he found another misplaced item. Her dad kept a straight face the whole time, even egging him on. "Are you new or something? It looks like you haven't a clue as to what you're doing." The doctor adamantly denied it, of course, but her father just cut him off. "Then what exactly is your problem?"

If she hadn't been so weak, she would've doubled over with violent laughter. Only her dad! That afternoon, he stayed with her, never leaving her side as she was stuck in bed. They watched movies together, and Ellora leaned on her daddy's shoulder, nuzzling into his safe arms. She tried to wrap her little arms all the way around him, fidgeting to get closer still. Kissing the top of her head, he'd asked, "You comfortable, Lor?"

Snapping back to reality was painful. The memory was so real she could still smell the Old Spice scent of his aftershave and feel the bristly prickles of his beard as it caught on her hair. Tears filled to the brim, pooling in her eyes, until her lids released them when she blinked. Behr looked down when he heard her sniffling.

"I dinnae think my singin' was that bad, love." He thumbed away Ellora's tears. His strong hands lightly stroked her cheek. Brushing her hair out of her face, he tucked it behind Ellora's ear, shushing her. "It's okay, love. I'm here."

Looking up, she hiccupped, trying to answer him. "I

miss them… *so* much. I wish I could have just one more day with them."

Understanding came to him. He kissed the top of her head, resting his chin there. Holding the woman he treasured, the woman who held his heart, he tucked her in tightly to his side. Ellora reveled in the feeling of his hot breath on her crown. "I know, love. I know. Just let it out."

After that, Behr rarely left her side. Ellora's nights were spent snuggled under his arm, relaxing comfortably on the bed, watching movies. For the most part, Behr was a complete gentleman. He did steal some kisses along her neck, but would regain some control just as Ellora would turn to kiss him back. She thought he was holding back because he didn't want to hurt her if things went further, but she wasn't so sure. He seemed hot and bothered one moment, then all guards would go up the next, leaving him detached. She hoped that was the reason, because if she was being honest with herself, Ellora was falling for him… HARD.

As she was contemplating this, Behr ran his other hand down the length of her arm, lacing his fingers through hers. She squeezed his gently and turned to face him. He was already facing her direction with a tranquil, inquisitive look on his face.

"So Lachlan tells me your stitches can come out tomorrow, yeah?" His suspicious grin made her think he was up to something.

Nodding warily, she answered, "Yes, they do. Lachlan says my skin was just as stubborn as I am and healed itself up pretty fast. Why? What are you up to, Mr. Buchanan?" Ellora's eyebrow rose in curiosity.

"Well, you've been stuck in 'ere long enough, so I thought I'd take you on my boat in the morn' and give you a private tour around the Isle. The views are breathtaking. I arranged to bring lunch with us. The fresh air would do you well, Lor. While we are out, I've arranged for some guys to come help seal and polish the floors for you. Perfect timing, eh, love?"

The giant man sitting next to her lifted her delicate hand, softly kissing her palm. For such a large man, he was always so gentle and attentive with Ellora. Looking into her eyes, he winked maliciously and nibbled her palm, then ran his tongue lightly across its seem. Ellora's stomach grew hot, watching him do to her hand what she wished he'd do to her lips. He looked up at her through his thick lashes. "What say you, Ellora? Do we 'ave a date?"

14

The stitches came out without any problems. Lachlan said everything looked as it should, and Ellora was cleared to go on Behr's little water adventure. He seemed as happy as Adelle was that they were going out. It warmed her heart to see how much people cared about each other here.

When she got back to Grady's, Ellora ran upstairs to change into a fitted tank with a pullover and her favorite skinny jeans. After she came down, she sat at one of the bar stools, savoring her cup of rich dark roast coffee -- her necessity in a mug. Two strong arms wrapped around her stomach, and the muscular ridges of abs pressed against her back, enclosing Ellora in a warm embrace. Her body already knew who it was the moment he walked in. His head came down next to her ear. "Ready to go then, love?"

Her smile stretched from ear to ear. "I've been looking forward to this since you told me you had a boat. I've just been waiting for an invite," she whispered softly back in his ear, letting her lips brush his lobe softly and loving the way he tensed up the moment her lips made contact with his skin.

He kissed her neck tenderly then backed up a step. Behr laced his fingers through hers, guiding Ellora off the stool. They shouted their goodbyes as he led the way out the door.

They walked down the pier sidewalk hand in hand. It was a remarkably clear, sunny day. A slight salty breeze blew Ellora's hair around her shoulders. The outdoors relaxed her. She was drawn to it. She took in a deep cleansing breath, loving the smell of the fresh sea air and the sun shining on her face. Behr slowed his pace so he walked in step beside his dark haired beauty. His large frame cast an impressive shadow on her side. He couldn't resist catching glimpses of his angel's reactions to the unrivaled beauty of the sun rising on the harbor. Her eyes were alight with an uplifting spirit that had them sparkling with perfection. They enjoyed their walk in a comfortable silence, the connection they shared through their joined hands the only communication either of them needed.

They made their way past Beaumont Crescent and onto Quay Street toward the boat terminal. Ellora felt excitement rise up inside her for the first time in a long time. She was going to have so much fun today... on the boat, and with Behr.

"See that one there, love?" Behr pointed to a large, white two-story ferry with an open wide rear section that could take in at least four good-sized vehicles. "She's mine." It wasn't a newer model, but her clean, sleek design was timeless and classy.

"She is beautiful, Behr." His chest puffed up with pride as he turned his dazzling perfect smile on her. He was obviously very proud of his boat, and it showed.

When they made it to the terminal, Behr opened up the door for Ellora to enter first. He nodded his greetings to his fellow boat and fishermen as they walked in. Behind the front desk sat Gavin.

"Hey there, lass. Glad to see you join the living! And it's good to see you out n' about, too, ya ol' grizzly bear. I was startin' to think you were in hibernation after all this time." Gavin punched Behr in the arm playfully, not even remotely effecting Behr. "Where are the two of you off to, eh?" Gavin came around the desk to grasp Behr's forearm, and shook it while patting him on the back in a brotherly fashion.

"Toss me the keys, lad. I'm takin' Miss Ellora Belle Sutherland 'ere on a grand tour of the Isle."

Gavin tossed an old set of keys overhand. Behr caught them with one hand in mid-air. "Aye, she's sure to love that. It's a grand day for it, that's for certain. Will you be needin' a chaperone, Miss Ellora? Or do you trust this Behr to keep his paws to himself, do ya?!" Gavin roared out a throaty high-pitched laugh, ducking Behr as he swung at him.

"It's best you keep that fool's mouth o' yours shut, or I will shut it for ya… permanently." Behr's threat sounded scarier than he meant it to be, but his crooked smirk gave him away. "We will see you in a bit, Gavin. Check in at

Grady's, a'right. They're sealing the floors today."

"Aye, brother, o' that you can be sure. I will see you both later. Go easy on her, Behr, will ya!" he shouted and winked as Behr cursed him under his breath.

Behr lightly grasped Ellora's elbow, while his other hand lowered to the small of her back, gently guiding her out the side door that lead to the docked boats. He helped her step up onto the impressive boat and onto a side cushioned bench. Then he started the process of untying and raising the anchors, prepping to start up the engines, and carefully backed out of the dock.

In no time at all, they were cruising at a relaxing speed, turning left out of Portree Harbor, heading north of the Isle of Skye. With the cool sea breeze blowing her hair back, Ellora took in the gorgeous view. The breathtaking cold looking water was a striking vivid blue, and the mountains of the Trotternish Ridge were a deep emerald green. The land was so spectacularly beautiful that they looked like the work of an imaginative painter envisioning a fairytale land come to life.

Behr was stationed behind the wheel, driving one handed, confident and completely at ease. It was an amazing sight to see him. She noticed right away that Behr's overall demeanor changed almost immediately once they were on the water. He was the most carefree and relaxed she'd seen him, since meeting him months ago. He smiled more, his eyes seemed brighter, and his laugh was carefree. It was safe to say Ellora loved this version of Behr. He was definitely a man of the sea. He belonged on water.

Behr caught Ellora staring at him. She was sure she blushed scarlet, since she could feel her face heating up. Ellora quickly looked down at her boots for a few seconds. When she thought it was safe, she peeked up at him through her eyelashes. His head was tilted to the side with a devilish grin, one hand lazily draped over the wheel and the other motioning with his finger for her to come over.

Ellora stood up and made her way over to him, much too quickly and a little too enthusiastically, but without tripping and falling, so that was a plus. Behr slowed the boat down and had it idling. He grabbed her hand and walked with her over to the rail on the side of the ferry.

"All right, love, how much of Skye's folklore 'ave you heard, huh?" Behr kissed the knuckles of the hand he was holding and stood behind Ellora. Wrapping one arm around her waist, he ran the other up and down the length of her arm. His roughened hands sent shivers down her spine. She loved how masculine he was. She leaned back into his muscular front, loving the safety his embrace promised when she was wrapped securely in his arms.

"Nope. You will be the very first to tell me Skye's stories!"

Behr looked down at Ellora as she looked up. His eyes seemed to darken as he searched her face. "Well, love, I feel honored to be your first." The deep timber in his voice vibrated through his chest and into Ellora's back, making her stomach do little summersaults. He broke eye contact first, lacing his fingers through hers and lifting both their arms, pointing toward a steep ridge climbing up the side of the mountain. "You see that tall rock there? The one that looks like a sitting king on a throne carved out of rock?" She nodded, looking at the majestic looking pinnacle.

"There were actually two of these pinnacles, and they are the preserved remains of an old married couple."

Ellora smiled up at him. She knew she'd like this story.

"Legend tells us of O'Sheen. One day, a local farmer heard cries for help while climbing up the ridge. He came upon a pair of legs sticking out o' the dirt. It was a Brùnaidh that had gotten trapped after an enormous landslide."

"A Brùna what??" Ellora giggled, looking up at him. Funny things happened inside her when she heard his thick accent use the ancient language. Behr smiled sweetly at her and kissed the tip of her nose.

"It means hobgoblin or a Fairy, love." Ellora's eyebrows flew up. This story was going to be jam-packed with folklore. She listened intently as he continued. "O'Sheen dug him out, saving his life. He was very grateful and vowed to repay O'Sheen for his kindness with a wish. O'Sheen was a very happy man, though, and wanted for nothing. So they struck a deal that they would meet in one year's time, and perhaps by then, O'Sheen would want something. They met once a year for many years after and became great friends."

Behr leaned down, kissing a path up the side of her neck, whispering suggestively, "O'Sheen met a beautiful woman in town and fell madly in love with her. They hastily married soon after, for they couldn't be apart, not even for one day. The Brùnaidh even played music at their wedding. Every year, still, O'Sheen walked up the ridge to meet his old friend, walking hand in hand with his love, enjoying the view of *their* Scotland." Ellora's heart swelled from the love this legendary couple had for one another. She listened to Behr as she watched the enormous rock that towered proudly high above the ridge.

"But, many years later, right after their last visit, O'Sheen's wife passed away unexpectedly. O'Sheen was so devastated and heartbroken after losing his soul mate that he soon after died of a broken heart, eager to reunite with her where they could be together forever. A year later, right on schedule, the Brùnaidh sat waiting at their ridge for his good friend and his wife. He became very worried when his friend never showed. He eventually got word that O'Sheen died of a broken heart, and he became consumed with guilt and sadness that he was not there when his friend needed him.

"He decided to honor O'Sheen by memorializing their love forever. With a small hammer, he chiseled away at an enormous rock, forming the shape of his aged friend and then one of his wife in the rock behind him. There they sat in rock form, perched high on the ridge, looking out at the Isle of Skye. The Brùnaidh named the mountain Storr, which is of Norse origin meaning Great Man. Over the centuries, his wife's rock formation has crumbled due to terrible weather conditions and the harsh forces of nature. Now, The Old Man of Storr sits alone, forever mournful."

Tears streamed down Ellora's cheeks as Behr finished the story and the boat slowly sailed past. She tried to hold them back, but there was no use. The heartfelt way Behr told this story had her feeling choked up. "That was a beautifully sad story," she managed to say in between hiccups.

Behr squeezed her tight and nuzzled his face in her neck. "I will take you up there someday, love. There are hiking trails that lead all the way up the mountain." He trailed little kisses down her neck to where it met her shoulder, his day old scruff dragging and tickling her.

Ellora tilted her head to give him better access. Though she tried hard to keep her wits about her, she failed miserably as each tender kiss had her further and further away from control. "I'm glad you told it. I'd love to hear another one."

He continued to kiss up and down the side of her neck, and softly nibbled on her earlobe as she watched the Mournful Old Man of Storr fade away in the distance. The moment seemed to stretch on peacefully like this, with just the sounds of the waves breaking against the boat and the occasional gulls squawking overhead. The boat bobbed up and down in a sensual rhythm that made her blood pressure rise with it.

This quiet solitary moment with Behr was so intimate, she was almost frightened to turn around. As if reading Ellora's mind, he stopped and slowly turned her to face him. He cupped her chin and tilted her face up to meet his eyes, which were dark and hooded with passion. His breaths were coming in and out rapidly, his chest rising and falling deeply. Ellora put her hands on his chest, hoping to calm him, but he held his breath for a beat and stepped closer to her. They were now standing chest to chest, stomach to stomach, and thigh to thigh. The full body contact had Ellora's whole being shuddering in anticipation.

His hands moved softly up her back. One hand ran through her hair at the nape of her neck. Instinctively, she wrapped her arms around his neck. They just stood there like that, staring into each other's eyes, moving their gazes to their lips and back again. The boat had them swaying back and forth like a slow dance. His eyes took her in one last time, before he slowly dipped his mouth down to hers. There was no one there to burst in and interrupt. It was just Behr and her.

Ellora started to feel nervous jitters, knowing they were going to kiss again. And this time, it wasn't just to make an ex jealous. She took a couple of deep breaths and sighed, letting her eyes close as he pulled her in closer. His soft, full, strong lips landed on hers. He was gentle at first, lightly pecking and nipping at her lower lip. Then gradually, he deepened the kiss, taking Ellora's lip into his mouth and sucking on it. He ran his tongue over her lips, silently begging her to open up to him, then delved in deeper when she obeyed.

Their tongues massaged and twirled together. Behr groaned in what almost sounded like agony as he pulled Ellora impossibly closer to him. *This. Right here.* Ellora thought. It was heaven on Earth to her! Right here, she was safe in Behr's arms, without a worry in the world. His kisses were expertly given. He gave so much passion in each kiss, touch, and embrace. He held nothing back, and she didn't want him to. Little moans and sighs started to escape her own lips as he stroked her back with his hands and stroked her tongue with his. Just before Ellora lost her mind and almost ripped both their clothes off in a frenzy, Behr slowed the kiss and pulled back a little, resting his forehead on hers.

They just looked into each other's lustful eyes in a daze, trying to catch their breath. His hot breath mingled with hers. Behr kissed Ellora's forehead, both her eyelids, her nose, and lifted up one eyebrow when she lifted her waiting mouth to his, anticipating his next kiss. Needing another kiss. His eyes flickered with amusement as he laid several playful kisses on her waiting lips.

"If we keep on the way we 'ave, Miss Ellora, we will crash this boat into the rocks and have to swim home, love."

Oh yeah... the boat... steering. Ooops!

Behr flashed Ellora a wicked looking smile. "This, is far and away the *BEST* tour I've ever been a part of!"

Ellora laughed heartily and pinched him lightly. "This *BETTER* be the best tour you've ever had! I'd hate to think what you've done with your other customers." Ellora gave him one more good pinch. He batted her away and jogged back over to the control station.

Ellora followed him to the controls as he gripped the wheel, unable to stop herself from smiling like a giddy little girl on Christmas morning. Behr got the boat back on track, heading further north along the Skye coastline.

They came upon a high mountain ridge with jagged folds, pleats, and columns climbing the cliff sides.

"All right, love, you see that pleated cliffside there?" She smiled and nodded, still too tongue-tied -- no pun intended -- to speak after their steamy kiss. "That there is Kilt Rock. Legend tells us the story of two giants, Fingal and Fiona, which goes a little like this…

"There was once a giant and his wife who lived on the north coast of Scotland, and their names were Fingal and Fiona. They lived quite happily, and the love they had for each other was unbreakable. One day, while Fingal was out, Fiona had an unexpected visitor drop by. Fionn McCool, an Irish giant, was travelling through Scotland to meet some relatives, when he spotted Fingal and Fiona's house. He stopped to ask for something to eat and drink. When he saw Fiona, Fionn became transfixed with her beauty, and made several passes at her." Behr wiggled his eyebrows, eyeballing Ellora. "But Fiona refused his advances and demanded that he leave. Fionn left, but not before declaring that once his business was finished, he would be back to fight for her, swearing he'd bring her back to Ireland with him." Behr locked Ellora in his arms and swung her around. She squealed at his antics.

"Upon her husband's return, Fiona told Fingal all about her visitor. She warned him that the Irish giant was much bigger and a fearsome warrior." Ellora shook her head as Behr lifted both his large arms and flexed. She appreciated this movement for a moment, as he, too, looked like a legendary folklore warrior chiseled out of rock. Ellora nodded in approval, making it obvious to him that she was studying his form.

"Fingal was insulted at the idea that he didn't have a chance against Fionn, and Fiona feared for her loved one's life. She swore to herself that she would protect him at any cost. Fiona had come up with a genius plan, and reluctantly, Fingal agreed to go along with it. During the next week, Fiona instructed her husband to build a giant cradle, and she began to knit a large blanket and a large baby bonnet."

"A little over a week later, Fiona was sitting outside, hanging her laundry out to dry, when she saw Fionn McCool coming toward their home. She called, 'Fingal, quick! Strip down to your underwear and wrap yourself in this blanket!' Baffled, Fingal did as she asked." Ellora laughed as Behr's voice cracked trying to shriek like a woman.

"She told him, 'Now, get into the cradle!' Aghast at what Fiona was asking of him, Fingal protested and began to leave, but as he passed by a window, he caught a glimpse of Fionn marching toward their home. Far taller than Fingal and clearly a toughened warrior, the sight of Fionn scared Fingal witless. Fiona was adjusting the knitted baby's bonnet on her husband's head just as Fionn burst in.

"'Fiona, I'm here to take you away! Where's that husband of yours? I'll win you fair and square!'" Behr got a little too into the story as he wrapped his arms around Ellora and dipped her. She looked up at his face, seeing his eyes were alight with adoration. Ellora silently begged him for another kiss, but instead, he continued the story, enjoying the effect he had on her. "Fiona offered Fionn tea and calmly set about preparing some refreshments, telling Fionn that her husband was out but would be back quite soon. As the water boiled for the tea, Fiona excused herself to bring the wash in.

"She came in and began unraveling a large wet table cloth. Once unraveled, Fiona walked past Fionn and out the door, shaking out and hanging the giant cloth over the cliff's edge to dry. Fionn asked her what she was doing, and Fionna told him she was drying her husband's kilt.

"'His kilt?' Fionn asked, alarmed at the massive size of the cloth. Fingal, who was hiding in the cradle, peeked out at Fionn, making the cradle creak. "What's that?" Fiona told him, 'my wee baby boy. You can hold him if you'd like.' So Fionn walked over to the cradle and stared at the gigantic, ugly baby sleeping inside."

Ellora burst out laughing, picturing an oversized ugly giant wrapped up in a blanket and bonnet, portraying a baby. Behr laughed along with her then continued.

"'How old is he?" Fionn asked, panic rising in him. If the baby was this big, the father must be massive. 'Oh! My wee boy is just a year old, and still growing,' Fiona added with a small smile. Fionn nodded and excused himself. Fiona watched from her window as Fionn McCool ran from the house and back toward Ireland, destroying the bridge connecting Scotland and Ireland as he went, to prevent a jealous husband of *undetermined* size from coming after him."

Ellora sat back, enjoying the story. Behr was so funny; he changed his voice to a higher pitch when speaking as Fiona, and very low when speaking as Fingal and Fionn. He even used sound effects! Behr was the *BEST* storyteller.

"Now, it is said that Kilt Rock got its pleated column shape by the giant, heavy, wet wash Fiona left on the cliffside, leaving behind the deep impressions." Behr lifted up his eyebrows, clearly amused with this story.

Ellora laughed and clapped her hands animatedly at the conclusion to the story.

"I have to say, Behr, these legends are pretty romantic and funny. I love hearing them."

"Ah, yes, Miss Ellora, ours is a romantic history! I'm very happy you're enjoying them! I know the perfect spot up ahead to drop anchor and have a scenic lunch. What'd ya say, Lor...? You up for a bite?"

"That sounds great, Behr. I am pretty hungry."

Behr turned the boat around, avoiding touring all the way around the Isle. "Aren't you going to take me on a tour all the way around Skye?"

Behr slowly shook his head, now looking past her to the horizon. "I don't go all the way 'round, not anymore."

Ellora lifted her brow in confusion, wanting to know why but feeling it wasn't her place to question him why. Without hesitation, Behr slung his arm over her shoulder and kissed her forehead affectionately as he started to explain.

"My father was a Captain, a very successful and well known fisherman in Portree. He used to fish and trap all over these parts." Extending his arm, Behr lazily pointed all around them.

"Well, the life of a sea man was a rough one for him. His health started to fail him in my teen years. So, naturally, he started training me to take over the family business that has been handed down for generations. However, I have never wanted any part of the lifestyle. Sailing far out to sea from the mainland, rough seas, and long seasons were not my idea of a good life. I remember seeing my mother cry every night, and I used to think that was normal. She was so lonely and worried all the time. Aye, their marriage suffered from it. I knew I would never let myself become the sort of man who left his wife and child alone to fend for themselves."

Ellora nodded, listening intently to his confession. She could definitely see that it wasn't a life suited for him. He cared about too many people to just pick up and leave everyone behind.

"I guess you can say I'm a bit of a homebody. I never wanted to stray far from Portree. Time passed by, as it always does, and my father put more and more pressure on me to take over the legacy. Aye, n' I almost did just that until Gavin's da came across a used ferry boat in need of a small restoration, some freshening up, and TLC. Sympathetic to my plight, he offered to sell it to me for crumbs, as long as I helped with the tourists once she was up and running. It was going to be a great income for me."

"In hearing the very disappointing news, my father flew into a fit of rage. I was accused of dishonoring a long family history. He gave me an ultimatum, and I chose my new life. He disowned me, stressing how ashamed of me he was and what a huge disappointment I was in his eyes. My mother, whether she agreed with him or not, went along with his decision like she always did. Soon after, they picked up and moved on the other side of the island, leaving me here. I moved in with Gavin's family, until the money rolled in and I was able to get on my feet, grateful for their kindness. When I tried to go after them to make peace, he said I wasn't a part of the family anymore. He declared my younger cousin his next in line. We agreed not to step on each other's toes. He stays on his side, and I stay on mine, which is fine. I'm happy with what I'm doing now. I wouldn't change it for the world. I would've never met you had I left with them anyway, and I can't have that!" He winked at Ellora and kissed the tip of her nose.

At that moment, she thought about how lucky she was to have had loving, supportive parents. Yes, they were taken from her far too quickly, but the time she *did* have, she wouldn't change for the world. Behr's parents, on the other hand, showed no love or support, and had abandoned him for the choices he made regarding his own future.

Wrapping her arms around his waist, Ellora squeezed him in tight to her. Laying her head on his chest, Ellora did her best to console him without making him feel pitied. "I'm sorry that happened to you, Behr. But I'm very happy you stayed. My time here wouldn't mean as much, or be as interesting to look at, without you." Ellora laughed when his eyebrows flew up in shock at her unexpected statement.

"So what you're tellin' me, Miss Sutherland, is that I'm your personal man candy in-charge of keeping your view acceptably delightful? Is that the way of it?"

"Yup! You pretty much summed up your role. There will be weekly checks to make sure you stay on point, so don't disappoint me or I will get myself some new eye candy!"

Behr swept Ellora up into his arms, lifting her off the ground. His laugh rumbled deep in his chest. Giving her a playful bite on the neck, he played along. "I won't let you down, boss lady. I look forward to your next inspection! Will that be a full body inspection?"

"Ha!! We shall see. If you play your cards right, then maybe." Ellora wiggled her eyebrows as she looked over his impressive body suggestively.

Just up ahead, past the last curved and pleated cliff column was a breathtaking waterfall. Ellora's jaw dropped. This island was absolutely magical, and it was the perfect spot to enjoy their lunch.

Behr killed the engine, dropped anchor, and went down below deck. He came back up with a cooler and a plaid wool blanket, then strolled over to where he left the object of his affection. Tucking the blanket under the arm he was holding the cooler with, Behr wrapped his free arm around Ellora's waist, pulling her in close to him.

They walked past the captain's cabin toward the back of the ferry to a wide open cargo section. Behr walked them right to the center of it, facing the waterfall, and placed the cooler down. He shook out the blanket and placed it down on the deck. Then he reached over, grasping her porcelain hand, and helped her get seated before plopping down right beside her.

"I brought a variety of things to eat. I wasn't sure what

you'd like, love. I hope its a'right." Ellora thought Behr looked so cute as he searched through the food he brought. He really wanted to impress her. It was incredibly hot.

"I'm sure I will love whatever it is you brought. I brought my hunger, so I'm ready to dig in." Ellora rubbed her stomach as it growled right on cue.

Sitting back, she watched Behr as he put together a beautiful picnic, and just took him in. All of him. He was so thoughtful and considerate by nature, and she could tell he'd taken the time to think of every detail on their outing.

She watched as he quietly took out two soup thermoses, some warm herb crusted bread, and several varieties of cheeses. Next came out a small seafood platter of a mixture of local cold sea food appetizers and dips. He then retrieved two small glasses and a bottle of red wine. Once at the bottom of the basket, Behr pulled out a wedge of chocolate cheesecake, and looked up at her through his eyelashes and wiggled his eyebrows.

"A proper date is not a date at all without dessert, eh, love?"

He searched over her peaceful face, taking in all her expressions as she lit up at the thought of chocolate.

"You got that right, oh captain my captain." Laughing, she saluted him. Ellora started to feel a little giddy nervousness creep up inside her at his mention of 'date'.

"Sooooo, this *IS* a real date then?" She half smiled and lifted her brows in question. "Not just a friendly date between two, um, friends? Right?"

Behr leaned into her, cupping her soft cheeks with his big hands. Before he even answered, Ellora was already certain of what it would be. His ice blue eyes told her all she wanted to know. He stroked her cheek with his thumb, a small smile and a caring gentleness shining in his eyes. He looked over every inch of her face longingly, committing it to memory.

"I told you once before, Ellora, that when something I want is in my sights, I go after it. Nothing in this world can stop me from going after you, love."

Ellora looked down, feeling a growing blush stain her cheeks with his very forward and honest comment. She'd only expected flirtatious banter. He took hold of her chin and lifted it so she was looking him square on.

"Ellora, I don't want to dance around the subject anymore. You know that I have feelings for you. From the moment I laid eyes on you, I've wanted you to be mine. I'm in no rush to push this on you either if you are not yet ready. We have all the time in the world to let this thing we have between us grow. You must know, I do not play around with a woman's heart. I do *not* like games. I am just a man looking for a good woman to stand by his side. From the very beginning, I have felt very strongly for you, Ellora. You are always on my mind." He motioned his hands back and forth between them. "And I know you feel this, too, love, just as intensely as I."

Her chest grew tight at his confession, and her heart swelled even more for him. She nodded.

"Yes, I do," is all she could respond with a soft whisper, and she meant it, too.

Behr beamed back at her, obviously very pleased with her admission, and nodded his head in approval at her quiet answer. While pouring her a glass of wine, he watched her perfectly plump lips as she took an appreciative sip. She sighed her approval before he drank from his own.

One would think Behr was an introvert when first meeting him, with his quiet reserved demeanor. Ellora definitely had. When in reality, he just sat back and observed, listening to what was going on around him. Behr made his decisions, then slowly let those around him into his life if he so chose. He rarely made any rash or sudden judgements without giving it some serious thought first. He expressed himself honestly and to the point, rarely saying something he didn't mean. Behr was a man who cared deeply for those lucky enough to be in his life, and wouldn't think twice about giving them the shirt right off his back. Ellora felt fortunate that he included her as one of the people he cared so much about.

They finished up their delicious lunch. Ellora slurped down her Cullen Skink, a traditional hearty fish and potato soup. It was delicious, and she was practically licking the remaining drops leftover from the thermos.

Behr shot cloth napkins at the beautiful slob in front

of him, playfully saying she was a "disgrace to ladies everywhere," so she slurped louder. Behr laughed loudly, shaking his head, declaring that he was embarrassed to be seen with her. Ellora purposely let it dribble down her chin. He laughed long and loud, the deep tone echoing off the rocky cliffs. She leaned into him with soup dripping down her chin and neck, teasing him. She faked hurt confusion.

"Mr. Behr Buchanan, are you saying that my terrible manners embarrass you so much that you wouldn't make out with me looking like this?" She sucked in her cheeks, making the fishy face, and puckered her lips at him. As she lunged at him, she wiped her soupy face on his cheek. The shocked look on his face was priceless. Ellora laughed hysterically when he fell back, trying to avoid the inevitable soup dribble attack. She enjoyed her goofy antics, feeling carefree, young, and happy.

Behr roared out in-between his gasping laughs. Turning the tables, he stalked toward her on all fours. "Ooooh, you're going to pay dearly for that, my little American she-devil!"

He leapt on Ellora as she was backing away, crawling like a crab. Squealing in surprise, she tried to kick and buck him off as he pounced on her playfully. He easily wrestled her down to the ground and straddled her.

"Aaaah, we've got ourselves a scrapper now, don't we? I know just how to deal with a wild woman..."

Ellora was out of breath from laughing so hard, and

tried at no avail to fight off this solid muscle that was Behr. He carefully pinned her down with his legs overtop of hers, and after grabbing both her wrists, pinned them over her head. She giggled as he zeroed in on her from the above her, looking to the navel that peeked out of her lifted shirt and smiling a menacing, devilish grin. Her stretched out form was completely vulnerable to him.

"Now, Ellora, you asked for this!" He brought his other hand down and started his attack.

"Aaaaaaaah!!!!!!" Ellora screeched out as Behr relentlessly tickled her ribs.

Tickling. Worst torture ever! She squealed, screeched, bucked, and wiggled all over the place. She must've even unconsciously bit the arm that held her down, because he let up a little, allowing Ellora to pull her right hand out of his strong hold and roll to her side.

"Ah, ah, ah, you're a wily one, you are!" Behr rolled with her, squeezing her tight against him. Her back was to his front, like they were spooning, before he started in on his tickle torture. Ellora wiggled and wiggled, and as a result of her constant squirming, her shirt shimmied up a few inches in the back. He stopped his onslaught abruptly. She could feel the emotional separation almost immediately. She wanted his caring warmth to embrace her again. Instead, she felt an icy chill coming from his direction.

Ellora looked over her shoulder. Behr gave a heavy mournful sigh, tracing his finger over the healing gash. He traced it so softly she barely felt him. As he looked down at her, his eyes pleaded with her, silently begging for her permission. She nodded once. This large, oppressive man bent down and gently trailed soft kisses along her scarring back. Surprisingly enough, Ellora actually didn't mind. His touch was accepting, supportive, protective, and loving all rolled up into one. He laid one more long lingering kiss, then lowered her shirt down. He slowly sat up, bringing her up with him.

"Are you ready to tell me what happened, Ellora?"

ehr held both of her hands, gently squeezing them for assurance. Ellora turned around to sit Indian-style, facing him. Her anxiety level rose to where she had an extremely hard time breathing. With watering eyes and several ragged breaths, she slowly nodded as fat tears rolled down her cheeks. She couldn't hide what happened anymore, and she didn't want to. Not from Behr.

He had been nothing but extremely patient with Ellora since the very first night she'd arrived. She struggled inwardly on how, or where, to begin. Shaking her head jerkily, she stuttered, "I... I'm not sure I know how to begin."

Behr scooted closer to her and wrapped his arms around her shoulders. He whispered in her ear, "It's okay. Just start from the beginning, love. There is no one else around, just you and me."

Her eyes darted around, not really focusing on anything in particular. Her mind was fuzzy whenever she tried to think about all the events that led up to her escape. It was like her thoughts were scattered and out of order.

"Well, I guess I should go back to before my parents passed away." Ellora could feel him nod his head as his stubble caught on her hair.

"Start wherever you can, love." She leaned into his hold and let her mind go back to a time she'd tried so hard to forget.

"Well, my father grew increasingly agitated working with his corporate shark partners. I remember hearing him talk to my mother about how they did not work honestly. They were corrupt, immoral, and used threats and blackmail to get what they wanted. They had no honor or values, which was *very* important to my father." Behr squeezed her arm supportively, agreeing with her loving statement about her father.

Ellora reluctantly removed herself out of Behr's all-consuming and loving arms. The separation instantly made her feel hollow and cold inside. "Behr, remember when I told you about the one man who demanded to take me out?" His caring and concerned expression turned rigid as he nodded once. "He is the very same man who's responsible for everything that's happened to me. He made several forceful passes at me, and every time, I refused him or ran, the more fixated he became with making me comply with his *needs*. Oh, Behr, I've never met someone so vile... so disgustingly creepy as this man. Just one look in his lifeless eyes, and you know you're in the presence of evil."

Behr closed his eyes and took a deep breath in. He would let her continue the story because she was finally opening up to him, trusting him enough to unload her deepest darkest secret she'd been keeping. But he had a devastating feeling deep in his gut that grew with each word uttered from her story. He had a pretty good idea where this story was headed, and he wasn't sure how he'd take it when he heard his angel speak the words. Already, he wanted to find this bastard and end him. No mercy and no second chances for the man who dared put his hands on the woman he cherished.

After several moments of sorting out the horrid events in order, Ellora continued. "Well, his advances escalated to the point where I pretty much clung to my father and any of the other colleagues we worked with, for fear of being alone. I was terrified that I'd end up coming face-to-face with him... Who knew what he would do if he ever got me alone? And I never wanted to find out."

Behr couldn't believe his ears. Anger burned hot inside him. Beads of sweat formed on his temples from the effort it took to hold in his outrage. *What man treats a woman like this?* "Ellora, why didn't you go to your father? To the authorities?

She looked down in shame. Her hair fell like a curtain around her face, hiding herself off from him. "I felt like it wasn't safe to tell anyone. He was very wealthy and had a lot of people who worked for him... including local police. He'd threatened my father, and he threatened me." Ellora shrugged her shoulders after the short statement. She would always regret not saying anything, not trying. Maybe her father would still be alive if she had. That, or maybe she'd be dead with them.

Behr's heart constricted when he caught a glimpse of the pain that was imprinted on her face. He could feel the regret pouring out of her as if he was feeling it himself. Behr pulled his broken angel into the safety of his arms. "I understand why you didn't. You loved them so much. You were just trying to protect them, even if that meant putting yourself in danger."

Ellora continued her story as her head rested against his chest. The sound of his heart comforted her. "Well, one day, the very thing I feared most happened… I found myself completely alone in the abandoned warehouse I was working in. He showed up like he *knew* I would be. That's when he pushed me up against the wall and… and… it was the first time he actually assaulted me." Ellora had a hard time verbalizing everything that was done out loud. She squeezed her eyes shut. An overwhelming ickiness crawled over her skin, and she felt extremely sick to her stomach. She was moments away from vomiting. Just the thought of Dalton touching her made her feel like she'd eaten a bucket of worms.

Behr pushed her back to look her in the face. His was red with fury. His jaw was clenched, and his eyes were completely dilated, making the blue irises disappear. Breathing raggedly, his chest heaved as he tried hard to keep his anger under control. Behr hissed out of clenched teeth,

"Ellora. Did he… Tell me he didn't…" Ellora quickly interrupted him before he could finish.

"No. He never got the chance. My father walked in, and I struggled out of his hold and ran out." She decided to skip the details of Dalton's attack that day and move on. It wasn't something either of them wanted to hear out loud.

"That definitely was the straw that broke the camel's back. My father handed in his resignation that very day. He came home a few hours later, while I was in the middle of preparing for my college admissions essays. I couldn't wait to get as far away from Dalton as possible. My dad stormed in, demanding that we pack our things immediately. We were leaving. We would head out that very same day. Afraid I'd lose the chance of a lifetime, I refused to go with them. The admissions cut-off was in a few days. Stubbornly, I demanded that I stay behind. I told him I'd catch up with them in a few hours, and that I'd be fine on my own."

Behr shook his head. He closed his eyes and ran both hands through his hair roughly. Ellora knew what he was thinking… that she was stupid for staying behind. "My father reluctantly agreed, but not before checking my car over, making sure that everything was running properly, that the tank was full and I had a spare tire, just in case. I thought his behavior was odd for him. He was acting paranoid, and he wouldn't explain why. He would stop what he was doing every once in a while and look over his shoulder or up and down the street, like he was looking for someone."

Ellora paused the story for a moment, wiping the tears that streamed down her face with the back of her hand. Swallowing the dry lump in her throat, she took a shaky breath in and closed her eyes tight. Behr felt her petite little body quake. Seeing the tears fall made him feel hollow inside. He wanted to shield her from all the hurt she'd ever felt. He wished he could take it all from her, and carry the pain of it himself. They sat facing each other, her legs over his and his around her. He rubbed her arms, trying to soothe her. After a moment she continued.

"They left that afternoon. I kept so busy I didn't realized that I hadn't heard from my parents all night. I... I got news of their accident the following morning." Behr let out a pained groan. He closed his eyes and dipped his head.

A mournful sob escaped Ellora as she thought about her last moments with her parents. The painful ache she still felt ripped her heart wide open. Behr wrapped the fragile girl in his arms, rubbing her back in soothing circles. He let her cry out. After several minutes passed, Ellora reined in any lingering emotions that over took her, regaining some control, and after a moment, she finally continued.

"I couldn't believe it." Shrugging, she pinched the bridge of her nose, trying to stop the burning tingling sensation that always came when she tried hard *NOT* to cry. Ellora shook her head side to side. "I still can't believe they're gone. I lost the only two people in the world who cared about me."

Behr cupped her face and rained kisses all over her wet cheeks and trembling lips. "I'm here, love. I care. You're not alone anymore."

Ellora was deep inside her head relaying the story. She didn't respond to Behr's loving declaration. She just continued the story.

"I met with our family's lawyer. He was the only man my father trusted, Mr. Jonathan Lawrence. He made arrangements for their funeral, and tried to tell me that he was going forward with his own investigation. Mr. Lawrence was taking a more thorough look at their accident. He had spoken with my father before he left, and there was definitely something in his tone that prompted him to look into the matter a little deeper before it was closed. He also tried to go over a possible change in the Will that concerned me if, what he found in his investigation, turned out to be exactly as he suspected. But I wasn't in the right frame of mind to listen to anything more. I was stricken with so much grief, I was sick over it and just walked out. I just didn't care."

Ellora sat for a minute, thinking. When she raised her head up, she saw grief mirrored on Behr's face. His concern for her was etched in his expression as he sat there with her silently, listening.

"After several months passed, I was approached by Dalton Ramsey Claiborne himself. He actually had the gall to come to my house after all that'd happened. He was accompanied with two men that looked like his bodyguards. They threatened, strong-armed, and bullied a scared, weak-willed and grieving girl into going back to work. He was desperate to have me back... to finish the contracted project that had been put on hold for far too long -- the very same project my father was in charge of finishing. I reluctantly agreed to go back to work the following week, but I only agreed in order to get them out of my house. There was no way I would ever step foot in that place ever again. I didn't care what happened anymore."

Behr nodded, prompting her to go on when she stared off, lost in her own thoughts. "Go on, love. I'm still here. I'm listening."

"Lots of investors started backing out of the project, fearing incompletion. I'd cost the company *LOTS* of money. That's when I noticed things getting... weird." Behr stiffened when he felt Ellora's body shudder with the memory she was reliving. "I noticed dark SUVs following me. I felt like I was being watched whenever I went out. Then there were the late night hang up calls that had me thinking I was losing my mind. So I had my cell turned off for several days and just hid. I was reminded of the frantic look my father had when he tried to uproot us and leave. That was the first time I started wondering if their accident was *really* an accident." Behr's eyes narrowed in understanding as his jaw ticked. His tension had him coiled up so tight he felt ready to snap. His nostrils flared as he grasped what she was implying.

"When I turned my cell back on, there were dozens of messages that I'd either ignored or missed from our lawyer, Jonathan Lawrence. I called him immediately and voiced him my fears, and made an appointment that afternoon to meet with him. I got myself ready, but when I walked outside toward my car, I saw that it was leaking some kind of fluid. It had left a large puddle. I was so paranoid I didn't think it was wise to drive it like that, so instead, I just called a cab to take me to Mr. Lawrence's office."

Behr's breathing started to escalate the further into the story Ellora told. He clenched his teeth and fisted his hands at his side. Ellora paused, but he looked her in the eyes and nodded for her to go on. He had to keep reminding himself to stay calm for her. It was harder for her to tell the story than it was for Behr to hear it. It'd do neither of them any good if he flipped out.

"When I arrived I told him all my fears, and he validated each one when he told me that it was no accident... My parents were murdered. He urged me to get out of there, to hide. I wasn't safe anymore. He handed me an envelope, which contained all the evidence he had collected along with some documents my father sent to him through the mail the day before his death. They contained incriminating and illegal events that he had compiled, collected, and saved while working with Dalton. He must've known something bad would happen. His findings were very detailed and thorough.

"I told him to keep it, just in case anything was to happen to me."

Behr interrupted with one word, "Ellora!" He brought her in tight to him and squeezed her tightly. She hugged him back until he brought her back at arm's length. "You better not *ever* think like that. Not ever again!" Ellora just shrugged. She still feared he would find her.

"That was the only evidence available that could be sent to the proper authorities if needed. I let him know that I was being followed and probably watched, so the less I knew about the evidence, the better. I started to panic, thinking that maybe they already knew. Maybe my house was bugged. Maybe his office was, too. I scribbled on a piece of paper the only place I knew I could run and hide, where no one would find me. I folded it up and gave it to him, and I told him not to open it until something happened. He would know when that was.

I took a cab back home to pack up my things. When I got home, I went up the stairs into my office to grab the necessary documents needed to hop on a plane out of there."

Ellora's heart started pounding out of her chest as she remembered what happened next. Her breath came in and out rapidly, and she rocked back and forth unconsciously. The nightmare of the moment still shook her to the core. She squeezed her eyes closed, remembering the jarring details.

Behr leveled her with his imposing glare. "What happened, Ellora?"

"When I walked in the office, I tried flicking on the lights, but they wouldn't work. I noticed once walking in further, that the furniture was upturned and lying over. I heard one footstep next to me in the dark, creaking the floorboard, and I froze. I thought, *oh my God, I'm too late. It's over. I'm dead.*"

Behr stood up when his pent up frustration and anger became too much for him to sit still. He paced the boat deck, but Ellora continued without pause.

"A man lunged at me from out of the shadows. I screamed at the top of my lungs, absolutely petrified by the sudden attack. I jumped out of the way and dashed across the room to get to the phone, but tripped in the dark over the debris that littered all over the floor. I grasped the receiver and dialed 911 as fast as I could. The office window was open a crack, so I continued to scream at the top of my lungs, hoping somebody -- anybody would hear me."

Behr's pace quickened as the climax of the story was rising. He clenched his fists like he was ready to go to war. But Ellora was in a trance, transfixed with the memory of that night. She had to continue now that the words flowed out of her like water bursting through a dam. She needed to get it out.

"That's when I was hit, hard, on the side of my head. It knocked me to the ground. He saw what I was holding and ripped the phone out of my hands. Then he slapped me a few more times in the face. I tried shielding the blows with my arms, but he grabbed them and pulled them to my sides, and sat on my stomach, pinning me down. He pulled out a six-inch blade that was serrated and had a curved point. When he held it to my neck, he pressed so hard I could literally feel that my flesh was about to break open."

"FUCK!" Behr bellowed out, losing his grip on his anger. All his muscles were flexed and tensed so tight he looked like a stretched out rubber band, ready to snap.

"He leaned in close to my face. I could only see his cold, black eyes. They were filled with a blood thirsty rage. His eyes dilated as he focused on me. He asked me where the documents were. He knew. I really was being watched. I just shook my head back and forth and lied. I told him I didn't know what he was talking about, and asked why he was doing this to me. Losing his patience, he wrapped his hands around my neck, squeezing my windpipe so hard I couldn't let out another sound. He just looked down at me with an enormously eerie smile on his face. He was enjoying what he was doing."

Ellora paused the story for a moment because Behr had become increasingly upset. Balling his hands into tight fists, his knuckles turned white, and his face reddened the more she told him. Reaching up, she grabbed his fist, opened it up, and laced her fingers with his. Ellora kissed his hand tenderly, giving him a moment to calm down. He took a deep long breath in and forced it out slowly. After schooling his emotions, he gave a slight nod, letting her know he was good, and to go on.

"Just then, we both heard a voice coming through the receiver. *'Ma'am! Ma'am! Are you all right? Help is on the way.'* My attacker reached over and yanked the phone out of the wall. In doing so, he loosened his grip on me, and I was able to use that one distraction to wrench myself out of his grip. I kneed him in the crotch and clawed my way up then dashed for the door. Before I could make it, I felt him punch my back, and then there was a dragging sensation. The force pulled me back a step. That's when it finally dawned on me that he'd plunged his knife into my shoulder and slashed down my back." Ellora unconsciously rubbed her shoulder. The memory was so raw and painful; she could still feel everything like it had just happened.

Behr sat down behind Ellora, trying to ease her growing anxiety and the shock her body was going through in reliving everything all over again. He wrapped his large arms around her fragile little body and kissed her all over her neck, shoulder, and collarbone. Nuzzling into her hair, Behr whispered her name like a prayer, "Oh, Ellora, love."

The strength in his arms gave her the strength to get through the story. "He stumbled from the force of the blow, and tripped on the debris on the floor. I used the adrenaline pumping through my veins to force my legs to move. My back felt like someone set me on fire. The pain was so intense."

Ellora pinched her eyes closed for a moment. She could almost feel her jagged scar tingling from the memory.

"I could feel my warm blood soaking my clothes and pants, coming out like a stream of water out of a faucet. I ran as fast as my legs could carry me in my weakened condition. When I made it to the top of the stairs, I heard his pounding footsteps close behind me, and him screaming my name over and over. I skipped stairs, almost hovering above them. I was going down so fast, praying I didn't trip. He was right behind me, getting closer. When he was close enough to grab me, I jumped the last few steps and over the landing carpet, just like I used to do so many times as a kid.

"The runner was loose, you see, and would often slide on the sleek hardwood floors and slip out from under you if you landed on it wrong. Knowing this, I leapt over it, while my attacker landed right on it and fell. Hard. I raced out of the house and jumped in my car." Ellora stopped the story abruptly, placing both hands on either side of her temples. "I can't remember what happened after that. I blacked out."

Ellora took a moment to settle herself. She was violently shaking, and her heart was beating erratically from telling the story. She was covered in goose bumps from head to toe, and the hairs on the back of her neck stood up. Behr took the time to calm himself down as well. He continued to rain kisses on her neck.

"I'm so proud that you fought back. You're the bravest

woman I've ever met."

Ellora shook her head and whispered, "The story doesn't end there."

Behr tensed up. "What... What happened?"

Ellora waited for her heart to settle. She was close to passing out. After several seconds of deep breaths, she continued.

"When I woke up, I was in the hospital. I felt relief that help had obviously arrived, and I felt momentarily safe. I saw someone that looked like a doctor standing at the foot of my bed, looking over my chart. I closed my eyes in relief. There were lots of people there, so I thought I'd be safe. That's when I felt a hard, heavy hand smack down over my mouth. My eyes shot open, and I saw *HIS* black eyes staring back at me once again. I blinked several times, hoping it was just a horrifying nightmare, trying to snap myself out of it. My lids snapped open, and he lightly traced the blade of the very same knife down the length of my cheek. He threatened that I had until my discharge time to tell him where the documents were, or he would cut me up piece by piece. He promised that it didn't matter where I was or where I hid... He'd always find me."

Behr realized why this extremely brave girl was so reserved and jumpy when she first arrived. She was expecting the devil to jump out and get her at any moment.

"The next day, I grabbed my stuff and snuck out of the hospital. I took a cab and headed to my safety deposit box at the bank, before heading straight to the airport. Twelve hours later, I stumbled into Grady's. Forever marked and hiding in Skye."

Behr dragged his hands through his hair roughly and raked them down the back of his neck, in a mixture of anger, shock, and frustration. He did this a few more times before standing up. He looked down on her for a moment or two with a fierce determination.

"Aye, love, n' that was the very best move to make. I will make sure those weak bastards *NEVER* lay a hand on you again! Not while I live! I will protect you. You will always be safe with me. I swear it." Behr paced back and forth across the back boat deck as he made this pledge.

Ellora swallowed the large lump in the back of her throat. "You see, that's just it. I live in a constant paralyzing panic, that it's only a matter of time before they find me and finish the job they started."

Behr stopped abruptly, pointing right at the trembling girl that made him want to take on the world. "Over *MY* dead body! They would 'ave to go through me first."

His voice thundered loud and deep. Ellora swore she felt the deck she sat on vibrate. He was definitely a daunting force to be reckoned with.

"Aye, and that is nae easy job. I fear nae man!"

Ellora whipped her head up at him. For the first time, she felt angry at him and frightened. That's what it was. She was frightened. The truth was out now, and there was no going back. Hot tears trickled down her face as she realized what she'd done.

"I don't *WANT* that! I don't want anyone to stand In front of me, shielding me and putting their own lives at risk, just like my father did. I'm just not worth it. I don't think I could live with myself, or with the guilt, if something malicious happened *AGAIN*! This is why I didn't want to tell anyone. It's just safer that way. I couldn't bear it if you, or anyone else I care about, ended up getting hurt or worse, killed, because of me. I don't think I could survive it a second time."

Behr's eyes widened in shock at Ellora's unexpected outburst, but slowly changed to understanding. He gave her a smile that could melt the ice caps.

"Oh, my sweet Ellora. 'Ave you nae figured me out by now?"

She lifted up one eyebrow and waited for him to continue. Behr shook his head in defeat and went on.

"I will go to the ends o' the earth for those I care about. I would tear down the heavens and charge through the darkest parts of hell, just to protect you. There is not a soul that could ever stop me, living or not." He narrowed his eyes on her, and Ellora's heart skipped a beat. "Including you!"

Ellora stood up to face him, a mere inches separating them. She held his face in her hands. Behr was still pretty worked up, and it took a few moments before he looked her in the eyes again. She tenderly stroked his cheek with her thumb. When his eyes softened, she spoke again, her voice a quiet whisper. "I will *never* feel completely safe again, not until they are stopped or caught. Only then will I feel safe enough to stop hiding."

Behr placed his hands on her shoulders and drew her closer, hating the separation between them. "You dinnae 'ave to go it alone anymore. That is the worst thing you could do. I will be by your side. Always."

Ellora smiled at him. "You are a seriously stubborn man. You know that, right? I guess I found another flaw."

He smiled back. "You 'ave no idea how stubborn I can be!" Behr placed several soft kisses on her mouth, trying hard to stop her tears and steer her away from the painful subject. It worked. Ellora hummed her approval as his kiss turned from sweet and tender to heart stopping and passionate.

"I don't have a choice here, do I?" She laughed lightly against his lips as he nipped her lower lip, kissed both her cheeks, and then shook his head *no*, pulling her into him. He tightly tucked her away in the safety of his arms.

At that moment, they made a silent pledge to let the subject drop. Funny enough, this moment and her confession didn't ruin their date. It only brought them closer together.

Ellora plopped back down on the blanket and snatched up the chocolate cheesecake. With fork in hand, she hacked into it and shoved a large piece in her mouth. With cake packed inside her cheeks like a chipmunk, she looked up to Behr. She held up the demolished piece and asked, "You want in on this, bodyguard?"

Behr's smile widened as he bent down and crawled over to the woman who owned him... mind, heart, and soul.

ominick drove back to Ellora's house to get a more thorough look at the scene of the crime. Now that he knew he was being followed, he raced all the way, hoping to lose whoever it was. He screeched up her driveway and skidded to a halt as he slammed on the brakes. Yanking the keys out of the ignition, Dominick plowed through the door, skipping two stairs at a time. He made his way to the trashed office at the end of the hall.

The lights were still out, but there was plenty of sunlight coming in from the large window for him to get a fresh new look at his surroundings.

He wasn't really sure what he was looking for, but knew what it would be when he found it. Dominick started rummaging through scattered papers that littered all over the desk and floor, but abandoned his efforts when he found nothing of importance. As he walked over to a small circular side table in the corner by the phone, he noticed the cord was yanked out and the receiver was off the hook.

Opening the slightly ajar drawer all the way, he found several leather bound books. He went through quite a few calendars, notepads, and date books, stopping when he found a frantically circled appointment for four forty-five to see a Mr. Jonathan Lawrence. Looking at the date, Dominick noticed that it was for the very same night that Ellora had been attacked and brought to the hospital. He ripped out the note, shoving it into his pocket.

While pacing her room, Dominick saw a crooked, framed family portrait dangling by a thread on the wall. Something flat and grey in color hid behind it. He narrowed his eyes, walking over to the wall in two quick strides, and took down the photo.

It was a wall safe. "Hmmmm, and where's the key," he muttered to himself as he ran his fingers over the lock. Where would he hide it if he was Joseph? He anxiously but methodically searched through his desk drawers. Hidden in the back, he found a single key, but knew by looking at it that it was too small for the safe. But he tried with success on the lock on the filing cabinet. There was nothing but past bills and old tax returns inside. He looked through bookshelves, cigar boxes, and matching keepsake boxes, with no luck.

Not finding anything, Dominick kicked a pile of papers in frustration, scattering them around the room. A string of curses fell from his mouth as he ran his hands through his hair. He blew out an angry breath, about ready to give up. Plopping down in the office chair, he absentmindedly rocked back and forth, laying his elbows on the armrest. He leaned his head sideways, resting it on his hand, and closed his eyes. Rocking back and forth for a minute, he tried to collect his thoughts. When he opened them up again, his eyes were drawn to the small 5x7 picture of Ellora and her father in a loving, sweet embrace.

The glass was cracked. He straightened up and leaned forward, reaching out, and seized the photo. Carefully, he pulled out the glass shards. He wasn't sure why, but he planned to give it back to Ellora if he ever located her. When he pulled out the last shard, the corner of the picture came with it. Dominick pulled it out all the way, and something shiny fell out onto his lap. It was the illusive key! He was pretty freaking sure this was *the* key to the wall safe. He jumped up, and with two long strides was at the safe. Holding his breath, he pushed the key in. It fit. He turned it until he heard a click, and then blew his breath out, relieved. At what, he wasn't sure yet. He opened the safe door to find a thick accordion folder.

Walking back over to the desk, he put his hand out and swiped it across the desk's top, scattering all of the unnecessary papers out of the way. Dominick sat down on the edge of the seat and turned the folder upside down, dumping out all its contents. Out poured photographs of high profile people in compromising, shady back alley meetings. There were documents with detailed accounts of how they'd blackmailed others into approving building licenses, and how they bribed their bank agents into handing out several loans without the appropriate approvals. Then there was another from Joseph, a letter backing out as the lead contractor and foreman for the condo renovation project, citing *'moral'* reasons. The last document was a letter from one of the investors, addressing Dalton, saying that if they could not have Joseph Sutherland as the acting man in charge of their project, then they were backing out and taking their money with them.

WOW! If this wasn't enough motive for attempted murder, Dominick didn't know what would be. Money equaled motive, every single time. He looked at the upper right corner of the page; the date was the week before Joseph and BonniBelle's car crashed. What it looked like was that *someone* was willing to dispatch Joseph, stopping him from walking away, or to stop him from letting anyone else see all the evidence he had collected. Dominick wondered how Joseph got his hands on these photos, or how long he'd documented the illegal activities that went down under Dalton's authority?

Taking out his iPhone, Dominick Googled Jonathan Lawrence, finding that he was a lawyer working out of downtown Syracuse. He saved the phone number and memorized the address. Mr. Lawrence was obviously one of the last people to see Ellora before her attack. She looked like she was frantic to meet with him. This man just *had* to know something. Dominick grabbed everything and shoved it back in the folder. He gripped the key, locked the safe, and hung the picture back up. Taking the key with him, he raced out of the house.

Looking up and down the street as he approached his car, he noticed a dark sedan parked on the street a few houses down. All the lights were off inside the car, but he could see the shadow of the man sitting in the driver's seat. His eyes watched Dominick in the rear view mirror. Dominick quickly unlocked his car and hopped in. "I don't fucking think so, asshole," he gritted out through clenched teeth.

He put the car in reverse and stepped on the gas, gunning it down the driveway. Turning the wheel, he aimed straight for the sedan and smashed into his bumper. Rolling down his window, Dominick shouted, "Peek a boo, bitch!" He put the car back in drive and raced away. That car had followed him from the precinct. He was positive of it.

He didn't want to lead Dalton's oversized babysitter right to Mr. Lawrence. Now, it would be harder for him to tail anyone with his bumper looking like a tin can. It was only a matter of minutes before Dalton would hear about this. Dominick was running out of time. He *had* to find Ellora before they did. He floored it as he got on I-81 South. He could almost hear a faint ticking of a clock as time slowly ran out.

Dominick burst through the doors of Jonathan Lawrence's law office and slapped the front desk with his flattened palm. He showed his badge to the secretary. "I'm here to see Mr. Lawrence about the Sutherland family. NOW!"

She smiled sweetly at him despite his sharpness. *Oh great*, he thought. *I don't have time to be suave.*

She spoke first. "It's about time you got here. We've been expecting you. Right this way, Mr....?" The polite woman extended her hand, signaling him to follow.

Dominick was confused now. "How were you expecting me if you don't even know my name?" She lifted up a no-nonsense eyebrow at him and just waited. He cleared his throat with a cough. "Detective Antonelli, Ma'am."

"Very good. Right this way, Detective. He will be right in. Have a seat."

Dominick was led into the office, where he sat in the very antique, buttoned leather club chair, anxiously looking around the room. His knee bounced up and down, an old habit of his when his nerves got the best of him.

Right when he started to get comfortable, a well-polished middle aged man with neatly styled salt and pepper hair quickly walked into the room, reaching out his hand. "Detective Antonelli, I presume."

They shook hands. "Yes, sir, Mr. Lawrence."

Jonathan walked briskly behind his desk, took a key out of his pocket, and unlocked a safe. "Unfortunately, we don't have time for pleasantries, do we? You're here because something has happened to Ellora, or is about to. Am I right,

Detective?"

Dominick just nodded, shocked that this man somehow knew already that something had happened. "Yes, she was attacked and fled the States. It is a race between me and the very same men who attacked her to get to her. I'm hoping you can help lead me to her. Please tell me you know where she is, counselor."

Jonathan just smirked. He took out another smaller safe and entered the combination. When he opened it, he pulled out an envelope.

"So I guess it's finally time to hand these off to you. They contain detailed accounts of the illegal activities that Joseph witnessed over the few years he was partnered with Dalton. Also, there's a revised copy of his will. He left all his assets to Ellora, which, in the event that anything should happen to her, no other party or person is entitled to the assets listed for fear of forged or doctored authorization. It's a lot to read, but I suggest you read it at another time. Because I suspect you are just about out of it."

Jonathan handed Dominick the envelope with the copy of Joseph's will, a letter stating all of his suspicions and fears, along with a copy of the evidence Dominick found in Joseph's safe. It certainly looked like he had covered all of his bases. He was obviously worried that something was going to happen to him and his family. Unfortunately for Joseph, he was right.

He handed the envelope back and informed the

lawyer that if anything bad *was* to happen to Ellora, he wanted him to send these documents straight to the FBI. Jonathan hesitated, but nodded, taking them back and locking them up. Mr. Lawrence walked back over to him and placed two objects in his hand.

"I backed everything up on this drive." He handed it to Dominic. "It doesn't hurt to have as many copies floating around as possible for some added insurance."

Dominick took it and shoved it in his pocket. "I agree." The other object was a folded up slip of paper.

"Don't read it out loud. It will take you to her."

Opening it, he read it and then shoved it into his pocket. After thanking Mr. Lawrence, he shook his hand and ran out of the building. He sprinted for his car, and sped off to the airport. He had to get to her NOW! The race had officially begun.

Dalton's man rushed into Van's Hardware store, heading straight to the front desk. Ellora had used her credit card here, and he wasn't leaving without getting some answers. Approaching the desk, a young woman with wavy auburn hair stood ready. Her name tag read Bree. He took the photo out of his pocket and held it up.

"Do you remember this girl coming in here about a month ago?"

Bree glanced at the picture quickly and shook her head. "Nae, can't say as I 'ave."

"Look *AGAIN!*" he demanded, shouting so loud she jumped where she stood. Her eyes widened with alarm. There was something really off about this foreign stranger, and she decided it was best not to tell him anything. "You must be crazy! Do you know how many people come in here in one day? You really expect me to remember a girl who came in here a month ago?"

He leaned in and grabbed her wrist, pulling her toward him. She went cold at his touch, shivering as his features seemed to take on the look of an extremely psychotic monster. His mouth twisted into a sneer, and his eyes were wild and as black as coal. She flinched when his grip tightened. Bree gasped as the pressure turned her fingers blue.

"Have. You. Seen. This. Girl?" He slowly hissed out each word.

Bree faked bravado, lifting her head high, brushing him off as she pointed to Isaac.

"He's the cashier. If anyone would remember, it would be him."

"If I find out that you've lied to me… I'll come back for you," he promised. Dropping her arm, the *man* slowly turned on his heel and made his way over to where Isaac stood.

Her shoulders slumped the moment he freed her from

his paralyzing glare. She didn't know why, but she slowly started shivering. There was something really wrong with that man. He horrified her. He was a walking nightmare come to life.

He was trying to find Ellora. She knew all about how she was helping Grady. Kristy had told her when they spoke briefly, the night she'd come in for a drink when she helped waitress. The girl seemed sweet, and obviously cared for Grady a great deal.

This terrifyingly creepy man definitely did *NOT* have good intentions, whatever the reason was that he wanted her for. She knew Isaac would not say a word either. He had a huge crush on Ellora. She just had to call the pub and let everyone know someone seemed to be hunting her down.

As The Man left Van's Hardware store, he was approached by a freckle-faced, bleach-blonde woman.

"I know what you're looking for. Aye, n' I can help you, too, if you help me out in return." She lifted up one eyebrow, knowing she had his full attention.

Dalton's man shook his head from side to side, as he cornered her against the building. "That's not how this works, sweetheart. Tell me what you think I want to hear, and I'll let *YOU* know what its worth to me."

ehr and Ellora strolled into Grady's hand in hand. Not a few moments went by before they would look over at one another. Their connection had deepened after their long day out together, which gave her hope that everything could be okay here. As they strolled through the pub, hoots, hollers, and approving nods followed them. Behr guided her to a bar stool, kissing the tip of her nose as she sat down. When Ellora finally had the power to drag her eyes away from his, she noticed the overjoyed looks on the faces that surrounded them.

"I see the fresh air did you both some good. I'd ask how your outing went, but the proof o' that is as plain as the nose on my face." Kristy's' warm gentle eyes looked over them fondly.

Grady lifted his head with pride. "I knew this was a match that would work from the very moment I laid my eyes on you two! Aye, you'd have to be a fool not to see it."

"Geez, are we that transparent?" Ellora snickered, embarrassed but happy that everyone seemed to approve.

"You sure weren't, Ellora. You're a tough cookie to crack. You are really hard to read, but Behr over here, he was as clear as water," Gavin teased, giving them a thumbs up.

Patrick, looking bored as he slid down the bar where everyone gathered, shook his head in disappointment. "'Bout time you stepped up and claimed this lady as yours. I was startin' to wonder whether or not you liked women at all." Slapping Behr on the back, he passed him a drink.

Behr just took the taunting, teasing, and attention in stride, shaking his head in amusement. A smile threatened to appear on his face. Looking down on Ellora, he leaned in, kissing the corner of her mouth. "Aye, you dinnae make it easy on me either, didja? Stubborn, cute little devil that you are. But you were well worth the wait."

After a few groans, and threats of puking from the others, Ellora stuck out her tongue and switched topics to the beautiful finished hardwoods. "Wow, Grady, they turned out perfect! They look brand new! What a difference they make in here."

"That they do. Shine up like a new prized coin. I couldnae be any happier with the work that's been done here. Turned out far better than I could've imagined, and I 'ave you to thank, Ellora. You've done a fine job. Your father is looking down on you with pride, my dear, as am I."

Moisture collected in the corners of her eyes at the very mention of her dad. Ellora could only let out a hoarsely whispered, "Thank you." After swallowing several times to force the knot she had stuck in her throat, she went on. "That means a lot to me, Grady. Thank you."

The room became thick with emotion, so she changed the subject again. "Well, now we just have to decide on a paint color that is not already taken by the other pier houses on the harbor."

Patty, ever the instigator, had to get a jab in. "Too bad pink is already taken a few houses down, lass, but dinnae be discouraged. There are plenty o' other colors to choose from."

Ellora lifted her brow. "Ha, ha, very funny, ol' man."

Grady walked around the bar and stood in front of Ellora. She turned in her stool so that they were face to face. She looked over this wonderful man's face who had become like family to her, and realized how much happier and healthier he looked since she'd first met him.

He looked down warmly at the raven-haired girl who'd brightened his stale world, like a father would his own daughter. Grady cupped her cheeks with his calloused hands. "My dear sweet child, I've thought a lot on this. Had Catie still been alive to see this day, I know her well enough to guess what her decision would be. She would choose the beautiful color o' your eyes, dear girl, because o' all the love and kindness you've shown us all. It means a great deal to me, and I am thankful for the night you stumbled into this bar when you did. You've brightened up all our lives, and given me another reason to keep on going. No other color in this world will do."

Adelle agreed enthusiastically. "A rich emerald green

it is then. No other building on the harbor has the color. It is perfect!"

Behr burrowed into Ellora's hairline. He kissed her earlobe, awakening little flittering butterflies in her stomach. Whispering low, his breath tickling the sensitive skin on her neck, he told her, "I believe in fate, love. This was all meant to be, just as you were meant to be in my arms."

With the approvals of the others, Adelle passed out drinks as they all toasted to second chances. With a thunderous "AYE," the night had started memorably.

As the pub started filling up with patrons, Gavin and Adelle glanced at each other from across the room. They silently agreed on something with a nod, then shouted out above the chatter. "We have a surprise for you, Grady, and you, too, Ellora. Word spread quickly through town about all the excitement that's been going on around here. Well, a few frat boys from the local college were in here the night of your fever, and they thought you worked yourself sick. While you were in the hospital, they said they wanted to help with your efforts, so they donated their pool table for the pub's entertainment."

Adelle walked over to a huge object tucked away on the left side of the bar, which had previously been empty. Grabbing hold of the sheet, she dramatically yanked it off, letting it fall to the ground. Vanna White had nothing on her. The table showed signs of wear, but it was obviously well taken care of. Adelle snatched up the pool stick, and with one brow raised, asked, "Anyone up for a game?"

"This is perfect! I love pool!" Looking up at Behr, Ellora silently questioned if he wanted to play. A soft kiss on her lips was the answer she wanted.

"DOUBLES," he shouted, scooping her up playfully as he made his way over to the table.

"Oh, you're *ON*, brother. You are so dead!" Gavin shouted back at his friend, jogging over to the table.

They did kill them, too. Adelle turned out to be quite the ruthless pool shark. After their embarrassing defeat, she proceeded to annihilate anyone else who dared challenge her.

The night had peaked, but a few townies stayed behind for one more drink, a good story, and a game of pool. The rest of them went about helping Grady with clean-up.

Ellora was in the middle of wiping down a table and collecting empty drinks onto her tray, when the hair on the back of her neck stood up in warning. An icy chill slowly prickled its way up her spine, like spiders crawling across her skin. Goose bumps broke out all over her body from head to toe. Ellora felt someone's eyes on her. She felt them burning a hole right through her, spying on her. She was too afraid to look in the direction she *knew* he would be in. This feeling couldn't be real. She must be imagining it. Raising her head slowly, she worked up enough courage to look up. Everything around her moved in slow motion, while Ellora remained frozen and shivering where she stood. Unable to think. Unable to breathe.

A few bystanders walked past her line of vision. When they finally passed, her eyes immediately zeroed in on the one stalking her. Ellora's heart pounded painfully in her chest. All the blood drained from her face. She couldn't move. Her feet were frozen on the spot. She recognized him. He worked for Dalton. His eyes narrowed on her. Now, everything around them sped up in a frantic pace. He'd found her safe haven. She thought she could disappear here. She was dead wrong!

Behr looked over at Ellora, and was alarmed by her pale, ashen grey color. A shockingly horrified look was plastered across her face. Her eyes were wide open and intensely staring, not daring to blink. He followed her line of sight to the man across the bar, in the dark, sitting on a stool. The man was staring daggers directly at her. Behr looked back at Ellora, and she looked absolutely petrified.

It was the man Ellora had been running from. He knew it had to be by the look they gave each other. Behr didn't think twice before rushing him. A sick feeling twisted in his gut. He had to get her out of there. He had promised to keep her safe from her attacker. Without saying a word, Behr smashed his fist so hard into his face it felt like it would go right through him. Behr's large fist practically covered the man's entire face. Blood exploded out of his nose and mouth, spraying in all directions. He flew off the stool and skidded across the newly polished floors.

"ELLORA, RUN!" Behr thundered out so loud everything in the bar shook, including Ellora. It effectively snapped her out of her trance. She jerked in response, dropping the tray and drinks. When Behr looked back, he saw Ellora sprinting out the side door as fast as she could.

"Gavin, Patrick, over 'ere NOW!" Behr charged over to the bloodied man, grabbing him by the shirt collar and lifting him up easily. He cocked his fist back to deliver another punishing blow. The man shouted frantically, shielding his face with his arms.

"Stop! I'm Detective Dominick Antonelli. I'm a former police officer from Syracuse, NY. I'm here to help. Was that her? Was that Ellora?" Dominick rushed out quickly to avoid being hit again from the beast that hovered over him.

Behr shook him violently. "Dinnae you dare say her name again! She's scared to death. Why are you in 'ere?"

Dominick yelled louder, "I'm here to help! She's in a lot of danger. There are some ruthless people after her who'll do whatever it takes to find her. I'm sure, if I was able to find her… they will, too. Don't let her out of your sight!"

Behr let go of his shirt roughly, and pointed to Gavin. "Watch him, I'm going after her.

Gerard came barreling around the bar, holding his hands up, halting Behr on the spot. He turned to the detective, asking, "Some folks at Van's Hardware called tonight, saying a man was there asking questions… wanting to know where Ellora was… Was that you?" Dominick's eyes grew wide, and that was the only answer Behr needed. He plowed through the bar, bursting through the side door. He had to find Ellora. Fast.

Dominick shook his head. "No. He's already here!"

I can't believe he found me. Ellora raced out of the door and down the narrow alleyway in between the two buildings. She didn't even know where she was going. She just knew that she had to run as fast as her legs could carry her. Despair filled her as images of the brutal attack she suffered months earlier flashed back at her. Her heart was pounding so hard she could feel it throbbing in her ears. Breaking out into cold sweats, she cried out, "This can't be happening. This will never end."

She was approaching the end of the alley which headed to the back of the buildings. Glancing over her shoulder once again, to make sure that no one had followed her out the side door, Ellora almost stumbled on the loose gravel in the darkened alley. When her head turned back around, a large figure lunged out of the dark at her.

His strong arms snatched the petite girl right off the ground and dragged her back in the opposite direction. Ellora screeched out loudly and immediately fought, kicking wildly. She scratched her attacker's arms that held her in his iron, unmoving grip, hysterically trying to break free. Taking in a deep breath, she let loose a loud ear-piercing scream. His other hand slapped down over her mouth, trying to silence her. His remaining arm snaked its way around her neck, locking her in a tight chokehold.

She fought back as hard as she could, tugging and pulling desperately at his arm. He slowly squeezed her airway. Ellora caught quick little breaths whenever he let up a bit. He was much larger and stronger than her, dragging her easily down the length of the back alley.

She managed to bite down on his arm once, HARD. He roared out as pain exploded in his forearm, loosening his grip on her neck. As he ripped his arm out of her clenched teeth, she hissed out an excruciatingly painful breath. Ellora spit out a piece of the flesh that she tore off. Taking advantage of the precious seconds she had free, she screamed as loud as her lungs would allow. She sucked in another breath and let out one more hoarse scream, before he knocked his fist into the side of her temple with a force so hard, she crashed to the ground. Ellora's head bounced off the pebbled path. Trying fruitlessly to crawl to safety, she groaned as bright stars flashed across her vision. Her eyes clouded over and slowly faded to black. The man grabbed her ankle, dragging her over to him, then threw her limp body over his shoulder.

Sharp stinging pain was what woke her. Ellora's cheek throbbed rhythmically like it was going to burst. She was being slapped repeatedly, and her head pounded with each strike. Trying to get her eyes to open proved to be more difficult than it should have. The assault stopped abruptly.

"I know you're awake."

Ellora jumped at the sound of his voice so close to her ear.

Concentrating hard, the dizzy girl managed to lift her heavy lids. She squinted as she opened them all the way. That's when she realized her hands were bound, when she tried to lift them to rub her eyes and couldn't. Pulling at her bindings, she tested their strength… zip ties?

Ellora sat in a short wooden chair with her hands behind her back. When her eyes opened all the way, she came face to face with the living nightmare she feared most in this world. Except, she couldn't just wake up from this nightmare and have it mercifully disappear. There was no escaping this time. He'd finally caught up to her.

As she looked around, she tried to focus on her

surroundings. To her relief, she realized that she was still in Skye. The building was empty inside, abandoned. Definitely a warehouse of some kind, it looked a lot like the old hardware store Behr brought her to. The walls looked to have a stucco finish, and there were several inches of undisturbed dust on every surface. Desperately, she looked around for something -- anything that she could use to fight back or break free with.

"Looking for something to kill me with? I admire your survival instincts, sweetheart." The man dropped a very heavy sounding duffle bag right in front of her. A cloud of dust blew up around them and slowly settled back down. The bag was quite large, at least two-feet by three-feet in length. She watched with dread as he unzipped the bag and took out several knives, varying in size and shape, along with box cutters, duct tape, and a large plastic sheet.

Ellora lost control of herself as her fear tore her calmness to pieces. *Oh my God, he really plans on slaughtering me.* And it didn't look like it would be quick, not with all the terrifying tools he laid out in front of her. She said a silent prayer, pleading for protection. Ellora knew she had to stall him until she could figure out how to get out of this. She bravely looked right at him.

"What is your name?"

Swiveling his head, he glanced over at the bound girl with a questioning brow. "Is that really the question you wanted to ask?"

They stared at each other for a tense moment. "You're going to kill me either way, aren't you?" she shot back at him. He just shrugged and nodded, agreeing with her statement. The idea didn't seem to faze him at all.

"My name is Giddeon."

"It was you who killed my parents... wasn't it?" Ellora hiccupped the question, barely able to get it all out. She couldn't hide the grief in her voice when she spoke of them. It still hurt so much, and she was possibly looking at the very same man responsible for their deaths.

Crossing his arms over his chest, he rose to his full height and faced the frightened girl. "Joseph's stubbornness and moral righteousness is what killed them both."

"THAT'S NOT AN ANSWER!" Ellora roared out with such an outrageously thunderous shout that she didn't even recognize her own voice.

Time seemed to stand still, with no reaction from Giddeon to her outburst. He just stood there, glaring down at her like a statue, motionless, unblinking, and void of all emotions. No guilt passed through his expression. His eyes looked cold -- dead.

Then he seemed to come to some kind of internal decision. His eyes narrowed on the sitting target and sneered with a hatred she didn't understand. What had she done to make this man hate her so much that he looked forward to ending her life? Ellora thought she was going to go crazy from the deafening silence in the room. Strangely enough, the man was more terrifying when he was quiet and still. She could almost see him contemplating her demise. Her body shook as adrenaline rose with the tension between them and the devastating anticipation as to what would happen next.

He nodded once. "Yes, Ellora, I killed them." With a deep timbre, his voice echoed around the empty room, every word uttered repeated back to her. The moment felt surreal.

"Why?" Her voice broke on the small word, her question incredibly heavy.

Giddeon turned. Slowly, he walked over and knelt beside the duffle bag. "Fear is a very powerful motivator... wouldn't you agree, Miss Sutherland?"

A deep sob escaped her chest as he took all the tools from the bag and lined them up in neat rows. Pulling out the curved blade she'd become intimately familiar with, he slowly stalked over to where she sat bound.

He got within inches of her face, and she could feel his hot breath trickle over her. Ellora turned her head in panic.

Reaching out, he grabbed her chin. He forced her to turn her head back around, tsk'ing, "Ah aaah, I want you to look at me when I'm talking to you. I want to see the fear in your eyes. That's my favorite part, after all." Ellora squeezed her eyes shut in defiance. Not only that, but she didn't want his evil eyes to be the last thing she ever saw.

His voice deepened, laced thick with anger that vibrated through him. He snarled,

"Look at me! Or I will plunge my blade into this eye..."
He tapped the blade on her left eyebrow. The cold steel made
her jump and flinch. He moved, tapping the other eyebrow.
"Then dig out the other."

Sweat beaded up on her forehead and trickled down
her temple.

"You find out what makes people tick, and use it to
bend them to your will. Fear and leverage... That's how
Dalton handles all business transactions. *THAT* is why
Dalton chose to hire your father. Joseph was great at what
he did. He was new to the States and, therefore, ignorant to
the way Dalton handled his business. Joseph was desperate
to make a name for himself and for the family he cared for.
Dalton loved to use families as leverage. He thought it would
be easy to *train* him to fit his specific needs. He just had to
keep his mouth shut and look the other way, no matter what
he saw. It was difficult for Joseph right from the start. He
witnessed Dalton's unorthodox methods that he liked to use
to force a decision, land a big deal, and get the job done... no
matter what the cost."

Ellora shook her head in disgust. She had witnessed
firsthand the vile things Dalton was willing to do just to get
to her, and could only imagine how ruthless he'd be when
his money was on the line.

Giddeon looked at the cause of all the drama in
disgust. He didn't understand how someone could be so
obsessed over a simple girl. "Things took a turn for the worse

when your father started bringing *you* on the job with him."
Giddeon said this with malice in his tone. "All the lines
blurred once Dalton set his sights on you, but the more he
went after you, the bolder Joseph became. He wasn't easily
swayed or manipulated after that. He challenged every
decision, questioned every deal and the methods used to get
them done. When Dalton started pushing himself on you..."
Giddeon flung his arms out, motioning to the frozen girl
sitting helpless on the chair, and continued, "Joseph had had
enough and was determined to take down the shark. I was
told to deal with his behavior, because it's hard to find a man
with his kind of natural talent. Because of *you*, your father
had more chances than most ever did. Dalton is a very
ruthless and impatient man, who *never* gives second
chances. I was instructed to instill some much needed fear
into him, so he would be frightened into falling in line.

Ellora just sat there and stared back at him. She was
surprised that he was freely telling her any of this.

"I was just supposed to hurt him enough to get the
message across. That's all. He was supposed to drive around
town, and the brake lines I'd cut would slowly leak out. He
would hit a pole or land in a ditch somewhere and be scared
straight. I didn't know he would get on the highway for an
extended trip... especially since he left you home. By the
time he needed to get off his exit, he was going almost
seventy miles per hour, without any way to stop." Giddeon
paused for a moment. Ellora let herself believe that,

maybe… deep down, he was sorry for what he'd done. "I never meant for either of them to be killed. That was not my intent. That was a major fuck up that Dalton was *NOT* happy with."

Those fleeting thoughts left Ellora when Giddeon's expression grew cold once again. "But what's done is done." He shrugged. "I had to scramble to fix my mistake, so the law wouldn't come down hard on Dalton or the company."

"Well, you did it! It was done! They're dead! You won! Why are you still trying to kill me? Why couldn't you just let me disappear?" Ellora argued, desperate to get out of this, to reason or bargain with him to let her go.

Amused, he turned his thin lips up to what should've been a smile, but took on a twisted sneer. "You're a feisty one. I now see why Dalton's entertained by you. Besides, I didn't *WANT* to kill you… at first. But you wouldn't cooperate with Dalton, and threatened to leave… just walk away. Just like that, you were going to leave the project unfinished." He shook his head at her like he was disappointed. "Which is very unprofessional, I must say. I was surprised at you! Your father would be, too."

Ellora flinched. She knew, deep down, that it wasn't true, but it still tore her heart open to hear the hurtful words.

"You'd already cost Dalton so much money from all the delays and stalled progress. But when you tried to run… He was more furious than I have ever seen him. He was willing to blow billion dollar deals, just drop everything else in his life to get to you. And just like your father, you just wouldn't do as you were told. So I was instructed to bring you back. No matter what it took. No exceptions. Because no one turns their back on Dalton Ramsey. He found out from his inside source at the local police station, that Joseph had documents that could take down Dalton and his entire empire. So he ordered me to find everything... and to do it quickly.

I kept a close watch on you, and would've just left you alone, knowing how much Dalton wanted to make you *his* woman, his possession. But you were getting closer to the truth that I was trying so hard to cover up. I just had to get my hands on the original copy Joseph collected of everything that had gone on behind the scenes, before it was my neck on the chopping block. Dalton would not let another failure or screw-up by me go unpunished."

Ellora started to wonder just how many people were under Dalton's thumb. How many were blackmailed into doing what he wanted done... when he wanted it done? How many were forced into doing grotesque, imaginable things, for fear of what Dalton had the power to do to them or maybe their families. She was pulled out of her thoughts when Giddeon continued.

"With your car disabled, it should've bought me enough time to rip your house apart until I found what I was looking for. You weren't meant to come home, not so soon, but once you saw my face, I had to finish you. Or he would've finished me. Self-preservation and all that. Nothing personal."

"Well, I don't ever plan on going back! I want to stay as far away as I can. I will disappear, so you see, I won't be a problem for you. I didn't even see the evidence! I've never even looked at it! You can go back and just say I'm dead! It would be better that way. My old life is dead anyways. You don't have to do this!" Ellora's voice rose higher and higher as she pleaded with him. She knew that, with the end of his story, her chances of trying to break free would be gone, as well.

Giddeon walked around behind the girl slowly, like a beast stalking his prey. Ellora craned her neck to the side. If he was going to kill her now, she wanted to see it coming. No surprises. With a quick upward stroke of his blade, he cut her hands free. Ellora was relieved for just a moment, as blood rushed back to her numb hands. For a split second, she thought she saw understanding in his eyes. She almost let herself hope that he would let her run.

Until he jerked her up out of the chair. He re-tied her hands behind her back with the duct tape. Grabbing her arm roughly, he dragged the stunned girl across the floor and dropped her hard on top of the duffle bag.

"Nope. Sorry, sweetheart. I'm afraid I can't do that. Unlike *you*, Miss Sutherland, I don't *EVER* walk away from a job. I *ALWAYS* finish what I start." Violently, he shoved her limbs into the bag.

Ellora panicked, crying out, "Oh my God! What are you going to do?"

"I have only one chance left to save my own neck and to redeem myself in Dalton's eyes, and that is to bring you back with me. Before the detective gets to you first."

Ellora wiggled, kicked, and bucked wildly, shouting at him, "I will never go willingly! I will always fight back!"

Giddeon just snickered madly at her useless efforts to fight back. "I figured as much. That's why you're going in there." He grabbed her legs and crushed them together. Her ankle bones ground together painfully while he tried to tape them together.

Ellora hysterically shook her head, repeatedly screaming, "No! No! No!" Trying to yank her leg out of his grip, she fought him as hard as she could. She knew she had to keep fighting and screaming until either she broke free, someone heard her screams, or he just got it over with and killed her quickly. This couldn't keep going on for the rest of her life. She wouldn't just lie back and take it anymore. She would fight back and keep fighting, no matter what the outcome.

Giddeon ripped off a piece of tape and stretched it out over her mouth. He pressed down hard and shoved her head to the side when he was done.

"You have two options, sweetheart. Just two. Taped, shoved, and intact... Or cut up and bagged in plastic. Either way, you are coming with me." Giddeon pointed down. "And you *are* going in there."

He grabbed Ellora's snarled hair so tight she felt several strands pull out. Heaving her inside the bag, he slammed her face to the ground. Screaming frantically through the tape, she tried kicking his legs out from under him. He just laughed at her weak efforts and gave a swift hard kick of his own directly to her gut. She winced in pain at the crushing blow. Tears streamed down her face, and her nose ran, making it hard to breathe through the tape. Giddeon took enjoyment out of kicking her again and again, knocking all the wind out of her. This effectively halted all of her struggles, as she focused hard on not throwing up after every blow. With no exit, she didn't want to choke on her own vomit.

"Stop fucking fighting me, little girl! I'm losing my patience with you. Dalton didn't say I couldn't bring you back cut up!" he snarled out, crushing her under his weight as he sat on her. Pulling out the dagger, he dragged the blade down her chest. "Stop fighting back, or I will mark you here..." He easily sliced through the thin material of her shirt with the razor sharp blade, all the way down her abdomen. The cut was just barely deep enough to leave a small trail of blood behind. Then he continued his threat, "So it matches the one I gave you here..." He pointed at her back with the blade still in his hands. That wasn't a warning... it was a promise! And Ellora believed every word of it.

She stared helplessly up at him, his black eyes sending

paralyzing chills straight to her soul. His evil stare and murderous intent froze the blood in her veins. She realized in that moment that he loved this. Giddeon didn't do these things because he was *told* to do them. He was hired to do them because he loved inflicting pain on others. He enjoyed every moment of it.

Finally, Ellora turned her head, pinching her eyes closed. She couldn't bear to look at him anymore. A mournful wail escaped her lips. She didn't know how much longer she could do this! Right when Ellora was ready to give up the fight, she got an overpowering sense of her parents' presence in the room with her. They would want her to fight, and to keep fighting, so long as there was still breath in her body, she wouldn't let Giddeon take her back to Dalton. Not after her parents had died trying to shield her from him.

Ellora breathed in and out faster and faster, hyperventilating with the mounting stress as she heard the loud echo of the heavy zipper dragging across the track. Giddeon slowly closed the duffle bag over her. This bag was her coffin… It signified the end. Darkness. Death. Seeing his black eyes before being engulfed in darkness was too much for her to take. Her panicked breathing was pulling her closer and closer to passing out. She *HAD* to get out of this bag.

A thunderous boom shook the building, followed by an ear-piercing crash. The powerful force of the blast knocked Giddeon back. Ellora's eyes zeroed in on the chaotic scene through the tiny opening of the bag. Shattered glass rained down all around them. Giddeon snatched the machete off the dirty ground next to him, holding it up with the curved dagger already in his hand. Jumping up onto his feet, he sprinted toward the source of the destruction.

Taking advantage of the moment, Ellora quickly rolled from the fetal position that she was in, over onto her back. Using the strength in her knees, she pushed hard on the flap of the duffle bag. The stress caused the zipper to slowly pull apart. When the flap was more than half opened, a manic animalistic shout roared out through the window, freezing her progress. It was haunting. An uncontrollable tremble shuddered down her spine at the heart stopping sound.

An enormous monstrous figure had smashed his way through the glass of the picture window, landing hard on the balls of his feet. He charged full throttle at Giddeon with no fear and no hesitation. The once settled dust stirred up around him. This ominous man was exactly who she'd picture as the much feared monster in a horror flick movie.

They collided into each other, officially starting their brawl. Giddeon swung his blades around expertly, crossing them in a downward X motion. The dark monster quickly dodged them both at the last second, before grabbing both of Giddeon's wrists and easily wrenching them out to his sides. Cocking his head back, he crashed it into Gideon's forehead with a sickening crunch. His head snapped back sharply. The monster let go of him, letting the backward momentum push him down. Giddeon used the fall to his advantage, and skillfully rolled back all the way. His legs went up over him until his feet came back around, landing underneath him in a perfect back flip.

Ellora stared on, stunned at his fighting skills. Even when he was hit, his moves were fluid and flawlessly executed. Giddeon brought himself up in a crouching position, poised and ready for the next attack, which followed immediately. The monster never let up. He kept coming at him. There was no hesitation, no pausing, and no stopping him from trying to walk right through this man.

Kicking the machete out of his hand, the intruder stepped forward, landing two devastating punches, instantly splitting Giddeon's cheekbone wide open. Giddeon's eyes darkened, and he smiled wickedly at his opponent. He seemed to love every moment of the fight as blood oozed out of the opened gash. There was absolutely no fear in this man.

His arrogant smile only angered the monster more. He lunged, ready to throw another dangerous blow, but Giddeon quickly dodged it. He answered with a jab, cross hook combo of his own, and followed it up with an uppercut to the midsection, before jumping out of the way of the monster's fists. Giddeon was the more skilled and methodical fighter, but the monster was obviously bigger and much stronger, which made the fight evenly matched.

Ellora snapped out of it and finally dragged her eyes off the battle. She went to work on her bound hands, still behind her back. She easily slid her arms over the curve of her rear end in this position. Pulling her knees tightly to her chest, she then slid her arms over her legs. Now, they were successfully in front of her. Grabbing the zipper with both hands, she yanked it open the rest of the way. She rolled out clumsily, carefully looking around to make sure the battling men were nowhere around her.

They were still going to war, right in front of the window… and her only exit out. If she could just sneak her way around them without drawing attention to herself, she could make a run for it. Lifting her hands up above her head, Ellora brought them down hard over her knee, ripping the tape off. Cautiously, she walked a wide circle around them, staying in the shadows and out of their sight. She slipped several times on the broken glass but slowly made her way toward the window.

Grunts, groans, and snarls ripped their way out of the warring men as they struggled to get the upper hand and gain control of the knife. The larger monster easily pushed Giddeon across the room, with one fist tightly wrapped around his shirt and the other gripping the wrist that held the dagger. Giddeon pounded away at the monster's face with his free hand, but it had no effect on him. The monster lifted him off the ground, smashing his body against the wall. It stopped his attack, and now blocked Ellora's escape.

She stood in the corner shadows, frozen in place, her eyes transfixed on the two brutal animals viciously battling it out in front of her. Outside, the cloudy over-cast dissipated overhead. The moon cast a bright light through the large open window and onto the fierce face of the monster. Ellora's feet froze in place. It was Behr! *Her* Behr. He was the ominous monster savagely fighting her most feared nightmare. Her mouth hung open in a mix of shock and awe. Behr had turned into an entirely different person when angry. His pure unadulterated rage and twisted expression frightened her for a moment. She didn't even recognize him.

Her need to run had vanished. She couldn't bring herself to leave him behind... she just couldn't. Ellora must have unconsciously walked toward him, because before she even realized it, she was dangerously close.

Seeing the movement, Behr whipped his head around, and that's when his eyes met and locked on Ellora's as she stood frozen. His eyes narrowed, zooming in on the bloody trail on her shirt. Gritting his teeth, Behr's eyes darkened with a murderous bloodlust. It flashed through his snarling expression, and he roared out so loudly the ground shook. "GET OUT! ELLORA, RUN!"

Giddeon took advantage of Behr's distracted attention on the girl, and brought his elbow down hard on Behr's eye, blindsiding him. He gained the upper hand when Behr instinctively dropped his hand to his eye. Ellora looked on in horror as Giddeon lifted his arm up high and plunged the dagger into him deeply. Behr stumbled back a few steps. The sound of air rushed out of his lungs from the blow, the force having knocked the wind out of him. A high-pitched screeching noise filled the room and continued to escalate higher and higher. After several moments passed, Ellora realized it was *her* screaming. *Not again, not him, not again...* is all she kept thinking as her screams continued in her state of shock.

Not another person she loved. Yes, she loved Behr. The realization washed over her. An overpowering, vengeful, rage bubbled up inside her. Anger and hate exploded to the surface, erasing any fear she had ever felt. Ellora couldn't live through this again. Looking around frantically, her eyes found the discarded machete on the ground.

Giddeon lunged at her as she snatched the weapon from the floor. She grabbed it just as he tackled her to the ground. His weight knocked the wind out of her, and she gasped for air as they tumbled together. They rolled several times from the force of the hit, before coming to a stop. Ellora struggled under the weight of his body. Her exposed arms were cut up from the glass shards littered on the ground. He pressed his forearm over Ellora's neck, cutting off her air supply. He easily overpowered her, grabbing the handle of the machete and forcing its change in direction, aiming for the center of her chest. She fought against her own hand as he turned the blade on her, inching its way downward, looking to hit its mark.

A rush of air escaped his lungs as he was forcefully yanked off of the girl. The air whooshed as his body cut through the space between them. Behr wrapped his hand around his neck, throwing him into the stucco wall, cracking it behind him. His other arm dangled limply at his side. Behr smashed his head into the wall several times, shouting, "I'll *KILL* you! I'll fucking kill you!"

Giddeon smiled ruthlessly, spitting blood onto Behr's face. "You're going to *have* to kill me. That's the only way I'll ever stop." Behr thundered out in anger. Fury vibrated through him. Behr squeezed his neck tighter, his gritty fingernails cutting into the flesh of his neck, and lifted him off the ground. Giddeon frantically kicked his feet, searching for solid ground. Behr grabbed the handle of the dagger still sticking out, and pulled it out in one swift tug. The fury and adrenaline coursing through him had him feeling no pain. Without hesitation, Behr punched it through Gideon's shoulder, causing a sickening gurgling sound to come from his mouth.

Voices shouted from outside of the window, and one by one, several men jumped inside. An unfamiliar voice called out to Behr. "We've got him. Let him go. We need him alive. He's not the mastermind. Stop, Behr. We need him." It was the stranger from the bar. Behr abruptly let go of his neck, dropping him hard on his ass.

Behr stumbled over to where Ellora sat on the gritty floor and knelt down beside her. "Ellora, oh, thank God you're all right. I couldn't find you. I'm so sorry, my love. I searched for you. I thought I'd lost you… then I heard your screams." Lifting her up effortlessly with one arm, he set the shivering girl onto his lap. He showered her with his kisses. "I thought I'd lost you." Ellora's eyes chose that moment to turn on the waterworks. She sobbed as Behr softly kissed away each and every tear off her dirt-stained cheeks, both her eyelids, neck, and finally her bruised lips. All the while, he chanted softly over and over, "Ellora, my love, I thought I lost you. Did he hurt you badly? I'm 'ere. I love you… I'm 'ere." He continued his heartfelt, emotionally devastated promises as Ellora urgently kissed him back. She was frantic to get closer to him.

"Oh, Behr, when I saw him plunge the blade in… I thought, I thought that was it. I thought he'd taken you away from me."

She wrapped her arms around him tighter. She couldn't seem to get him close enough. Cupping Ellora's face delicately, he let out a breathless sigh. "I couldn't go on living if he took you from me. You 'ave my heart, and I cannae go on living without it." Grabbing his shoulders, she tried to pull him even closer to her, but stopped at the painful groan Behr let out.

"Oh, Behr... You're bleeding really badly! I have to get you to the hospital." She sobbed harder as the scene played over and over in her mind of Giddeon plunging the dagger into Behr. His clothes were now drenched in blood. Ellora placed her hand over the wound, pressing hard on it to stifle the bleeding.

She shook her head. "Oh, Behr, I'm so sorry! This is all my fault! Because of me, I almost lost another person I loved. This would've never happened to you if I wasn't' here." Her body trembled as tears rolled down her cheeks, leaving drip stains on her face.

Behr shook his head no. Pain etched deep in his features at hearing her broken devastation. "Oh, my love, it was me who went after him. I had to keep the promise I made you." He kissed her softly on the lips until her sorrow subsided, then continued. "I crashed through the walls o' hell to get to you, and fought the Devil himself to keep you safe. I will never let anything happen to you, not while I live. I'll be by your side... always. Ellora, I love you. No one will take you away from me. Not ever again."

The police came soon after, taking Giddeon into to custody. Ellora found out that the man in the bar was a detective trying to warn her and protect her. He was sent here thanks to her lawyer's help. Boy did Behr do a number on the poor man's face. Detective Antonelli was investigating Dalton for her parents' murders and Ellora's attack. He swore to her that he wouldn't stop until he had him rotting under lock and key. It would take time, but he promised he wouldn't hurt her again. The detective followed the Scottish authorities to the prison in town.

With the help of Lachlan, Behr was stitched up and ready to go within a few hours. He was lucky that the strike was in the 'safe pocket' below the shoulder and above the armpit. He took the whole process in stride, and only kicked up a fuss when Lachlan ordered him to wear a sling for a bit. Actually, *threatening* him was more like it. Reluctantly, Behr let Ellora put it on for him.

She, on the other hand, had to stay overnight for observations. According to Lachlan, Ellora suffered a concussion and had several other minor cuts and bruises that needed to be cleaned and patched up. She would be cleared to leave if all looked well in the morning. She just had to take it easy for a few weeks. Or, in Behr's opinion... for the rest of her life. He made her promise -- no more death-defying adventures until further notice. Which, of course, she enthusiastically agreed to. Behr stayed by her side the whole night, kissing away all her lingering fears, and never giving her a chance to think about what could've happened.

The next morning, she was cleared to go, and she

couldn't wait to get out of there! She'd seen enough of hospitals to last her a lifetime. Grabbing Behr's hand, she tugged him close to her. Raising up on tip toes, she kissed the spot below his ear. Ellora ran her nose across his day old scruff, loving the way it scratched at her smooth skin. It always seemed to awaken all her senses.

"C'mon, Behr, let's get you home so I can get you out of these clothes."

He flashed her a wicked grin and lifted his brow. "Aaah, now that's what I'm talking 'bout. Do you plan on tucking me into bed then, Nurse Sutherland? Or is your plan to take advantage of me?"

She giggled as she tugged him out of the double doors to the hospital. "You have blood all over you. You look like a gladiator." Ellora nudged his hip with hers, winking at him.

"I'd say I'm due for a sponge bath then, yeah?" He rubbed his hands together like a naughty little greedy boy, and she loved every minute of it.

Ellora laughed as she pulled on his stained shirt, drawing him in for another kiss, wrapping her arms around his neck. Behr held her tight with his good arm. He grunted out his frustration with the sling as it created a gap, preventing them from getting as close as they wanted to. Taking over the kiss, Behr's strong lips were demanding and needy. His hand pressed on the small of her back, pushing her body into his. Ellora raked her hands into his hair, tightly tangling her fingers through it, pulling him harder to her. Behr's tight muscles tensed and twitched at all her loving attention. She still feared that if she let him go, she would lose him. It would take a while before Ellora would be able to shake that feeling.

When Behr finally broke the kiss, the very dazed girl looked into his dilated eyes that mirrored her own passion. Ellora couldn't hide it from him anymore. She knew he would be able to read her like an open book from then on. Looking down at his moist lips, her voice dipped low and husky. "Hmmmm, a sponge bath, huh?" She deliberately looked him up and down suggestively and nodded. "I think we can work something out."

That was all the confirmation he needed. Throwing her over his good shoulder, he jogged down the walkway. She squealed in surprise when he slapped her ass playfully. "Aaah! Behr, what are you doing? You're crazy. You're supposed to take it easy! I'm telling Lachlan on you!" She laughed good heartedly as he continued to carry her down the walkway.

"Some things just cannae wait, love!"

"He'll be coming back at any moment!" Ellora shouted out, getting the group's attention.

Everyone rushed around, making sure all the preparations were in order. Kristy and Gerard had been cooking all that day next door, getting ready for the big event. Behr, Patty, and Gavin were in charge of hanging the new sign and all the electrical hookups. Lachlan and Ellora were rearranging the layout of the tables and chairs for a much better flow, to make the place appear roomier. The pub had been painted inside and out. The paint color chosen by Adelle for the outside was coincidentally called *Mystical Emerald Isle Green*. It made the pub stand out from all others, especially with the truly mystical Trotternish Mountains as a backdrop.

Adelle did a genius job at collecting vintage signs and old photographs of Skye. The sly minx also snatched up copies of Grady and his wife, Catie, from years ago, standing in front of that very pub when they had just opened their doors. She'd had the photo blown up, matted, and framed. It now hung front and center behind the bar. The eclectic mix gave the pub a relaxed, warm and inviting atmosphere. It encouraged patrons to relax and hang out awhile.

Adelle was in charge of keeping Grady away all day, while they applied the finishing touches. They rushed to put everything back in place, in a big hurry.

After a whole day house hunting with all her pickiness and indecision, Grady was officially done and ready to go home. Poor old man, Ellora was sure Adelle had worn him out. He was probably exhausted.

They got a frantic call from Adelle, giving everyone a heads up, so they all scrambled to finish. Luckily, the whole town was on their side in keeping him away. Delay after delay helped give everyone at the pub precious extra minutes to finish up.

Lachlan and Ellora grabbed the large tarp from out back, running it out front.

"Here, Behr, hang this loosely so we can easily remove it when they get here."

Behr climbed down from the ladder, bending over to give the object of his affection a brief kiss on her plump lips. He grabbed hold of the tarp and placed several more kisses on her forehead. "Thanks, love. You've done an amazing job. The old man might just give himself a heart attack when he's seen all you've done. Too much excitement for one man. He'll love it!"

"Oh, everyone here should be thanked. I've had so much help. I couldn't have done any of it without y'all. "

Behr nodded his head. "Aye, you could've. This never

would've happened had you not come and kick-started everything, shifting us all into gear. Grady's depression and grief kept him from moving forward. You were his hope, Ellora. Because o' you, he's found a reason to go on living, not just existing. Aye, you 'ave done the very same for me, as well, love."

With watering eyes, she heard him speak the truth. "I feel the same way about him, this place... "Ellora choked down a big breath as she swallowed the knot in her throat, then continued, "and you. I feel the same way about you, Behr." Running his thumb across her pouty bottom lip, Behr cupped her face and kissed her softly. They were interrupted with the news that Grady and Adelle were a block down and around the corner.

Behr and Patty sprinted up the ladder. Behr used his stronger arm to help Patty quickly pull up the tarp and hang it just so. Afterwards, everyone picked up ladders, tools, and cleanup supplies, dumping them in the alley behind the pub to hide them from view. The townies were all instructed to sneak in through the side door in the alleyway. They filled in quickly, doing a good job of keeping quiet. Kristy was helped inside, bringing enough food to feed an army, then ran out front to meet up with the rest.

Adelle skipped around the corner excitedly, over to where they all stood. Grady stepped cautiously closer, confusion clearly written all over his face. He eyeballed the tarp suspiciously. "What's goin' on, guys? The place burn down or what?"

In a singsong voice, Adelle hugged him tightly, announcing, "Welcome to your grand re-opening!" Kristy pulled the already loose tarp down, letting it cascade to the floor around him, revealing the brand new sign.

Grady's Pub

Come for the beer

Stay for the stories

"Oh my word! How did you... when did you do this? This is incredible. I'd never have imagined this!" The tears filled his kind old eyes, spilling out at the corners. "I would've never dreamed it would look this beautiful! Not in a million years."

Patty walked over, roughly clapping him on the shoulder. "Let's not sit out here crying like a wee baby. Come on inside. I need a drink."

Nice. Real subtle, Ellora thought as she rolled her eyes at Grady's crass friend.

Patty forcefully pulled him into the new doors. Grady looked at the artful details of the refurbished stained glass that had been expertly set inside the panels. The rest followed close behind.

"*!!CONGRATULATIONS!!*"

All the townies shouted, making Grady jump back in surprise. Moira from Cafe Ariba Bistro hustled over with a tray of mugs and passed them out to everyone. They all toasted, "To Grady! May you live to be a thousand years old, and never close your doors!" Everyone lifted their mugs and shouted a thunderous "AYE!" then drank up.

For the first time in a very long time, Ellora was looking forward to her future in this town, and developing a deeper relationship with the man she'd easily fallen in love with. These people were her family now, and Skye, her home.

EPILOGUE

Giddeon knew he was in deep shit now, but he couldn't stay there. He'd rather be in an American prison than in this shit hole. He used his one phone call to contact Dalton, knowing he should still be at the office at this hour, and growing more and more anxious as the line continued to ring. He really needed his help getting out of this fucked up situation. With Dalton's connections, it shouldn't be too hard. Right when Giddeon was sure he'd have to leave a message, the line clicked over.

"Dalton Ramsey Claiborne here," he drawled out dryly.

"Dalton! It's Giddeon. I only have a minute..."

"Did you retrieve her? Is she still alive?" Dalton cut him off. Giddeon had beads of sweat form on his forehead, thinking, *Oh shit! Here we go.*

"Yes. She's alive. She's still hiding in Skye."

"DO. YOU. HAVE. HER?" Dalton all but shouted over the line, creating an echoing ring in Giddeon's ears.

"No. I need your help. I've been caught. The local police have arrested me. I need your help getting me out, and then I can get her. I swear, I'll get her this time."

Silence stretched out over the line. The longer the silence lasted, the higher his anxiety rose. He had *really* fucked up, and Dalton wasn't happy.

"I see." Dalton stretched out the syllables in a cold and calculating way. "There must be some misunderstanding. I think you have dialed the wrong person. However, you sound like a man who could use some good advice... You have made your bed, and now you're going to have to lie in it! Whatever it is that you've done, I'm sure you will *suffer* the consequences dearly for your actions. If I were you... I would just disappear. Before someone else makes you as such." The line went dead after Dalton's under current threat.

That was his way of warning him to hide, or he would be hunted down as well. Giddeon was now on the same level as the girl he'd hunted, except Dalton never favored him. He was dispensable, replaceable, and utterly forgettable in his eyes.

Giddeon slammed the phone down hard on the receiver repeatedly. Curses flew out of his mouth. *"FUCK!"* Giddeon rained out punches on the concrete wall, leaving blood splatter behind. The pain eased the numbness inside him, instantly making him feel a euphoric calm, making him feel *something*.

The detective behind him just laughed condescendingly at his outburst. "You ready to talk yet?"

Walking over to the bars, Giddeon leaned his forearms on them with a relaxed cocky air. Gone was his violent rage. Resting his head on the bar, he looked out at the detective and laughed.

"It's not me she has to worry about. Not anymore."

"You're damn right she won't!" Dominick shouted in his face. "Your ass is going to rot in prison for the rest of your fucking life, once I bring you back!"

"You really think prison scares me?" Giddeon slowly shook his head side to side and leveled him with his lifeless eyes. "What a fucking joke. You have no idea who you're dealing with, do you? No? What I meant was, I failed. I'm no longer a threat to her. It's over for me. I will never make it back. I will disappear like all the rest, written off as a disgruntled ex-employee. It's not over for Ellora, though. It's far from over for her. We have all just started playing a very dangerous game to him. The more she runs, the longer he will continue to hunt her down. And he won't *ever* stop. Not until he either captures her or kills her. He will just keep sending one guy after another after another, until he gets the outcome he wants. Dalton has claimed her, and there is no stopping him now." Giddeon lowered his head and narrowed his steely eyes on the detective.

"This is just the beginning."

Dalton ended the call then pressed the button for his assistant. Susan walked into his office brusquely.

"Yes, Mr. Claiborne? What can I do for you, sir?"

"Susan, I need you to get my agent on the line immediately, the one who handles international properties please. I am interested in acquiring properties around Scotland. Have him set up some tours. Tell them I want them ready by the time I arrive. Book my first class seat for the next available flight out of here."

"Scotland, sir?"

Dalton glared at her. He didn't like to be questioned. His annoyance was made clear in the tone of his voice, giving off a dangerous warning. "Yes... I have a few loose ends I need to tie up there."

Confused, she looked up. "What is it for, sir? Why not send a rep up there? You are needed here, and you are booked solid with board meetings all week to discuss the future of the Reno Project."

Dalton stalked over to her, gritting his teeth menacingly. She averted her eyes downward, knowing full well that he didn't like being questioned. She had seen what he'd done to other employees, even witnessed what he'd done to those who'd wronged him. When Susan started to quake in fear, he smiled, clearly enjoying her discomfort.

"Let's just say, I will be going for business... *and* pleasure."

To be continued in the Forever Marked Series with
Book 2: Beyond Redemption

ACKNOWLEDGMENTS

To my Lord and Savior. I can do all things through him who strengthens me.
~Phillippians 4:13

To my loving Hubby. I sacrificed countless amounts of time and energy away from my family, in order to write this book. Your love and support means everything to me. Thank you for putting up with me. I love you so much Eggie. I did it!

Womb-mate! Thank you for listening when I told you I was doing something new and crazy. You pushed me to write chapter after chapter so you could be the first to read it. You were the first person to truly believe in me. You were my biggest fan-girl from the very beginning! I love you twinny twin.

Thanks mommy for reading to us at an early age. I'm so happy I was born in a family of book lovers. Daddy!!! Your over exaggerated storytelling and crazy antics helped fuel my imagination.

To my Chicken Soup Chicks! Thank you for welcoming a crazy nut job newbie like me, into your group. For putting up with all my questions and uncertainty. You all are the best group of people on the planet. I'm truly proud and blessed to call you my friends. I can't imagine waking up and not talking to you all on a constant basis. We have many inside jokes, shared stories and endless memes. I look forward to meeting you all in person someday. It will happen.

To my amazing Beta readers/critique partners: Sam Destiny and B. A. Dillon, Thanks for putting up with all my exclamation marks!!!! Your patience, advice and hard work you've invested on FM has been an unforgettable learning experience. I'm so grateful to you both and I cannot thank you enough for all of your support and for believing in me. Love your faces off!

To my PA Tori the terminator Carlson. You are a machine. Thank you for all your help and being so bodaciously amazeballs. You rock. The end.

Kendra! Thank you so much for putting up with my crazy messages and excited nervousness. Your work blew me away.

Airicka Phoenix. Thank you for my awesome book cover and banner. I'm so in love, you did an amazing job and I had a blast working with you.

Sarah Ann... My beautiful mind mate. You helped keep me sanely, insane. Our job as government spy decoders is waiting for us! And remember... They're just noodles.

To my extended family on both sides who were excited with me and supported me through this exciting journey. Love all you crazy guys. To my oldest friend Shannon who couldn't wait to read it. Love you, hun.

And last *but certainly NOT least* Thank YOU, my amazing readers. You are epic and I love you. Thank you for going through this journey with me.

I'd love to hear from you, good or bad. Your feedback will help make the next book better. THANK YOU!

ABOUT THE AUTHOR

I grew up in Upstate New York, but my heart belongs in Arizona. If given the chance, I'd gladly trade in frost burn for sunburn. I grew up causing all kinds of trouble with my twin sister/partner in crime. My wild over-exaggerated story telling grew along with my love for reading. I am a proud wife and mother of three beautiful daughters, and two fur babies.

With the support of my hubby and the encouragement of my womb-mate, I put pen to paper and let my imagination run free.

I love coffee, peanut butter cups, Angry Orchard, and OF COURSE reading! I enjoy all genre. Paranormal, thriller, romantic suspense, dystopian… you name it.

I'd love to get to know you all, so hit me up. I love to gab. Go ahead. Don't be shy! Where to get ahold of me:
Facebook:
https://www.facebook.com/authorLadyJ
Goodreads
https//www.goodreads.com/LadyJ-author
Twitter: @LadyJ_Author
Instagram: @ladyj_author
Email: LadyJauthor@yahoo.com

Keep reading for a sneak peek at
B.A. Dillon's A Vision in Time!
Available now!

A VISION IN TIME by B.A. Dillon

Prologue – Mia
Simple Gifts

I have never been more grateful for a week off, time with family and friends, and this delicious dessert table layered with so many goodies. My co-worker, Scott, made his ten-layer chocolate cake again, but what I'm really scoping out is Emma's apple pie and homemade ice cream. The sugar keeps calling me back to the table.

This is truly a Thanksgiving to remember. Luke's injuries have healed enough to be released from the hospital, but Emma is still hovering over him like he's a child. She looks incredibly tired, and I have to wonder why we didn't decide to postpone this event until the weekend. Luke's dad, Charlie, offered to host Thanksgiving this year. My mom and I tried to change his mind while we were pacing the hospital waiting room a few days back, but he wouldn't hear of it. He said we would be celebrating, and here we are. Luke, Shane and Isaac, along with the rest of the Street Crimes Division of the Tampa Police Department, managed to bring Javier Rivera's operation to its knees. Thank God! People who mess with kids need to leave this planet.

Emma is a rock. I am so in awe of this woman, it's easy to understand how Luke fell head over heels in love with her. Last year she struggled with terrible nightmares. Finding Luke and surviving his latest undercover stint almost makes me believe in happily ever afters. When I see her try to hide a yawn, I decide it's time to intervene. "Ok, that's it pal. You and Luke need some rest. You are officially diverted to the guest room for the next couple of hours."

"Mia, I need to finish wrapping up all the left-overs, and then I promise I'll sit for a while," she mumbles through another yawn.

"Nope. Not buying it. My mom and I can handle it. And, if you continue to argue with me, I'll call in reinforcements and bring in the big guns. I have KJ's phone number."

"Leave my son out of this. No need to call KJ. I'll take Luke into the guest room and rest a bit, but get Katie and Julia to help you. I'm a little worried about your mom. What happened to her today?"

"Emma, I don't even know how to answer that. When we were getting ready to leave my condo, she walked right into the sliding glass door. That's how she got the bruise on her forehead. She claims one of the girls closed the door on her when they were feeding the cat. To be honest, I'm more than alarmed. The other day she asked me to pass the salt, and it was sitting right in front of her. We've experienced so many incidents over the past few months; I'm petrified to let her drive my kids anywhere. Last Sunday, she fell into her pool. That was the last straw. I'm taking her to the doctor tomorrow for a full physical."

"Yeah, I think you have reason to be concerned. Let me know what I can do to help."

"Well for now please go rest."

"There's one more thing we need to talk about," she mumbles again through a yawn, but then looks at me with a most serious expression.

"What?" I voice with a noteworthy attitude. Emma continues to stare straight through me, waiting on me to start talking. "What, Emma?"

"Come on, Mia . . . the elephant in the room? We need to talk about what happened Saturday. You need to talk about it. I bet you haven't said one word to anyone."

"Wrong. I had a brief conversation with my mom that day, but . . ." Biting down on my bottom lip, I search for a way to change the subject. "My mom knows. My mom understands."

"But your mom is dealing with whatever is going on with her vision, and doing her best to stay strong for you and your girls. Mia, talk to me! We all witnessed whatever that was firsthand. Did you give a statement to Isaac?"

"No, and before you say anything else, I'm not going to. At one time I thought Isaac might just be the perfect guy for me. I've had a major crush for months. Now he looks at me like I have three heads! Let this go, Emma. I'm really okay." I begin to search the room for an escape, or any reason to get away from Emma's concerning gaze. Continuing, I make one last ditch effort to shut this conversation down. "I had some kind of vision. It helped the guys find Luke and prevent a catastrophe. Be grateful, and let it go."

"Mia, because of you, Luke is here today. The two of us, with the help of those incredibly handsome guys over there, saved him. I owe you, friend. Someday, I'll figure out a way to properly thank you. But for now, here's Dr. Johnson's card. She can help you, Mia. Her practice is all about helping people like you and me interpret dreams and visions. Shelley Johnson saved me, which in turn saved Luke. My dreams were memories, Mia. She guided me, and helped me find answers. You had a full-blown vision, and you nearly passed out. Call her." As she turns to walk away, she gently slips Dr. Johnson's business card into the back pocket of my jeans. Now I feel like I'm carrying a hundred pound weight.

Typically when this crew gathers together, we're a party in the making. But today has been rather subdued as everyone attempts to process the events of the past few weeks. Isaac has been huddled up with Luke's dad for most of the afternoon. The two must share some special bond. Charlie has been an incredible host today, spending a tremendous amount of time with my mom. It was sort of cute watching them play cards earlier. I think that's the most fun she's had in weeks. Just maybe we'll get through the holidays unscathed, and we can all relax and enjoy ourselves.

As I head into the dining room to make one final clear of the table, I can feel him behind me. Isaac Miller isn't just a good-looking man, he's every woman's dream. This guy is so gorgeous I have to wonder why he doesn't have a Miss America blonde on his arm at all times. He's tall, but not too tall, maybe six foot two. He seems to wear his sandy brown hair high and tight, the norm for this All American country boy who doesn't seem to understand the word casual. I'm not sure I've ever seen him in a t-shirt. I wonder if his wardrobe only consists of long sleeve dress shirts. I bet he's a man who likes wearing a designer tie. But I've always believed a man's eyes are the windows to his soul. One look into Isaac's green and gold flecked irises spikes my blood pressure, sends my heart racing, and puts me into a tumultuous cycle of lust. Crap! Two dates. Two simple meetings for coffee was all it took to send me spiraling out of control. But then the calls stopped, and he claimed work was to blame. Saturday he called me babe and held me like I was someone special. But here we are again, tip-toeing around like we barely know each other.

"Mia?" Crap! Now what? "I'll help you. I've been hoping to get you alone for a few minutes." Crap! Alone for what?

"Great! Can you grab the last two bowls? I just sent Emma and Luke into the guest room to rest, and it looks like everyone else just got roped into a rousing game of Go Fish with my girls." Rounding the corner of Charlie's kitchen, I barely get the platter of turkey on the counter when I feel his arms come around me. Before I know it, his mouth captures mine with a deep and frantic kiss. Just when I'm about to lose myself in his kiss, I remember my children, my mother, and my closet friends are less than twenty-five feet away. "Isaac! What are you doing?"

"If you have to ask, then I'm doing it wrong," he chuckles against my neck. "I've wanted to do that since Saturday. We need to talk. We have so much to talk about, but I'm hoping talking will lead to more. Actually, let's start with more first."

Not able to break away, his lips meld to mine once more. This time as his lips rest on mine, I feel his hands tremble as he cups my cheeks. Without thinking about the eleven people in the living room, I pull myself closer to his body, needing his touch. When I feel him begin to pull away,

I nearly whimper. Barely audible I whisper, "Isaac, I . . . I need to . . ."

"I know what you need, beautiful. We need some time alone. Is there a way to make that happen tonight? Besides, we have a lot to discuss. I let my new job take over my life and forgot for a moment how much I want to know you," he whispers before kissing me soundly once again. "I've been worried about you. When you 'saw' Luke being held by Rivera, my heart nearly stopped. I need to know you're okay, babe," he murmurs while running his tongue up my neck.

"Oh, God! Isaac, please . . . I don't want to talk. Please, I don't want to think or talk about what happened yet. Let's just be spontaneous tonight. That is, after I figure out what to do with my kids and my mother."

"So what you're saying is you just want to use me for my body?" he murmurs moving to the other side of my neck.

"That's what I'm asking for. Right now, that's what I need." I plead as I kiss the sensitive spot under his jaw. With my mind traveling a million miles an hour, I desperately attempt to come up with a babysitting scheme.

"Mom!! Mommy!!" Sophie wails from the living room.

There's nothing like motherhood to dampen the mood. "Guess it's not gonna happen tonight, handsome," I murmur as I graze my lips over his.

As his forehead drops to mine, he exhales a heavy breath right at my mouth. "Damn! Rain check?"

As I turn to step into the dining room, I sigh, "Here's

hoping it pours tomorrow."

Chapter One – Mia
With a Little Help from my Friends

There are three things I love about today. One – the spread laid out at this barbeque is absolutely amazing. Scott and Brandon, the best cooks among us, along with the rest of the gang, really outdid themselves this year. Two – knowing that summer vacation is just a few weeks away, makes having to go back to work this week almost bearable. And finally – the best part of today – having the chance to avoid kids for a few hours and hang with adults. Katie and Shane's annual Memorial Day barbeque is most definitely the highlight of my three-day weekend.

There's only one problem, and her name is Emma Finch. I can feel her eyes burning straight through me before she even delivers one word. And then it's out, one simple question that I have no intention of answering. "So, you want to tell me what's going on?"

"I . . . Emma, there's nothing going on." I stammer attempting to change the subject. Emma is an intuitive little bitch. Damn! How are we gonna keep this a secret? "It's great news, huh? Katie and Shane will make terrific parents. I know they've waited a long time to have kids. They must be ecstatic."

"Yes, yes, they're thrilled, as am I. Now, quit trying to

change the subject. You can keep telling yourself that nothing is going on, but I can feel the sexual tension. If the two of you keep pulling all of that into our space, I'm gonna have to take Luke home early tonight. For the record, Isaac isn't as good at hiding his feelings as you are. He's a nervous wreck . . . keeps giggling like a little school girl."

"Emma, honestly I don't know what you think you see. I'm incredibly jealous though as you are one lucky woman. Luke looks at you with such love. That look is a beautiful thing."

It's more than beautiful; it's a true happy ending. Who would have guessed that a chance meeting at this Memorial Day barbeque a year ago was the beginning of an incredible love affair. Luke Myers simply stole Emma Finch's heart, and they fell madly in love. Emma looks great, finally at peace after the pure hell she endured last fall. It's amazing what true love can do. Her nightmares are gone, and they've made a life together. Watching the two of them makes me want my own happily ever after. I want what they have. What am I saying? No I don't! I've opened myself up to that nonsense before – only to get burned. I have a life full of love with my girls and my mom. Who needs a big strapping man anyway? Ughh!

"Mind if I steal her away, Mia?" Lost in my own thoughts, I have no idea what Luke just said. "Mia?" Luke asks again while pulling Emma's hand to his lips.

Barely audible, my response is clipped. My mind

wanders back to Isaac sitting across the room and I find it difficult to tear my gaze away. The green and gold of his eyes almost makes them look like marbles. Man, I'd love to run my hands through his soft sandy brown hair. "What? I'm sorry. Sure, take her away! She asks too many questions anyway."

"Mia, don't go anywhere. We have a lot to talk about." Emma conveys with a raised brow.

"Luke, can you do something to shut her up?"

"With pleasure." Before I know it, he tightly wraps his arms around her while whispering messages of love in her ear. Lost in their own little world, their lips lock and the two lovebirds only have eyes for each other. Finally – an escape.

As I'm walking away, I just know Luke's proposing soon. If I were a gambler, I'd bet he has a very special night planned for her this evening. Why do I know this? There it is again. Those visions keep popping up in my head all the time. Wish I knew what's in store for my future. What am I saying? No – no I don't!

Making my way to the patio, I'm delighted to find a cold beer, a comfortable chair, and a moment to gather my thoughts. Isaac has been overly attentive tonight, behavior I'm sure everyone has noticed. Ten minutes ago I made it perfectly clear with just a sinister look to tone it down. I told him exactly what I wanted from him on Thanksgiving. We agreed friends with benefits worked for both of us. He needs to get it through his thick head that our secret affair needs to stay exactly that – top secret.

"Anyone up for a game tonight?" Katie asks while wrapping her arms around her husband.

"Just not Pictionary . . . apparently I suck at that game!" Emma laughs.

"Sweetheart, I saw right through that terrible drawing of a 'Smart car' last year which led me directly to your gorgeous self. You all can play Pictionary because I'm taking my woman home early tonight." Luke coos while gazing at Emma. Damn – there it is again. He's proposing tonight. I know it!

"I think we should find a new game anyway. Luke has the upper hand in Pictionary, and he cheats, too. What other games do you have, Katie?" Isaac suggests while winking at me. When we meet later, after he gives me three orgasms, I'm gonna kill him.

"What about 'Battle of the Sexes'? What do you think ladies? Let's divide into teams and kick some guy ass!" My best friend, Julia, hollers from her perch next to the keg of Yuengling.

Just like last year, Katie and Shane lead everyone back inside to avoid the heat and looming thunderstorm heading our way. It's clear from the moment we head back inside that avoiding Isaac isn't going to be easy. Every time I look his way, I'm on the receiving end of a smile, a wink, or a look that soaks my panties. His stare from those gorgeous marble eyes is enough to cause me to lose my resolve and let the cat out of the bag. Before I can find a seat with the girls, my phone signals a text.

Isaac: Answer your phone and then go outside.

Me: What?

Isaac: Mia! Answer the phone and go outside.

As soon as the message flashes on my screen, I see Isaac turn and head into the kitchen as my phone begins to ring. "Sorry guys, my sitter is calling and I need to check up on the kids. I'll be right back." Darting outside, Isaac is on the line and directs me to the walkway on the side of the house.

"Isaac, what are you up to? Emma's already suspicious. If we're missing at the same time, she's gonna give one of us the third degree . . . and it will probably be me." I seethe into my phone.

"Don't panic, just reboot the computer." The guy is steady as a rock. All. The. Time.

"What? Isaac, what am I doing out here?" allowing my inner bitch to emerge.

"You're not a patient person, are you? Let me talk you through it." I hear a door slam, and before I know it, Isaac is stalking toward me from the front of the house.

"Isaac, are you crazy? Everyone in there is gonna start asking – " And before I can finish my thought, his mouth is on mine, and his hands are lifting the hem of my dress. Kissing me deep and hard, my breathing rockets out-of-control and I feel that roller-coaster dip in my belly. One hand skates over my breasts as I arch my back in need.

Pulling back and trying to regain my senses, I whisper, "Isaac, what the hell are you doing to me?"

"I hope giving you the first of many orgasms today. I have to know. Do you want me the way I want you? Because I've been thinking about being inside you multiple times today," he asks as his hand finds a better location between my thighs.

"You are crazy! How the hell am I supposed to go back in there? Oh God!"

"Damn, Mia, you're fucking soaked for me!" Completely mindless now, it's all I can do to urge him closer. "We're out of here in an hour. Figure out an excuse. I'll duck out in the next few minutes with a work emergency. Meet me at my place by six. And Mia, don't bail on me again. Cause I'll come find you and drag you to my car, and I won't care who sees or knows about us. Do you understand what I'm saying?"

All I can do is nod while biting his lower lip, completely thrown by his moving fingers and caveman antics.

"Mia? I need words, beautiful."

"I'll make an excuse and check in with my sitter and my mom. I'll meet you at your place by six," I whisper in a daze.

"Good girl." And then his tongue is back in my mouth reminding me why I would agree to almost anything he suggests. "I'll call you again. You go back in first. Try to play along this time and not look at me like you'd like to kill me! That's why Emma is suspicious."

Massaging my hand over his rock hard erection I whisper, "Emma's suspicious because you've been giggling like a nervous school girl all day. Her words, not mine."

"Careful, beautiful. I may just have to spank you tonight." Looking directly into my wide eyes, my hips jerk as he slips two fingers inside me. "We'll make this quick. I can't let you go back in there unsatisfied." Whimpering, all I can do is moan. "You think about this all the time, don't you, Mia?" Nodding and jerking my hips toward his fingers, I hear, "Answer me, Mia."

"Yes, all the time. Damn you!" Feeling a smile on his lips and a growl at my neck, I know Isaac is as turned on as I am. The lust in the air and one long, firm push against my inner walls sends my body over the edge quickly, "Oh, God, Isaac, don't stop! Do. Not. Stop!" The overwhelming sensation sends my body spiraling out of control, and it will be a miracle if no one heard me. While I work to catch my breath and slow my racing heart, I feel Isaac use something soft to clean up the moisture traveling down my legs. Giving him a quick look of concern, I stop his sweet gesture to send him back inside. I'm such a bitch. "We've been gone a long time. Better get back in there, handsome. I'll say thank you in a big way later tonight," I mumble while offering him a sincere smile.

"Answer your phone. Walk back to the patio and

pretend you're talking to the sitter, and for God's sake don't make eye contact with me when I come in the front door. I'm gonna have to stay outside for a while in order to face everyone in there," he mutters while attempting to straighten his pants.

"See you inside," I mutter from drooped eyelids. "Got a prediction for who might win 'Battle of the Sexes'?"

"Yeah, me. I'm definitely spanking you tonight," Isaac growls through a pained look. "I'm never making it back inside if you continue to taunt me. Go! Now!"

Laughing lightly, I begin to straighten my sundress and smooth my loose curls that have fallen from my once neat ponytail. "See you inside, handsome." As my phone begins to ring, I decide to ignore the first few rings, and wait for the fourth ring before I pick up. My mood just went from mediocre to exemplary in a matter of minutes. I spend a moment or two pacing the patio with the phone to my ear before walking back inside. "You listen to Alexa, honey. I'll see you in about an hour." I walk inside from the patio and find all the girls have gathered in the kitchen.

"Everything okay, Mia?" Emma questions while studying my expression carefully as she steps away from the group making her way to the sliding glass doors.

"Yeah, the kids were just wondering when I'm coming home. Alexa is the best babysitter ever! I'm so glad she's made herself available this summer and that the girls love her so much. She's also really great with my mom. I know her parents are happy I'll be keeping her busy over our summer break," I answer while wrapping an arm around my friend.

"I'm just glad we were able to help her out this year, and negotiate a truce between her and Ashley. Alexa almost seems like herself again." Stepping aside to make my way to the kitchen, Emma halts my movement abruptly. Leaning in she whispers right at my ear, "By the way, I'm not buying this little act you're staging. For the record, Isaac is a good man and he deserves the love of a good woman. You can keep denying it all you want, but I don't need a vision to know there's some major pull between you two. Six months ago I gave him a big speech about treating you right. Now it's your turn. I don't know what's going on with you, Mia. He likes you a lot. Don't mess this up."

Looking up I find one of my best friends with genuine concern in her caring expression. "Emma, I love you. You're one of my closest friends, but you have this all wrong. I'm not looking for a knight in shining armor. I'm a bitch. A busy bitch at that." Unable to reel my emotions in, the stresses of single parenthood begin to flow like a powerful waterfall. "Some days motherhood just sucks! Sarah and Sophie are fighting like alley cats all the time, and my mom's sight is deteriorating rapidly. The Medicare social worker is trying to push back her three-month immersion program at the Florida School for the Deaf and the Blind to mid-June, so I can finish the school year. I'm completely out of sick days and I'm under water, Emma. I don't have time for a happily ever after." I explain while offering a pleading look to let this go.

"All right Mia, I'll let it go . . . for now," she offers with a loving smile while guiding our path into the kitchen. "What can we do to help?" She asks loud enough for the rest of our friends to hear.

Rebecca's head pops up from the girls' conversation, "What's going on, Mia? Talk to us. If you can't talk to the four us, who can you talk to?" Rebecca's question brings me a moment of peace, and the realization how much I really need my friends. Shaking my head, I look up to find Emma, Katie, Julia, and Rebecca all studying my expression with warm smiles. They've moved us into a tight circle as I feel Emma grasp my hand. The five of us are as close as five women can be. We're more than co-workers, more than friends . . . we're sisters of the heart.

"Mia, I don't know how I would have functioned the last two years without all of you. We're not just friends, we're a family. We are the people we choose to be a part of our lives. You're struggling, Mia. We love you, and all we want to do is help," Emma croons as her grip tightens around my hand.

"Yeah, pal, I'm not working this summer so I have tons of time to hang out and help with the girls," Katie responds with a smile and wink. "Besides, I need some mommy-on-the-job-training!"

Keeping my game face in check, I offer the girls a wide smile as Isaac returns via the front door. Watching him adjust his jeans one last time causes a bubble of laughter to spill over my lips. "I love you guys! There's just so much to do, I don't even know where to begin. I guess I could use some help packing to get ready for my big move. The girls and I have lived in the condo for five years. There's so much stuff. I only have the month of June to transfer my entire life to my mom's place." As I look up I see Luke, Shane and Isaac have joined the circle and are watching me with concern.

"No need to hire movers, Mia. With three trucks, the three of us can move all your stuff. Your mom's place is right around the corner from you, right?" Shane offers.

"And my dad will help as well. He needs something to do besides popping in on Emma and me!" Luke laughs. "My dad can move your mom over to St. Augustine next week. That way, you keep things on track according to the schedule the doctor gave you, and you and the girls can finish the school year peacefully." Luke suggests while wrapping his arms around Emma.

"Luke, that's an incredible offer. I know my mom and Charlie developed a great friendship this past year over their love of gardening and playing bridge, but that's way too much to ask." I laugh while shaking my head. This is overwhelming. I will not cry.

"Nonsense. Besides it gets him out of our hair for a few days," Luke chides.

"I'll organize the moving weekend! Everyone pull your phones out and look at your calendars." Julia hollers to everyone as I grab my purse feeling completely overwhelmed. When I look up, everyone is scrolling through their phones and I have a small pocket calendar in my hands.

"What is that?" Rebecca asks while laughing. "Mia, are you ever going to use all the extras your phone has to offer?

"Nope! I like my paper calendar. I always have, and I always will. I despise technology!" I answer through clenched teeth. "And no one better say a thing about it!" With that, everyone begins discussing dates as I cross into the kitchen barely able to breathe.

"Take a breath, beautiful," I hear Isaac whisper. "You've got a room full of people who only want the best for you and your family. They're just trying to help you. Let them." Isaac demands through hooded eyes. Pulling me aside, he continues, "Luke's dad is great. He saved me from myself many years ago, and that's a story I'll share with you someday. Let him drive your mom to St. Augustine and get her settled. I'll take you over there this summer once she's established her routine, and we'll spend the weekend there. And before you start delivering your typical rant about not needing anyone's help, know that my offer is purely selfish. I've had dreams about you waking me up with your mouth –"

Pulling us from our private moment, Julia screeches

from across the room, "Mia? How's the first Saturday after school's out for the official move? Everyone is free, but this only works if you're free as well." Before I have a moment to even think or react, everything is arranged. Luke's dad, Charlie, will be driving my mom over to St. Augustine next weekend; Katie and Rebecca have offered to watch the girls so I can check in with my mom a few weeks later; and the move has been completely orchestrated by Julia. Holy hell, I just agreed to go away for an entire weekend with Isaac. I think I'm gonna pass out.

Bringing me out of my panic attack, I feel Emma's arm come around my waist as her hand gently strokes up and down my back. "I know. Sometimes all this love is a bit overwhelming, and maybe unbelievable. But Mia, we do love you and want what's best for you, your mom, and your girls. It's really that simple." Everything about this moment makes me want to run away from all these people and cry for days, or grab on to each one of them and never let go.

"I know. Someday, someday I might trust you enough to share my entire story, so you'll understand why this is so difficult for me. I made a big decision a long time ago to only rely on my own strengths. My entire life has been full of so many let-downs, it's almost impossible for me to trust anyone. But I think I trust you. I want to believe everyone here is for real. I'm just not completely there yet." Finishing my monologue, I'm pulled back into Emma's embrace and my eyes well up with tears.

Sensing how uncomfortable I am, Emma pulls back and shouts, "Are we gonna play 'Battle of the Sexes' and kick some ass, girls, or just stand around all day?"

In a matter of seconds, the mood easily shifts back to party atmosphere, and I can't help but smile at this group of people who somehow managed to crack open my heart and pour in a little love. A vibrating phone in my pocket reminds me that the tall, muscular, green-eyed cop, who nearly brought me to my knees an hour ago, still expects me in his bed tonight.

Isaac: My bed. Two hours. I owe you three more.

Me: Only three?

Isaac: Do you want me to drag you out of here in front of them?

Me: I'll be there.

Purchase on Amazon:

http://amzn.com/BOOWLKLW3G

Follow on Facebook:

https://www.facebook.com/BADillon520

Keep reading for a sneak peek at:

Tagged For Life by Sam Destiny

Dedication

Sometimes you just gotta let yourself fall and not be afraid.

In the end you'll fly.

To the brave people that fall hard and fly high:

You are brave.

Stay that way.

Prologue

29th Nov. 2014

Tessa,

My beautiful, amazing Tessa.

It's kind of scary knowing that you are close to me and

yet so far away. But then, close is always a question of definition, isn't it?

I've had a lot of time to think over the last couple of days, and frankly, all I really worried and wondered about was how to start this letter. 'Hey' doesn't seem to cut it. 'My love' might scare you off, right? And everything else wouldn't be enough. I figured your name was the best thing to express what I wanted to convey. I can still feel it on my tongue. I can remember the way it would roll off and how it always filled me with such warmth.

That moment before you'd look up at me, was always filled with anticipation because I had a feeling every time you raised your eyes to mine, you were more amazing and I was falling just a little bit more for you.

I know what is between us in the sense of distance and trouble, but I won't lie, when I think of you I feel tall enough so I can look over it all and see you.

There's nothing I want more than to tell you I hope you flying back home hasn't changed any of the things you felt for me. You just... Remember? We both know how that sentence should have ended. You just love me. I can't wait to hear the words from your lips. You keep me going right now. Do you even realize that?

We never exchanged contact details and I don't know why. Maybe things had been just too head-over-heels in the end? Maybe you didn't want to because you thought that I needed to focus on other things. Maybe you thought I wouldn't contact you. Either way, I figure I need to fight for this harder than I have ever fought for anything. That sure means something because I am a soldier. Anyways, I got your address from the front desk. Remember that you needed to sign it? Well, technically the solider did that for you, so maybe it slipped your mind. It certainly vanished from mine. Either way, thankfully Tank reminded me of protocol.

It's too funny how he suddenly changed his tune about you because he thinks you are what will keep me sane. Little does he know that sane is not what you do to me.

When I think of you I cannot help but feel all warm. I want to be rough with you even while I'm soft. I want to mark you mine even while I hope you'll mark me yours. I want to own you while I want to be owned by you.

I've never been one to write letters. I always hated that there was no response or no chance to see what the person reading thinks while doing so. With you I don't mind. I guess it's because I can always tell myself the letter got lost.

Or someone kept it from you.

I don't know how good I'll be with writing, or how often, but I want to try, because the need to pick up the phone and call you is overwhelming. Not that I have your number or anything...

No matter what's coming our way, Tessa, remember that I'll always be your soldier. Remember that you are the woman who cracked my heart wide open. Remember that you are all I want. There are moments when I think that you are maybe MORE important than anything else. Does that scare you?

It sure as hell scares me. And proves one thing:

I love you.

Jazz

Chapter One
October 2014

Tessa Rowan checked her list for the hundredth time. It wasn't every day that she would be traveling to the US to meet all her crazy online acquaintances. Aimie, Hilary and Emma were going to be there once she arrived. Three weeks of fun, friends and festivities. She hated that her best friend wouldn't be able to join them, but Evy had just gotten a promotion and wasn't ready to leave yet.

"What if we don't get along?" Tessa asked again, hearing her best friend sigh. She was trying to help her pack, but she didn't offer much useful advice. Instead though her best friend seemed distracted.

"It'll be fine. The good thing is none of the girls have met before. I mean this will be new for all of you. Imagine how I'll feel next time I come along. You already know each other and I will be the outsider," she complained and Tessa turned back to her, placing her hands on her hips. As if she'd let her bestie feel left out.

"Please, as if I'd ever give you the chance to feel unloved," Tessa mumbled, grabbing a pair of jeans. For some reason, she was nauseous. In less than twenty-four hours she'd be sitting in a plane, getting away. For years she had thought about that trip and finally it was becoming reality.

"I know you'd never do that, but still, I want to go with you," Evy fussed and Tessa rolled her eyes.

"And I want your ten thousand plus paycheck every month," she replied, and Evy grinned, sitting up. That definitely was something she really liked. This probably was one of the few moments where her best friend didn't look pensive.

"Okay, so I checked you in online. You'll have a window seat throughout almost every flight. In LA you'll have to hurry since I'm not able to reserve a seat from there to Monterey. Not that it will matter, because by then you'll be ready to drop."

Evy was damn good at her job as a travel agent and therefore, Tessa didn't have to arrange anything. She had just pulled out her credit card and paid for whatever Evy had gotten her.

"Thank you, I can't say that enough."

Her best friend just waved that off, giving her a hug before finally starting to fold Tessa's clothes and helping her pack. She had so much stuff that she would need six very strong guys to carry her bags. Half of it would stay in the US, since Tessa had agreed to bring chocolate and other goodies with her, but she sure would fill the space with new items in no time.

"I want you to message me once you've landed and found Wi-Fi. Remember, roaming costs are enormous. You want to avoid them, trust me," Evy explained and Tessa felt a little as if her mother had gotten a twin. Between those two it wasn't hard to feel twelve years old again: "*Wear a sweater. It's California, I know, but it'll be October nonetheless.*" Her mother was worried out of her mind, and Evy wasn't far behind, even though her best friend would never officially admit to being concerned.

"Keep an eye your bags. You'll most likely have them checked in all the way, but your handbag and carry-on definitely need watching. There's a lot of pickpocketing in LAX, but I'm sure you can keep your stuff together. Split your money. Everything you have should be in four different bags. It's safer for you. Plus, the credit card; keep it where you can reach it and not lose it. I don't know, sew a pocket into your bra or something," Evy went on and Tessa turned, cocking her head.

"It's not my first flight. Even though my last trip to the States was more than a decade ago, I still know overall what I need to be aware of. Besides, I plan on keeping my credit card with me at all times. It's the only thing that can save my life after all," Tessa winked, hoping that once she'd start her trip, her calm would finally return.

Thinking about which handbag to take for the flight,

and which to pack for use in the US, she threw her favorite black one into the luggage since it was too small for a trip like that.

With combined forces they closed the two suitcases and then sat down on them, sighing. This was it. She had her clothes ready and all she had to do now was wait for morning and her trip to begin.

The moment it was time to say goodbye, the tears started streaming down Tessa's cheek. It made her realize how quickly life could be over. Even though airplanes had amazing statistics when it came to delivering their passengers safely to wherever they wanted to go, there were enough accidents to bring Tessa to remind Evy that she loved her more than anyone on this earth. She was the sister heaven had refused to give to her.

"I'm going to miss you like hell. No matter what'll come, you're the best friend a girl can wish for. I'm gonna text you whenever I can. And I'll facetime you every night. You work forever anyways, so we'll have all the time in the world. Please, try to get out of work earlier than you did the last few days though. Actually, don't. It might make you regret not coming, and regret is something you shouldn't be feeling. We'll make sure the next get-together is here, at our home," Tessa promised, seeing how Evy wiped away her own tears.

"Stop making it sound like we'll never see each other again. I want you to get out, clear your head and have fun. I know you need it."

And it was true. Tessa's life had run in circles for the last three years and her usually calm demeanor had changed into a short-tempered, frustrated one.

Besides, Tessa knew she needed to get away from her monotone routines in order to find out what she was missing. Hanging with the girls seemed to be the perfect way to get her head back in the game and think about what she wanted from life, because even though she always used to have a plan, life seemed to take an entirely different turn. Twenty-nine was by no means old, but she wasn't the exactly a teen anymore, either, and kids seemed to be a fantasy that didn't belong in her reality any longer. After all, just the timeline already was difficult: finding a guy and getting to know him enough to maybe plan a baby ... that could take years. And then you never knew if you'd even get pregnant right away ... nah, children most likely weren't in her cards anymore, especially since finding a guy seemed impossible. Once burned, twice shy; that was definitely Tessa's motto since her ex-boyfriend had managed to crumble her self-confidence into little pieces again and again.

Perfect, none-cheating guys existed only in books. Romantic gestures were a creation of the female mind because they were deprived of the flowers-and-candles-reality. Maybe all stories had spoiled Tessa for any real guy out there. She had no idea and didn't want to think about it any longer.

"We both know I do," she agreed and then kissed her best friend's cheek another time before hugging her tight. Her luggage was checked in, her tickets were safely put away in her handbag and her credit card rested between her Starbucks- and her health-insurance-card.

"I want postcards. A million. And pictures. A million-and-one," Evy whispered before releasing her.

"Everything you want, I promise," Tessa laughed and then stepped back, knowing she needed to go now or she wouldn't ever leave without stowing her best friend away in her handbag.

Passing through security, Tessa thought about the last time she had been so excited and obviously it had been too damn long because she simply couldn't remember it at all.

Purchase on Amazon:

http://amzn.to/1G3qBIW

Follow on Facebook:

https://www.facebook.com/SamDestinyAuthor

74037451R00189

Made in the USA
Columbia, SC
24 July 2017